KINGDOM
OF WITHOUT

KINGDOM OF WITHOUT

ANDREA TANG

SIMON & SCHUSTER BFYR

NEW YORK · LONDON · TORONTO · SYDNEY · NEW DELHI

SIMON & SCHUSTER BFYR

An imprint of Simon & Schuster Children's Publishing Division
1230 Avenue of the Americas, New York, New York 10020

For information about special discounts for bulk purchases, please contact Simon &
Schuster Special Sales at 1-866-506-1949 or business@simonandschuster.com.
The Simon & Schuster Speakers Bureau can bring authors to your live event.
For more information or to book an event, contact the Simon & Schuster Speakers
Bureau at 1-866-248-3049 or visit our website at www.simonspeakers.com.
Interior design by Hilary Zarycky
The text for this book was set in New Caledonia.
Manufactured in the United States of America
First Edition
2 4 6 8 10 9 7 5 3 1
Library of Congress Cataloging-in-Publication Data
Names: Tang, Andrea, author.
Title: Kingdom of without / Andrea Tang.
Description: First edition. | New York : Simon & Schuster Books for Young Readers,
2023. | Audience: Ages 12+ | Audience: Grades 7-9. | Summary: Seventeen-year-old
Zhong Ning'er, a wily young thief, must use her wits to survive in
an alternate, futuristic Beijing.
Identifiers: LCCN 2022054903 (print) | LCCN 2022054904 (ebook) | ISBN
9781665901444 (hardcover) | ISBN 9781665901468 (ebook)
Subjects: CYAC: Robbers and outlaws—Fiction. | Friendship—Fiction. | Beijing
(China)—Fiction. | LCGFT: Steampunk fiction. | Novels.
Classification: LCC PZ7.1.T3757 Ki 2023 (print) | LCC PZ7.1.T3757 (ebook)
DDC [Fic]—dc23
LC record available at https://lccn.loc.gov/2022054903
LC ebook record available at https://lccn.loc.gov/2022054904

For the original JAMME crew: Esther, Margaret, Mallory, and Jade, who believed in me from the start, and made me truly proud to be an Asian American storyteller

DRAMATIS PERSONAE

Zhong Ning'er	钟凝儿
Cheng Yun	程韵
The Red Yaksha	红夜叉
Ge Rong	盖熔
Pan Zhenyi	番振亦
Ke Zi'an	柯子安
Ran Feifei	冉霏霏

The Lark	百灵鸟
He Bailing	贺百灵

The Beiyang Court	北洋政府
The Emperor Huiming	辉明皇帝 (袁琨)
The Emperor Xuyuan	续元皇帝 (袁懿祁)
The Emperor Hongxian	洪宪皇帝 (袁世凯)
The Brocade Guard	锦衣卫
The Gendarme	北洋军
Minister Cheng	程大人
Cheng Wei	程霨

CHAPTER 1

Phantoms

Getting around the city with only one leg, one arm, and not a single drop of Complacency to compensate for a pair of inconveniently missing limbs was—to Ning'er's dismay—way harder than she remembered.

The wooden stick helped a little. You had to cling to the little things where you could. Sometimes literally. So Ning'er clung to that flimsy little cane with all her might. It might not be a real prosthetic, but it had kept her upright for two blocks straight, which Ning'er counted as a win, however feeble. She shook her head. What a way to spend a Saturday night in the Sixth Ring, mere blocks from dirt-cheap nightlife. Instead of trolling for free drinks, here she was, dragging her two-limbed—and honestly, probably pretty delirious—body toward the cave of a workaholic who hated drinking and was also almost definitely going to yell at her.

Ning'er sighed. It was a satisfyingly self-pitying little gust of air. "You absolute fool," she reprimanded herself, clucking her tongue, which no doubt made her look even more like a mad-woman than she already did. "Sell your illegal prosthetics, Ning'er." She grunted as her stick scraped along the poorly paved street. "Don't take the courtesy drugs the back-alley doctor offers for the pain, Ning'er." Her balance wobbled precariously for a moment, then held. "You don't want to end up back on Complacency like your old man, Ning'er." Gingerly, she took one step, planted the stick, then took another.

It had been a very long time since she'd had any fewer than three decently functional limbs. Even before Ning'er had pawned her prosthetics—so, maybe an hour ago—she'd been used to getting herself banged up. It came with the territory when you lived in the Sixth Ring. If it wasn't a bar fight in some seedy dive, it was wear and tear from hard labor or getting caught out after curfew by an aggressive patrol android. But usually, Ning'er's body had the good sense to only fuck with one major injury at a time. And three good limbs outnumbered one bad one.

There wasn't much you could do with one leg, one arm, and a wooden stick, though.

It would have been a dreadfully depressing state of affairs, if not for three things:

One, the guy who was—with any luck—about to yell at her was also a guy who could fix pretty much anything.

Two, his workshop was a reasonably easy walk from the butcher shop clinic that had torn Ning'er's prosthetics from her body, so at least she didn't have to travel too far.

And three, as she dragged her sad, sorry carcass onto the workshop doorstep, she saw a light flicker on inside.

A moment later, the latch on the door clicked.

"Took you long enough," Ning'er rasped, before she pitched forward.

Powerful, well-tattooed arms caught her with the ease of long practice. The stick clattered aside. "天啊," sighed Ge Rong. "Ning'er, haven't you learned anything from the last time you sold my work on the black market?"

"First of all, how dare you automatically assume the blackness of the market. I could be a reformed citizen." Ning'er attempted to pull herself upright with her remaining arm. "Maybe I became the mistress of a billionaire playboy and sent the prosthetics to his wife as a consolation gift."

Ge Rong caught her before she could fall again, scooping her over his shoulder like a sack of rice. "I don't think trolling the taitai population of Beijing counts as reforming."

"Put me down," Ning'er commanded the back of Ge Rong's smock. He smelled like paint and metal shavings. "I feel very patronized!"

"You should have thought about that before you embarked on your newfound career as a Second Ring gold digger." He dumped her unceremoniously onto one of his workshop stools, then paused. "You didn't really, did you?"

Ning'er scoffed. "Please. Would I be here if I had actual legal means to get them replaced?" Goddamn, she'd forgotten how much phantom limb syndrome actually hurt after years of high-end prosthetic use. Her head sagged against the wall behind her. In a smaller voice, she confessed, "I needed the money. That dive where I've been playing barkeep pays absolute garbage."

Ge Rong had his back turned, already rummaging through his inventory. "You can't keep working shit jobs, then paying a literal arm and leg just to make rent, kid."

"Ha ha, cute."

"I'm serious." He turned around, a prosthetic in each hand, screwdriver tucked behind one ear. Ning'er didn't know whether to be horribly embarrassed or grudgingly touched that he kept spare samples of her exact size on hand. "Do you know how many amputees in the Lower Rings have to wait months at second-rate engineering shops just to make do with poor fits and worse mechanics on their prosthetics? And here you are, selling yours whenever you're broke because you have the luxury of—"

"You. You are my one and only luxury in this life, A'rong."

Ge Rong sighed. "I suppose that's true, after a fashion," he agreed wearily. "Doesn't mean it's good, or right. What happens to all the tips from that bar of yours?"

"What tips?" Ning'er quipped. Her shoulders slumped. "Business is slow. For obvious reasons."

Ge Rong at least had the good grace to wince at the reminder. "Supply chains?"

"Supply chains." Ning'er gave a ghastly little flourish with her free hand, miming a toast with a glass of imaginary wine. "Liquor shipments are completely unpredictable now. We nearly had a riot last week when we miscalculated for the post-work rush and ran out of bottom shelf beer. Management says we might have to shut down." She pulled a face. "Or start buying even shittier beer. Literal worst part of those stupid earthquakes."

"I don't know about that," said Ge Rong dryly. "It's possible that the farmers whose homes, crops, and foreseeable livelihoods were permanently destroyed have it a tad worse."

Ning'er scowled at him for just a split second before relenting. She sighed. "Noted."

"What about your baba?" Ge Rong squatted before her. With careful, steady hands, he rolled up her empty trouser leg. "Maybe he could help you out."

"My old man? Who sold my original arm and leg for a Complacency hit? The very same baba who landed us in this predicament in the first place?" Ning'er snorted. "Yeah, pass. Ouch!" She hissed as the tiny cybernetic cables of the new prosthetic bit into the spot where her thigh ended.

"Sorry, I'll fix that." Ge Rong's screwdriver danced between deft fingers, readjusting the cables until the sting subsided. "What about finding other work?"

"You mean other customer service gigs? All dependent on shipping lines, so currently also fucked by the earthquakes?"

Ge Rong sighed. A brief tendril of guilt snaked through Ning'er at the weariness in his eyes. A'rong sighed a lot around her. He probably deserved a little less exhaustion in his life than what Ning'er regularly wrought, but he'd never done wrong by her. Risked more than he had to, in fact, to keep her on two functioning feet. Ge Rong was a real, once-in-a-generation talent. Those beautifully tattooed hands had earned a small fortune from the Second and Third Ringers who could afford his art, and probably a larger one from nouveau-riche Fourth Ringers affecting airs. He could have set up shop among his wealthy clients, renting a penthouse in the Third Ring, or buying a nice big apartment in the Fourth.

Instead, here he lived, in a shitty studio in a shitty Sixth Ring neighborhood, misusing his talent and resources to craft knockoff prosthetics for penniless miscreants like Ning'er. It was the kind of do-gooder nonsense that would destroy his career and earn him a hefty jail sentence if the court ever found out. Yet he'd never once turned Ning'er away from his workshop, no matter how many times he threatened and lectured.

"Well, you'll have to figure something out, one way or another," said A'rong. "This is the last set of prosthetics you'll have from me." Apparently, in addition to being an art and engineering savant, Ge Rong was also a mind reader.

He moved on to Ning'er's arm, massaging the long-abused muscles of her shoulder to prepare for new prosthetic cables. He took a deep breath—Ning'er would bet her remaining organic limbs that he'd rehearsed in front of a mirror for this exact argument—and added: "You can't keep selling your own limbs, and I can't keep doing illegal biohacks to keep you afloat."

"Why?" Ning'er didn't normally like to push, but she knew more about Ge's operations than most. "Your high-and-mighty supplier put a moratorium on charity work?"

"The Red Yaksha is my supplier, not my sovereign," said Ge Rong, a little tartly. He clipped the cables into place, ignoring Ning'er's yelp of protest as the cybernetics latched on to her shoulder. "No, I'm the one cutting you off. Barkeep's privilege. You should know all about that."

Ning'er stuck her tongue out at him. Experimentally, she gave her new metal fingers a little wiggle. The movement was crisp as ever. Ge Rong's handiwork was still excellent. It twisted something inside her heart. "You said you were cutting me off last time, too," she couldn't resist pointing out. "And the time before that. What, you think third time's the charm?"

"Fourth," said Ge Rong, utterly devoid of humor. "And last."

"Because the supply chains are just gonna magically un-fuck themselves?" Ning'er blew out a gust of frustrated air. "Come on, you're smarter than that! Or have you somehow missed the protests that blow up every time the court sits on their pretty hands while the price of rice skyrockets? There are already rumors about imposing more curfews on the Lower Rings to squelch the protests, which is going to be super great for keeping a bar afloat—"

"There are other jobs out there."

"That will hire a street urchin with no secondary school diploma, and no hope of a university degree? A'rong, you need to stop believing that—"

"My supplier needs a thief."

Ning'er stopped mid-rant, the words frozen in her lungs. "One, I don't do that anymore," she said when she could breathe again. "And two, your supplier, you can't mean—"

"The Red Yaksha?" A'rong raised his eyebrows at her. "I told you, he's not my sovereign. When he wants something, he pays. Handsomely."

Ning'er sucked in a slow breath, contemplating her options. The Red Yaksha was the most beloved hero of the Lower Rings: the anonymous savior who lurked, shadow-like, beneath the cover of night to steal from the Upper Rings and feed the poor. Ning'er might have dismissed his existence as bullshit if it hadn't been for the scandalous hack on Chrysalis—the biggest manufacturer of android parts and state-of-the-art prosthetics—the same year Ning'er lost her organic limbs. The leak had been well-timed— whoever orchestrated the data theft had targeted cybernetic blueprints and components. Possessing a decent prosthetic wasn't technically illegal in the Lower Rings, though the means to make them were well-guarded by draconian intellectual property laws that kept Upper Ring manufacturers rich.

But Chrysalis's manufacturing secrets had found their way to Ge Rong's workshop. And all of it, according to the rumor mills, had been the handiwork of the Red Yaksha, savior of the Lower Rings, bane of the gendarme, and enemy of the imperial court.

"Who is he?" Ning'er asked at last. She held up her hand—the flesh-and-blood one—before A'rong could feed her some bullshit answer. "No, really. Under the mask, who's the Red Yaksha?"

A'rong was already shaking his head. "I can't tell you that."

"But you can tell me to work for him." Ning'er folded her arms. "That's not fair, A'rong. Besides, like I said, I'm retired."

The side of A'rong's mouth quirked. "So come out of retirement."

"For some creepy dude in a mask? Pass."

"He built you your limbs."

"You built me my limbs," Ning'er corrected pointedly. The metal fingers of her new arm screeched against the palm as she closed her fists. "Anyway, I'm clean now. I—I'm not like my old man. I haven't touched Complacency since I quit thieving."

A'rong's eyes went soft. "You don't need oxyveris to do your job."

"Don't I?" Ning'er pulled a face. "We're talking a day at the office that involves scaling buildings, and breaking and entering, and making off with expensive things. So, last I checked: yeah, I need Complacency."

"That stuff enhances you physically," said Ge Rong. "It doesn't do the work for you."

"Same difference, isn't it?" Ning'er couldn't quite keep the edge out of her voice. "Without my regular dose of oxyveris, I was just another Sixth Ring amputee who couldn't afford real prosthetics."

"And now"—Ge Rong knocked pointedly on her new arm—"you've got the prosthetics."

Ning'er swallowed hard. "I've never thieved without Complacency," she said quietly. "The only reason I started taking it in the first place was because I needed to work. You know that, right?"

"I know," said A'rong quietly.

"Fuck." Ning'er pinched the bridge of her nose. "I'm being stupid, aren't I?"

And just like that, the tension broke. A'rong laughed, the sound light but laced with sincerity. "You're many things, Zhong

Ning'er, but you've never been stupid." He looked at her—really looked at her this time, his gaze soft, as he laid a big, calloused hand on her shoulder. For a fleeting, stupid moment, Ning'er wondered how her life would have turned out if she'd been born a daughter of Ge Rong's family. How different would things be if Ge Rong had been her real brother? Would they still be having this conversation—weighing the risk of one desperate crime over another—if Ge Rong had been Ning'er's blood, instead of the father who'd gambled his own daughter's body parts away for a drug that nearly killed them both?

It hurt to think about. She stared at the hand on her shoulder. The intricate tattoos on A'rong's knuckles blurred with the abrupt, embarrassing prick of heat in her eyes.

"Just give the job some thought," said A'rong. "You owe yourself that much, at least." Gently, he swatted the back of her head. "And don't let me see you back in my workshop missing any new limbs for at least another month, you hear?"

Ning'er didn't quit thinking about the Red Yaksha during the whole walk home.

The thing was, A'rong was right on some level. Basic politeness probably dictated a debt of gratitude to the do-gooding phantom of the Lower Rings, if only because it meant girls like Ning'er got access to the same prosthetics rich kids got for pocket change. But Ning'er had never trusted the unknown.

Flickering streetlamps hung low over the shadow-strewn streets. Ning'er sighed up at the shoddy lights. Another infrastructure headache that no one would bother fixing, because no one ever bothered fixing anything in the Sixth Ring. The guttering orange glow played over the yellowing screens plastered to the sides of decaying buildings. The only one still legible was a dramatic shot of a young gendarme officer, strikingly handsome even in faded colors under poor lighting. The infamous Young Marshal. Ning'er sighed, glowering at the boy in the picture. His portrait was accompanied by some stupid, tone-deaf slogan, plastered in bold characters beneath the image, urging the citizens of the Xuyuan Emperor to serve their liege in exchange for his glorious protection. As if a seven-year-old who'd been crowned as a toddler knew shit about protecting his citizens.

She must have walked past the poster of the Young Marshal a hundred times. The son of a wealthy minister, his rise through the ranks of the gendarme—not to mention the favorites at the imperial court—was notorious. Rumor had it that, at just eighteen years old, he'd be named the youngest lieutenant in the Brocade Guard any day now. If it bore fruit, he would be making history: the Brocade Guard were the elite of the elite, the hand-chosen enforcers who represented the throne itself. No one had ever been chosen before their twentieth birthday.

With a place in history secured, not to mention the favor of the crown buoying his career, the Young Marshal would no doubt continue his family's fine work of exploiting the misery and labor of the poor for the comfort of the Upper Rings. He was a monster, in every sense.

He was also, unfortunately, preposterously good-looking. Whoever ran the Emperor's propaganda machine had chosen their poster boy well. Ning'er couldn't count the number of times she'd wanted to deface his stupid portrait, only to pause, unable to bring herself to ruin that beautifully rendered face. Besides, it wasn't like drawing an unflattering mustache on the Young Marshal's flawless visage would actually destroy his accompanying political power. If only.

Tonight, she paused for just a moment, scowling up at those famous features: the dark swoop of thick, expensively cut hair falling over expressive, long-lashed eyes. A mouth like a girl's, almost too full for its jawline. The face of an angel that belied its bearer's cruelty.

Ning'er stared a few seconds longer, metal fist clenching and unclenching. Then she spat at the foot of the flickering screen and kept walking.

The only source of light in Ning'er's apartment when she unlocked the door was a single blinking notification on the screen of the cheap monitor by her window. Ning'er frowned. That was weird. Pretty much every citizen—even in the Lower Rings—owned a monitor. They provided you with the basic informational necessities of daily life: the weather outside, headlines, reports on emergency curfews or restrictions on travel between Rings. But Ning'er had already cleared her alerts. She shouldn't have gotten a new one unless—

Ice filled her veins. With a snarled expletive, she raced toward the monitor. "Shit, shit, shit, 妈的—"

Too late. The notification blinking brightly at her was all her worst fears made real: her balance sat at zero. The entire contents of her meager bank account—all twelve thousand kuai she'd earned off her old prosthetics—had been withdrawn. Which meant only one thing. Only one other person still had access to the codes on Ning'er's personal account.

Ning'er sucked in a deep, steadying breath. Then another. The first person ever to take her in off the streets had been an old man who ran a bookshop near the park where Ning'er had been sleeping. She'd been huddling under someone's forgotten picnic blanket for warmth when Mr. Yu had found her and offered her a few coins and a spare cot in the bookshop in exchange for some clerical work. "Breathe," he'd said when she began to hyperventilate, certain that her life would never be more than this: never planning her life beyond one day, then the next, entirely dependent on the mercy of strangers. "Breathe, little one. Through all the trials that the universe hurls upon us, the only thing that will carry you through is breath. So breathe. Your own breath sustains you when nothing else does."

That had been years ago. Ning'er had been twelve, a child still, really, and easily mollified by small kindnesses and dime store wisdom. But Mr. Yu had been wiser than most, and from time to time, when she felt well and truly backed into the worst of corners, Ning'er thought to herself: so long as you live, you have your breath. So breathe, Ning'er. Breathe. It means you're still alive.

Now, for several minutes, all Ning'er did in that tiny, dingy studio was breathe. Inhale. Exhale. Repeat.

When her heart rate returned to normal, she pulled a chair up to her monitor. Slowly, she opened a search box and began to type. At dawn's first light, she was going to have to pay a visit to her father.

Old Man Zhong had, once upon a time, not been an entirely shitty parent. Ning'er tried not to spend too much time thinking about the almost-good days. There had been a time when he'd smile at her, really smile at her, and his eyes would still be his. She'd still called him Baba, back then, and he'd called her his 宝宝, precious one, his darling daughter. He used to swing her high up on his shoulders after a hard day at work, laughing as she shrieked with delight. They'd never been rich—hell, they'd never even really entertained fantasies of scraping together a life beyond the Sixth

Ring. But they'd been happy, for a time. No matter what cruelties the Lower Rings visited upon them, Ning'er had felt certain and secure in the cozy cotton blanket of Baba's love, steady as the modest roof over their heads. And for a few golden years, that had felt like enough. That had felt like it would last forever.

The factory accident had changed everything. With injuries that bad, and no prosthetic supplements cheap enough for the Lower Rings, the only thing that kept Baba upright and working was oxyveris: better known as Complacency. So the doctors had prescribed more, and more, and more, until eventually, Baba wasn't really Baba anymore.

You always paid a price, in the Lower Rings.

While Ning'er was best at ferreting out information when she had boots on the ground and solid evidence between her fingers, tracking her father down wasn't hard. Old Man Zhong had never been great at covering his footsteps, and drugs always made him worse. He left a digital trail everywhere he went.

This time, it led right to a cheap apartment building just three blocks from Ning'er's. She tamped down the irrational wave of hurt that he'd been living a stone's throw away from her for the better part of a year and never once tried to see her. It was for the best. She knew what happened when her father showed up. If she was lucky, he'd just scream at her, blaming her for the ruin of his life, cursing the wait before his next dosage.

After all, if he hadn't been providing for Ning'er, he'd never have taken that factory job. He'd never have gotten hurt. And if he hadn't needed to provide for Ning'er, he wouldn't have needed to mask the injury in the only way Lower Ringers could. He'd never have touched Complacency.

She hated that, deep down, she blamed herself too.

It was worse when she saw glimpses of his old self. The way her baba would smile at her, sweet, like he really meant it, lucid as he ever got. He'd try to hold her. And then he'd cry. The crying was always the worst part, worse even than the promises he'd shower on her: 宝宝, *I'm sorry, I'm so sorry for everything. I'll do better. I really mean it this time. I'll do better, and make it all up to you. I haven't taken oxyveris in three days, and I'm already doing so well, don't you see? I just have to keep it up, and we'll go back to how it was. We'll be happy again. I promise, I promise, I promise.* He would promise, and cry, and cry, and cry. His arms would make a desperate vise around her back as his tears stained her shirts and dribbled down the metal casing of her prosthetics.

Once upon a time, Ning'er used to cry, too. She stopped, eventually, deadened to the sting of disappointment. Fighting against the tug of Complacency, once it truly sank its claws into you, was a lost cause. A day, a week, a month later, and Baba would be on it again. And if he couldn't pump himself full of enough drugs to keep him working, money would start vanishing from Ning'er's accounts once more.

After all, to the court, it didn't particularly matter that Old Man Zhong had once sold his twelve-year-old daughter's limbs for a gram of Complacency. It didn't matter that he'd left her on the side of a street to die in the rain. It didn't matter that she almost certainly would have died if it hadn't been for people like Mr. Yu the bookseller, or later, Ge Rong.

All that mattered was that Old Man Zhong and Zhong Ning'er shared blood. Under the law, he was still her father, and she was still seventeen years old. And without legal adulthood, her father could do whatever he wanted with her money. It had gotten Ning'er pretty good at coming up with extra password authentications and clever blocks on her accounts, but between extra hours tending bar and the stress of finding another customer for her prosthetics, she'd gotten lazy.

And this time, her laziness had cost her. She could strangle her past self for being so goddamn careless. Her only hope of recovering her lost funds would be getting to her father before he got to his next dose. If he still had the money, there was a chance—a small chance, but a chance all the same—that she could wrestle it back from him. Ning'er had a whole emergency arsenal well-honed and practiced. Threats, or bribes, or a good old-fashioned guilt trip—none were certain weapons, but all were on the table.

Her father usually took a while to answer the door, wherever he was staying. Old Man Zhong didn't like visitors and was dead asleep more often than not. So when the designated door slid aside halfway through her second knock, Ning'er had to bite back surprise.

For a scant few seconds, she wondered if she'd pulled the wrong address from the public databases. The man standing before her looked worse than usual, his eyes bloodshot and beard overgrown. Ning'er's heart sank. "Ba," she managed. "Did you . . . did you already spend the money?"

The apartment's occupant swayed slowly on his feet without answering. He looked, briefly, like he was going to topple over. Automatically, she offered a steadying hand. It was the metal hand, which turned out to be a mistake.

He swatted the prosthetic aside, his entire body recoiling from the sight of her artificial arm. "Leave me alone."

"I plan to." Ning'er shoved her way past him into the apartment. "As soon as you give me back what's mine."

The slap caught her full across the face. It startled her more than it hurt, but she gasped with the force of it, sliding sideways into one of the cheap plaster walls. Her palms broke her impact, but her father was already railing at her.

"Yours?" he snarled. "Yours? Who was all that Complacency for? Who had to work to keep that roof over your head all those years?"

Ning'er turned from the wall. Her cheek smarted, but it had been a lucky shot. If it came down to a physical fight, she didn't intend on letting her father win. She strode toward him, metal fist clenched at her side. "And who gave up her original limbs to keep that roof over yours?"

A desperate, broken expression spread across his features. "Ning'er, I only ever wanted to provide. You have to understand, we didn't have anything, and you were too young to—"

"Shut up!" roared Ning'er. She didn't want to hear it. "You took my money! Like you were entitled to it, just like you were entitled to my arm, my leg—"

"You have no idea what I sacrificed!" her father whimpered. "You think you're so much better than me because you had the luxury to get off Complacency and have the audacity to talk as though that's your money? After everything we lost?" He raised his hand again.

Ning'er caught his wrist before he could strike her a second time. She'd used the metal prosthetic again, deliberately this time. She couldn't help but relish the tendril of fear that crept into his gaze when she tightened the chrome-reinforced digits on his skin, almost hard enough to bruise. "You have no idea what I had to do to put that money in my bank account," she hissed. "And if you touch me again, I'll make you regret it. Unlike you, I keep my promises."

His mouth took on a bitter set. "Oh, you will, will you? And

I wonder, what would the android patrols have to say about a daughter's assault on her own father?" He plucked his hand from her suddenly slackened grip. "They wouldn't appreciate a violation of their precious protocols, I imagine. You wouldn't want me to report you now, would you?"

Ning'er hated that he was right. Abruptly, she turned from him, palms raised. "You know what? I'm done. At the end of the day, if it comes down to a choice between me and Complacency, I know which one will win." She hated the telltale heat building behind her eyes and nose, but she barreled on all the same. "I'm done playing the fool. I know a lost battle when I see one. Enjoy the next six months before my eighteenth birthday. I won't bother you again after that."

Something alien flickered across her father's face. If Ning'er didn't know better, she might have thought it was regret. "Ning'er, wait, don't go. I—I lost my temper. I'm sorry. I'm sorry, you know I'm not really like that—"

He tried to cup her face between his hands. Ning'er jerked aside.

"Don't touch me!"

He flinched away, as if he was the one who'd been hit, not her. "Okay, I won't touch you. But you have to understand, this isn't me. I never wanted . . . I never wanted to be this person."

Ning'er hesitated on the threshold of the doorway. Her heart twisted at the way hope—it had to be hope, right?—bloomed in her father's bloodshot eyes. For a moment, he looked almost like his old self. "All I need is a chance, Ning'er," he pleaded. "The last stash I bought, it was no good, cut with all kinds of garbage, almost killed me when I tried to use it on an overnight shift. If I just had one more month's supply of the good stuff, the better brand of Complacency, I could get back on my feet, find better work, buy a half-decent flat for both of us—"

Ning'er stopped hesitating. "Goodbye, Baba." She slammed her way out of his apartment before she could waste more time imagining things that weren't there.

"Ning'er," he called. His voice had gone feeble again, slurred. "Ning'er, wait, come back here! Please! Don't leave me alone here. I need . . ."

Ning'er didn't actually give a fuck what Old Man Zhong thought he needed. She couldn't afford to. She picked up her pace, pulling herself well out of earshot, walking so fast she was practically running. Her organic leg had a cramp in the calf by the time she hit the bottom of the apartment stairwell, but Ning'er barely registered the pain. She wouldn't be able to concentrate on the actual problem at hand, not with her father's voice getting into her head.

And heaven above, what a monster of a problem. Rent was due this week, and the landlord would only give her a grace period of two weeks before immediate eviction. It would take well over a month to earn back the money Old Man Zhong had stolen and squandered, and selling her prosthetics this soon after the last set was out of the question. Even Ge Rong's patience—and recklessness—would only extend so far.

When Ning'er was a block from the apartment complex, she turned abruptly on the street corner, whirling on her heel, arms flung akimbo. "Fuck!" she yelled at no one in particular. A little old auntie hobbling across the street with her groceries shot Ning'er a mildly judgmental look.

Ning'er ignored the auntie and kicked a pebble across the street. Fear and fury rocketed her pulse into a hot buzz beneath her skin. "Fuck!" she yelled again. "Fuck, fuck, fucking fuck!" A few passers-by glanced over at her, cautiously alarmed, but most continued about their business. She could imagine what was going through their heads: just another Sixth Ring girl down on her luck, one among thousands of desperate, wretched souls clawing their way through the filthy underbelly of Beijing. Don't look at her. Don't look at any of these other poor, pathetic bastards. Keep walking. Just keep walking, if you know what's good for you, if you want to survive the Sixth Ring for one more day.

Breathe, chided Mr. Yu from the depths of her memory. *So long as you live, you can breathe.*

Ning'er breathed, angry little puffs as she exhaled again and again, resisting the urge to throw herself into the street and start punching the ground out of sheer, desperate frustration. No matter how bad things had gotten before, selling her prosthetics had always served as a rainy-day failsafe. Now, she'd finally run out of luck. Ge Rong would be so disappointed.

Ge Rong. Ning'er froze mid-exhale. All at once, their last conversation flooded through her head. His job offer.

Or rather, the Red Yaksha's.

Ning'er always kept a comm-link in her pocket. It was the cheapest model she could find—clunky and prone to malfunctioning, with a shitty display screen you still had to flip open to talk to anyone—but it still felt like an unnecessary expense sometimes. Since Mr. Yu had passed, the only person who ever called her was Ge Rong, and paying for a plan to talk to one person was a preposterous amount of money for a Sixth Ring barkeep to spend.

In this moment, though, as she pulled Ge Rong's link line up, Ning'er had never been more grateful for the frivolous plastic contraption.

He picked up on the third ring. "Ning'er?" Concern flooded his voice. "Is everything all right?"

"Nope," said Ning'er. Her throat caught. A beat passed, then a second, before she managed to say, entirely too brightly, "My father stole all my money and spent it on Complacency, so I am, in fact, deeply screwed right now—"

His breath hitched. "Excuse me?"

Ning'er barreled on. "But we're about to change that." Giddiness had taken the place of the rage from earlier. This was stupid. She knew that. It was possibly even stupider than trying to confront her father. But with eviction imminent, she'd run out of time for smart.

There was a pause on the other end of the line. "Tell me you're not going to sell your limbs again."

"Something like that." Ning'er offered a savage smile at the streets to the Sixth Ring as she spoke. "Tell your Red Yaksha that if he's still shopping around for a cat burglar, he's got one. I'm in."

CHAPTER 2

The Changing of the Masks

Travel between the Lower Ring Roads was a bitch and a half compared to the smooth-running luxury cars and leisurely checkpoints in the Upper Rings. You had to budget at least a half hour of extra time in case the eternally malfunctioning trains were running late, and then another half hour on top of that in case one of the guards decided to hassle you at a checkpoint. Still, there was something a little romantic about inter-Ring travel. None of the Lower Rings would ever hold a candle to the finery of the First and Second—they weren't meant to. The Upper Rings were reserved for the court and their hangers-on, where money and politics mixed in the lap of luxury. But even the Fourth and Fifth Rings felt fancy enough to a Sixth Ring girl.

The stratification hadn't happened overnight. Like most divisions, it had been a creeping, gradual change. Historically, proximity to the First Ring—the imperial palace—had always been most desirable and therefore hardest to afford. The closer you lived to the palace, the easier your access to its parties, the hunting grounds of corporate sharks rubbing shoulders with ministers while plotting the future of fortunes and empires. The closer you lived to the palace, the easier it was for your children to attend the exclusive tutoring centers that specifically prepared students for the civil service exams—the same exams that led to elite, cushy ministry positions at court.

Even the Lower Rings started sliding into line, over time. The Fourth and Fifth Rings hadn't been so different from the Sixth, once upon a time, but anyone with the money to do so flooded the Second and Third Rings as soon as they could afford the housing. It was a tale as old as time: the monied folk moved to the more desirable Rings, the original inhabitants got pushed further and further out, and so on and so forth, until at last, the poorest denizens of the city got stuck on the outermost, least desirable outskirts. The ministers could spout all the pretty talk they wanted about bootstrapping, but anyone with sense knew the truth: once you found your way to the Sixth Ring, your shot at making it out was as good as dead.

People resisted at first, but it was like trying to swim against a tidal wave. Petitions were ignored. Protests simply resulted in the construction of gated walls between the Rings. And riots were quickly stamped out by cyborg brigades.

The point being that, when Ge Rong gave Ning'er the address for a fancy high-rise nestled in the bourgeois comfort of the Third Ring, she couldn't quite calm the resentful little flutter of excitement in her belly. Back when she'd made extra income burgling the homes of the more fortunate, most of her thrill had come from sticking it to clueless rich people. But there was also something romantic about running free across the slick, fashionable balconies of high-rises and seeing people below who actually looked, comparatively, content.

This time, though, she knew something was wrong. It struck Ning'er, right in the gut as soon as she landed, soft-footed, on the balcony of the address A'rong had shared. Déjà vu, almost, but worse.

The pit of her belly went cold. She knew this place. The filigree along the railing of the balcony, the pale curtains billowing in the afternoon breeze.

She never forgot a house she burgled.

"What the fuck, Ge Rong," she muttered, sotto voce, as she stepped through the unlocked door. The place was empty, just as it had been the night Ning'er had broken in. The lights out, the rooms silent. That should have been a comfort. The apartment's occupant was probably off at some overpriced teahouse and had forgotten to lock their doors, confident in their own invulnerability. A lot of people felt invincible, nestled in a pretty little neighborhood just inside the Upper Rings. It had made burgling their homes that much easier.

But you didn't manage to stay in the business for as long as Ning'er had without developing a healthy sense of paranoia.

She looked up.

Her body moved on its own, all coiled muscle memory, before her brain fully processed what was happening. She tucked herself into a roll, shoulder jarring against the balcony floor. No time to wince at impending bruises. Someone—broader, stronger than Ning'er—landed in the exact spot she'd been standing a moment before. In the blur of motion, she made out a black face mask, coupled with plain, functional clothing that hugged the figure. Probably some kind of deranged hired security. Fucking great.

Their fingers bit into the flesh of Ning'er's arm.

"Oh, no you don't!" The fingers of her prosthetic clamped over her organic ones in a gable grip, and she twisted her hips as she wrenched free. She tried to run back out to the balcony.

Her would-be captor had other ideas. They dove toward her, one hand seizing her ankle. She kicked free, only to stumble straight into another pair of arms. The mask had brought friends.

The owner of the flat must have hired the goons after the first time Ning'er broke in. Maybe to dissuade future intruders. Maybe simply to kidnap the original thief if she was ever stupid enough to make a return.

And here Ning'er had played directly into their hands.

"Goddammit, A'rong." She wiggled one leg behind her new captor, trying to make space. Easier said than done. Would-Be Kidnapper Number Two had a solid bear hug on her. "You couldn't have picked literally any other apartment to set up a meeting in, huh?"

Her kidnapper didn't answer, but they did falter. Maybe they knew A'rong. Or maybe they just hadn't expected Ning'er to talk to herself while being kidnapped. Which was admittedly probably a weird thing to do.

It gave Ning'er the distraction she needed. Squatting down, she gave her adversary's knees a tug. With a squawk, they went sprawling. Ning'er wasted no time and booked it back out the door.

"Wait!" the first kidnapper yelled. It was the first thing either of them had said, aside from "Aah!" or "Mmph!"

"Like hell!" Ning'er yelled back without looking behind her.

Her hands found the railing. Her heart skittered on a halfbeat. She'd never done this without Complacency thrumming through her veins.

Well, fuck Complacency.

She vaulted, flung her legs through the air, and jumped. For a moment, freewheeling through the air, her pulse hit overdrive. Even with drugs buoying your brain, nothing ever beat the sensation of your tender, mortal body falling. The terror. The exhilaration. The spike of possibility that you might—just might—miss your landing.

Her outstretched hands swam through air. Her heart plummeted. And then her palms were scrabbling for purchase on the ledge of the neighboring building. The metal casing on her new hand shrieked but held. Grunting, she pulled herself onto the roof, ignoring the scrapes and cuts now oozing from the other.

For a moment, she considered turning around and waggling her tongue at the hired goons. Probably too unprofessional. Besides, the last thing she needed was them trying to follow her. One of them could get lucky.

Instead, she ran, her feet working double time to carry her as far as possible from that accursed high-rise. She had a far more important task at hand: yelling at Ge Rong.

Ge Rong looked surprised to see her. This, remarkably, pissed Ning'er off even more. She hadn't known that was possible.

"What the hell!" she yelled as soon as he cracked open the workshop door.

He opened it the rest of the way. "Hello to you, too."

"Fuck hello!" Ning'er stomped past him. "Was that your idea of a joke?"

"Ning'er—"

"Did you know?" Kicking off her shoes, Ning'er rounded on Ge Rong. "Did you know the asshole who owned that apartment would hire a couple goons to lie in wait for me? I could have been murdered! Or worse, fed to the gendarme, or those stupid pet androids of theirs, or even—"

"Ning'er!" A'rong had his hands up, and his face was doing several things at once, eyes wide, eyebrows practically acrobatic. "Stop."

"Why!" Ning'er yelled in his face.

"Because," said a new voice behind her, "Ge Rong has company."

Ning'er turned in slow motion. For one absurd moment, she thought she was standing face-to-face with some bizarre new invention. The thing was, the new voice's owner was no stranger, not really.

Everyone in Beijing recognized the mask of the Red Yaksha. It was pretty minimalistic, all things considered: the bright-red paint job, two protruding horns, stylized gold paint forming a snarling mouth and markings along the eyes and nose.

Just, you didn't really expect to find a face like that at your best friend's workshop. Fully dressed in a red cloak and everything, the whole nine yards.

The Red Yaksha tucked his hands into his pockets. Some part of Ning'er's brain noted that it was pretty sensible to have gotten pockets sewn in, even if the cloak itself was pretty dramatic.

"Nice job escaping that apartment," said the Red Yaksha. He sounded younger than she'd have expected. She couldn't tell if he was smiling behind that painted face, but amusement hung thick in his voice. "Zi'an and Zhenyi are both pretty strong."

It took Ning'er an embarrassing number of seconds to put two and two together. "You hired those goons to kidnap me?" She rounded on A'rong. "Why would the Red Yaksha try to kidnap me? You said he was hiring!"

"I am," said the Red Yaksha. "But I had to do my due diligence."

"By kidnapping me?"

"By ensuring that you were a good-enough burglar to escape someone trying to kidnap you."

Ning'er opened and closed her mouth several times before choosing a new target for her ire. "Did you know about this?" she demanded of Ge Rong.

A'rong looked very much as though she'd just pointed a gun in his face. "Um," he said.

"Yes," said the Red Yaksha helpfully. "It was a condition of the hiring process."

"I wasn't supposed to tell you!" A'rong blurted out.

"That part is true," the Red Yaksha conceded. "It's not much of a test if the escape artist knows all the obstacles in advance, now, is it?"

Ning'er took several deep breaths. She didn't particularly want to. She could think of several things she'd rather be doing than taking deep, calming breaths. Yelling at A'rong some more, for example, or punching the Red Yaksha in his stupid face, mask and all.

But she was also broke, owed rent, and was probably about to lose her only other job because of an earthquake-smashed supply chain. Yelling at A'rong and picking a fight with the Red Yaksha would solve none of these problems.

So instead, Ning'er breathed.

"Who are you?" she asked when her temper was under control. The question was directed at the Red Yaksha. You couldn't really force eye contact with a guy who hid behind a mask, but Ning'er did her best anyway, glaring him full-on in those painted-on eyes. "I won't work for a guy whose real face I can't even see, and I certainly won't steal for him."

"Ning'er." A low warning note had crept into Ge Rong's voice. "That's not—"

The Red Yaksha held up a hand. "It's a fair ask. Trust in exchange for trust, right?"

Slowly, carefully, he tugged the mask free from his features.

Ning'er took a step back without really meaning to. She'd

seen that face a million times on the way to and from A'rong's workshop, cruel and bright and beautiful, as he stared out at her from posters plastered on the walls of decaying buildings. She'd spat at that face just last night.

But this wasn't pixels flickering across a broken screen. This was the Young Marshal in the flesh. At least, she was pretty sure it was in the flesh. Ning'er resisted an urge to reach out and poke him to see if he was real.

The side of his mouth curled. "Surprise," said the Young Marshal.

Ning'er didn't take the hand he offered. "You're the Red Yaksha? Didn't you declare him your archnemesis or something on live television?"

"That was my father," said Cheng Yun. "And technically, he declared the Red Yaksha an enemy of the court, which sounds far less silly and much more official." He paused. An odd expression tugged downward at the corners of that pinup-boy mouth. "Obviously, he doesn't know what's behind the mask."

"Heavens above." Ning'er sat down heavily on the edge of one of Ge Rong's drafting tables. A'rong stood in silence, his expression carefully neutral, but Ning'er had known him long enough to recognize the nervous fidget in his hands. He was looking at the Red Yaksha—the Young Marshal—as if awaiting some sort of cue.

But the Young Marshal was only looking at Ning'er. "Still want to work for me?" he asked.

"Depends," she managed. "What could possibly be so important that both the Young Marshal and the Red Yaksha would hire a Sixth Ring girl to steal it?"

"Her," said the Young Marshal in soft tones. "Her, not it."

From his pocket, he fished out a handheld holo-projector and clicked a button.

A young woman burst into life before them, flooding Ge Rong's workshop with light. Oxygen stilled inside Ning'er's lungs. Ning'er hadn't seen that face since she was twelve: the golden-brown complexion striking against the feather-white dress that hugged the curves of the girl's well-muscled shoulders. There had been a time when Ning'er had thought she was a force of nature itself: devastatingly powerful and terrifyingly beautiful, unyielding as a tempest in monsoon season. It was a wholly different flavor of beauty from the Young Marshal's. Where the court's poster boy was lithe and angular, mesmerizing but untouchable, the girl of Ning'er's memory had filled a room, her warmth palpable even trapped behind the cold screen of a holo-projector.

Until, like all beautiful things that passed through Ning'er's life, she too had shattered.

"The Lark is alive," said the Young Marshal. As the girl in the hologram turned to laugh, seemingly carefree, at the camera, her features cast themselves over Cheng Yun's. For just a moment, his face superimposed with those ghostly features; the girl's silhouette cast over his own, the Red Yaksha looked like a man possessed. "So I'm here to hire a thief to steal her."

CHAPTER 3

The Tale of the Caged Bird

Once upon a time, much to her chagrin, Ning'er had believed in heroes and hope and figureheads, and all the other nonsense she'd slowly, quietly learned to put away, along with all her other sentimental, childish frippery. The thought of those days embarrassed her now. Worse, they made her feel stupid. She'd been a different person back then, the same foolish Ning'er who used to think her baba would quit Complacency one day: the product of a child's naivete, and of a wrongheaded, desperate desire for something better than what reality doled out to the Lower Rings.

But even the most pragmatic girls weren't immune to a need for occasional escapism. Back in those days, when she'd wanted to forget her own miserable reality for a little while, she'd watched the television broadcasts of the Lark's rallies.

Few really knew where the Lark had come from. Rumors, naturally, thrived. Some said that she'd been a simple farmer's daughter from Hebei who'd come to Beijing and set the hearts of the people on fire. Others claimed she'd been a child of privilege, rebelling against restrictive Upper Ring parents in the most spectacular way imaginable. Only denizens of the Sixth Ring knew the real story: the Lark had been one of theirs. He Bailing, a nobody, born to poverty and seemingly destined to die in it. Until she'd decided not to. Until she'd started using her heaven-granted talents: a hard-muscled charm tempered by the almost incidental loveliness of an attractive young woman still in bloom, a self-taught knowledge of political science and history, and perhaps the most dangerous weapon of all: her voice. When that nobody spoke, oh, how people had listened. It had carried her higher than any poor girl should rightfully have risen: all the way into the Third Ring, where she made a name for herself by talking to anyone who would listen.

As it turned out, a lot of people wanted to listen. Hence, the Lark was born.

But no one born in the Lower Rings ever really shed their origins entirely, and the Sixth Ring always recognized their own. No matter how high the Lark ascended, how beautifully she spoke, she never stopped looking hungry.

It was why Ning'er had started watching her broadcasts in the first place. She'd never seen a girl so mesmerizing, so powerful, so perfect, look so ravenous at the same time. But at the end of the day, Ning'er wasn't sure if the truth of the Lark's origins actually mattered. What mattered was her timing.

The ideas the Lark spouted off weren't unique to her. She wasn't the first to condemn the callous, lazy incompetence of the old emperor, the heartlessness of his ministers, the rumors that they'd lined their pockets with bribes from Second Ring businesses to keep themselves in power at court while Beijing fell to ruin around them. But the Lark had been blessed with two gifts that had eluded most others: first, a wonderful gift for oration. And second: she had a marvelous sense of timing.

After all, the Lark's rise had begun in small ways: an impromptu speech at a dingy Fifth Ring pub filled with drunken patrons, all too happy to cheer for a pretty girl who dropped pretty words at their feet. Then bigger venues: clubs, then small auditoriums, and finally entire outdoor rallies that drew teeming crowds. Everyone had heard directly from the Lark, the young woman with the remarkable voice whose words spoke for everyone, from the poorest beggars to the crown prince himself.

Which led to the second boon: she had a marvelous sense of timing. When the Lark's pretty songs trickled into the ear of the boy who'd one day rule the kingdom, all of Beijing had waited with bated breath, afraid to hope.

And then, sure enough, one day, the old emperor died—and the young, bright-eyed crown prince had taken the throne.

For a little while, his rule had felt like the favor of heaven itself. His dead father's crown had barely touched his head when he'd begun planning reforms. The budget for the gendarme and their android patrols were slashed. Plans were drawn up for the walls between the Upper Rings and the Lower to be replaced with public transportation that would grant access to every corner of Beijing for all citizens. Education reforms were written into law so that Lower Ringers had an equal shot at accessing the schools that might earn them positions at court. The Huiming Emperor wanted to hear from everyone.

And then Huiming—young, healthy, and robust—sickened seemingly overnight. Despite the physicians' best efforts, he was dead inside a year with no heir to his throne. All he'd left behind were two nephews. The elder prince, at twelve years old, was at least old enough to have a mind of his own, but his younger cousin was a mere child of two.

Was it any wonder that the clever, puppeteering hands of an influential cabal of Beiyang ministers crowned the two-year-old? The backlash was immediate, half the court righteous in their support of the child emperor, the other half aghast that the same ministers who'd campaigned against every reform Huiming and his Lark had ever championed would place a toddler on the throne.

At this point, the Lark promptly lost her mind.

It was one of those moments emblazoned in the national memory. Ask anyone from any Ring in Beijing, from the Second to the Sixth, and they'd remember where they'd been that fateful hour. The sunlit afternoon when the Lark had gathered her followers—everyone who'd ever loved and believed in her pretty words, everyone who'd ever looked at the young Huiming Emperor and thought, for just a moment, of hope—and marched on the gates of the First Ring, where the palace sat like an oyster waiting to be cracked wide open.

The Lark's words weren't so pretty now. Her words said things like murderers and traitors. Her words declared the Beiyang ministers enemies of crown and country and demanded justice for a fractured kingdom.

Ning'er had been in Mr. Yu's bookshop, craning her neck to watch the broadcast footage on the screen behind the register. The final moments of a girl in a bright-red hood over a white dress—contradictory colors: one the color of celebration, one the color of death. Her grim, half-feral smile, her arms outstretched toward the teeming crowds as she stood at the walls of the imperial city.

For a few precious moments, the Lark and her people had been a breath away from the seat of Beiyang power. The heart of the court. Frozen with anticipation, all of Beijing had watched, wondering if this was it. If this teenage girl might breach those stalwart walls and save Huiming's dream after all.

The moment had shattered with those first few screams

piercing the air from the unfortunate souls at the head of the crowd.

The thing was, they'd expected the gendarme. Hell, the gendarme were practically old friends. Every time a speech at a bar got a little too rowdy or a rally attracted more spectators than expected, sure enough, a regiment of soldiers would show up, sometimes with an android or two on retainer if the squad leader was feeling too lazy to get their own hands dirty.

This, though, was not the gendarme.

The camera had caught the shift in mood so precisely: the way that sunlit smile slipped off the Lark's face. The crack of gunfire. How hard the camera itself shook as the lens pivoted toward the telltale black and gold of Brocade Guard uniforms as they streamed out of the palace gates and enclosed the city square.

Rumor had it that if you ever saw the Brocade Guard in the flesh, you'd never live to tell the tale. On paper, they were just the emperor's personal guard. In reality, there was no "just" about it. They were trained young to wreak death and devastation, and groomed not to care so long as it was in service to the throne.

And so the slaughter had begun.

No one actually saw the Lark fall. You could search all you liked through the footage—and many had—but you'd never catch a glimpse of the bullet that clipped Bailing's wings. Afterward, they couldn't even find a body amidst all the chaos and grief. But everyone knew she'd died, just like the rest of the rebels in the square that day. She couldn't have survived, not a massacre like this one. There were pictures after, sometimes in documentaries, sometimes in some grim art piece, but always, always as a warning to all of what happened to people stupid enough to hope for better tomorrows: the streets of the First Ring, painted red with the blood of the emperor's citizens. The Brocade Guard had been ruthless and efficient. With thousands dead, what was the body of one girl, even if she'd nearly toppled a regime? You didn't get prizes for nearly. And in this case, nearly just meant another death for the historians to tally.

Or so Ning'er had thought.

She turned toward Ge Rong, searching those familiar features for some laughter behind his eyes, some hint of the joke being played. She found none. "Is it true? Is she alive?"

Ge Rong didn't say anything. He just closed his eyes and bowed his head.

Ning'er looked at Cheng Yun. "Where's your evidence?"

Apparently, it was a question he'd been waiting for. "See for yourself." He clicked his thumb on the holo-projector once more.

The laughing 3D hologram of the Lark vanished into the dark, snuffed out as suddenly as she'd appeared. A new image replaced her, glowing, if possible, even more brightly than the red and white of her deathday clothing had.

Ning'er squinted. "Is that a map?"

It very clearly wasn't just a map. The scrolling diagrams projected above them depicted roads and tunnels and even buildings, but there was more: neatly typed characters, pulled from what were clearly encoded email missives, with dates, times, locations.

"It's your evidence," said Cheng Yun in steady, grim tones. Ning'er checked an instinctive wince. It was his Young Marshal voice, the one she knew from TV. "I've spent the past three years gathering these docs. I've probably cozied my way up to every clerk in the city with database access clearance. I wanted to be sure. Now I am. The Lark isn't dead. She's imprisoned. And I know where she's being held."

While he spoke, Ning'er's gaze scanned, thief-quick, over the seemingly endless sprawl of documents gleaming around them. It wasn't enough time to get a load of the details, but it was enough to get a gist. She'd stolen enough to know authentic documentation when she saw it. Cheng Yun was telling the truth. It was like taking a full body impact on hard ground after a long fall.

"For the sake of argument, let's say that I believe you," she said at last. Her metal fist clenched and unclenched, trying to release the tension coursing through her body. She used her flesh hand to steady it. "I do have to ask the obvious questions. Nothing personal, you understand, but I like to know what I'm getting into before I consider signing on for a new job. If the Lark's really alive, and you know where she is, then why hasn't she escaped already? Why does no one know what really happened to her? And why has no one—no one but you, apparently—tried to set her free?"

Cheng Yun held up three fingers before Ning'er could press her interrogation further. "One. Just because she's alive doesn't mean she's conscious. There's a missive somewhere in that collection of docs that says she's very likely being held in suspended animation in a laboratory in the Fifth Ring owned by Lilium Corp. Two. Sometimes, the Bureau of Communications is actually competent at their job—especially given the number of ministers that are bought and paid for by Lilium. And three." He paused for a moment, eyes fluttering shut. When he opened them, there was something raw and resigned in his face. "The few people who figure out the truth and try to act on it tend to meet . . . messy ends. It's the nature of the way Lilium's executives keep their secrets."

Unexpectedly, something inside Ning'er flared up at that last bit. A competitive streak, perhaps, the wily cat burglar sensing a challenge. "Well, there's a first time for everything." Ning'er loved being first. She folded her arms. "So, how am I getting paid?"

"The collective behind the Red Yaksha has money set aside to pay a burglar's fee, but . . ." Cheng Yun hesitated. "Most of it would come out of the stipend I receive from my parents."

Ning'er's eyebrows climbed. "Come again?"

"My mother left me a trust fund before moving overseas. The rest is from my father."

Silence blanketed the room. Everyone knew who the Young Marshal's father was. Minister Cheng was a divisive personality, especially in the Lower Rings. After all, he'd been one of them, once upon a time. He'd clawed his way out of a Sixth Ring gutter and risen to prominence young, emerging on the dual prongs of charisma and ambition, and passed the civil service exams with flying colors. After that, he toed the line to a T, orchestrating crackdowns and spilling gendarme forces into the Sixth Ring to police the poorest neighborhoods, but he delivered the orders with such pretty words and softspoken tongue that you could hardly believe it wasn't all for the greater good. *Why put your lives, your limbs, your families at risk by trying to change such a stubborn system?* he'd coax. *Easier to work with the world than against it. Why not study hard, keep your head down, and take the exams? Why not earn the ear of the throne, rather than fighting against it, and put yourself into power the right way? The clean way, the proper way?*

Ning'er had to admit that seeing Minister Cheng's press conferences on the panoramic screens, broadcast from skyscrapers all over the city, those handsome features all clean-cut and larger than life, with his big earnest eyes and dimpled smiles, it was hard not to be a little entranced. To want, just a little bit, a little guiltily, for the charming honey-voiced man to be right about everything. He made you want to believe in him. He was a little like his son that way.

"Paying your thief with your courtier dad's money, huh? Nice." Ning'er raised her eyebrows at Cheng Yun. This job got shadier and shadier by the minute, but there was something blackly hilarious about this whole situation. "I hope you realize," she added, before she could think better of it, "that there are easier ways to enact your teen rebellion against your dad. Having a sex scandal, for example."

She winced as soon as the words were out of her mouth. *For shame, Zhong Ning'er,* she wanted to scold herself, *you know better than to sass an Upper Ring boy. See if he bestows a nice payday on you now, why don't you?*

To his credit, Cheng Yun didn't pout or threaten or complain about her manners. Instead, he cracked a smile, albeit a grim one. "By all means, if having a sex scandal will free He Bailing, I'll get right to it."

It felt strange, hearing Cheng Yun use "Bailing" as the name it was. After all, the Lark hadn't always been a title. Once upon a time, it had been the name of an ordinary girl with a big heart and big dreams in a dying kingdom, before her supporters had turned that name into a title and the girl herself into an icon. A martyr. The way Cheng Yun said it— so quietly spoken, the syllables gentle as a lover's caress—gave Ning'er pause for reasons she couldn't entirely articulate.

Before she could try, Cheng Yun pressed onward: "You wouldn't be alone. We have a team in place—a demolitionist, a hacker, even a medic. But I can't do anything with them without the right thief to chart the route and do the deed."

The right thief. Ning'er sucked in a long breath. Breaking a political legend out of a secret laboratory prison was a long way off from relieving Upper Ring taitai of their jewelry boxes. "I've never worked on a crew before," she said instead, because that sounded better than *Everything about this job awakens a usually well-buried fear of failure and catastrophe deep within me.*

Cheng Yun's eyebrows rose. "You're worried that you can't do the job."

"I never said that!"

He folded his arms, expression critical, as he tilted his head. "You're not what I expected."

Ning'er bristled despite herself. "Oh? And what did you expect? You know, when you tried to kidnap me."

He ignored the dig. "Someone bolder, I guess. Not every thief in the city has the nerve to steal from my parents, and you managed to get away with it scot-free, less than two years ago."

"I never—" Ning'er began, aghast.

"You never checked out who actually owns that Third Ring apartment, did you?" Cheng Yun's eyebrows climbed. "Perhaps that explains it."

Well, shit. "Your dad owns that place?"

"Not quite." Cheng Yun's lashes lowered. "My mother."

A horrific pause ensued. Ning'er cleared her throat awkwardly. "So, when I stole all that jewelry—"

Cheng Yun waved a dismissive hand. "She won't miss it. She hasn't been in the country for years, and even when she was, she hated deigning to venture beyond the Second Ring, and considered the Third barely a step above the Lower Rings." He shrugged. "Last I heard, she'd just been gifted a much larger flat in Paris by some European lordling she's been attending galas with. Which, luckily, means that that apartment is effectively mine now."

Ning'er stared at him. "Well, not that I wouldn't love to unpack, you know, all of that—but you still can't ask me to work with people I've never met before."

Cheng Yun cracked a grin. What a positively disconcerting expression, sitting right there on the face from all the posters. "Oh, but you have." He hummed. "Well, a couple of them, at any rate."

"That's ridiculous," said Ning'er, forgetting herself a moment. "How on earth could I have . . ." She trailed off. Two and two clicked together in her head. "Oh, no," she said in a small voice.

"I think, before we make any hiring decisions," said the Red Yaksha delicately, "that formal introductions to your kidnappers are in order."

CHAPTER 4
The Crew

T his is the dumbest job interview I've ever had," muttered
Ning'er.

She'd been sent to the Fourth Ring this time, which
did little to salve her mood. The commute wasn't as bad as a trek
into the actual Upper Rings, but it was still a pain in the ass. She'd
had to triple check the bus schedule to make sure she could catch
one early enough to account for the inevitable wait at the gate
checkpoints between the Sixth and Fifth Rings. And by the time
she'd gotten past those, she'd had to sprint just to make the next
bus out to the checkpoint at the Fourth, and so the whole process
began again.

It had been, all in all, almost two full hours of Ning'er's life
for comparatively little ground traveled, and she was extremely
over the whole business by the time she finally arrived at the designated location.

Her assigned destination was no luxurious high-rise, boasting
elaborate glass walls and balconies overlooking the city, but still,
the place reeked of money. It was a café, modestly housed, the
signage posted outside a nondescript building on the very end of
a street corner. The insides, though, showed off the price of the
rent in its sizable floor plan, populated by expensively lacquered
tables and a line of patrons who had the look of couples on dates
trying to show off sophisticated yet offbeat taste to their partners.

Which, strangely, made Ning'er feel a good deal more self-conscious than she had during her last, disastrous jaunt.

It was one thing to take in the thrills and luxuries of the more comfortable under the cover of darkness, where Ning'er herself was never seen—and if she was, that meant bigger problems than feeling embarrassed over her poverty. Here in broad daylight, though, with little else to distract her, Ning'er was acutely aware of the sidelong glances at her careworn sweater and the holes in her once-sensible boots. One particularly fussy-looking hipster actually huffed at her, then loudly whispered something judgmental to another girl. The words "let anyone in these days, don't they" were pitched perfectly to be heard.

Ning'er, preoccupied with scowling back at the woman as hard as she could, nearly jumped out of her skin when a warm arm draped itself over her shoulders. "Hey, 服务员儿," a baritone drawled under her ear. "Direct me and my lady here to our reservation, please, would you? We have a private room with our friends."

It took Ning'er a beat to realize the arm's owner was addressing one of the baristas, who bobbed his head, carefully blank faced. "Right this way, young master Ke."

"Excellent, excellent. Come along, then, dear." Before Ning'er could plant her feet on the floor and an elbow in her accoster's ribs, the baritone dipped lower still, a murmur just under her ear. "Relax. A'yun sent me to help you . . . shall we say, blend in. Let's follow the good man, shall we?"

Ning'er craned her neck, even as she found herself gently herded down the café corridor. The guy who'd materialized in her personal space—Cheng Yun's associate, very clearly—looked every inch the devil-may-care Fourth Ring university boy trying slightly too hard to look like he was here to show you a good time.

He dressed smart, in a well-starched button-down calculated to stretch over the breadth of his shoulders, but he offset the clean-cut vibes with shatter-cut hair, slightly too shaggy to be perfectly on-trend for the prim and proper business set Ning'er usually associated with boys who dressed like him. A pair of thick-framed glasses—unclear whether for function or fashion—perched over a surprisingly pert little nose.

"I know how to blend in," Ning'er muttered, careful to pitch her voice low, well outside the barista's earshot. "I don't need to be handled."

"Sure, but you're a cat burglar," her unwanted keeper murmured back. "Not a grifter. No disrespect to your skill set, but it depends on not avoiding notice. Right now? We're going to be seen, like it or not, so our best bet is to set the terms of how. Sixth Ring girls alone get watched for shoplifting. On the other hand, Sixth Ring girls on the arm of some meathead rich boy playing sugar daddy with his spoiled buddies? Nothing to worry about."

Ning'er wasn't so sure about that. She willed herself not to scowl, lest she blow their cover, flimsy as it was. In an establishment like this one, half the staff were probably Sixth Ringers themselves, commuting every day through the layered checkpoints that divided the neighborhoods. Flouncing around on the arm of a Fourth Ring boy probably wouldn't endear her to them, and the last thing she needed to do was piss off the waitstaff.

"Ah, thank you, Wen!" Ning'er's escort called ahead to the barista as they turned the corner.

The barista—Wen, apparently—glanced over his shoulder, looking the pair of them up and down. Ning'er braced herself for a pursing of the lips or a narrowing of the eyes. Instead, the barista's mouth twitched. "Popular as ever with the ladies, Zi'an."

Ning'er's escort dimpled handsomely. "What can I say? The ladies love a man who's, shall we say, socially involved." In a lower voice, he added, "You'll cover for us?"

The barista nodded slowly, his face giving nothing away. Just as quietly, he said, "You're in luck. It's a slow day—no Beiyang bootlickers that we know of hovering around, but you can't be too careful. I'll make sure you aren't disturbed."

"Excellent—I owe you one. Thank you, truly."

The barista shook his head. "No thanks necessary. The Red Yaksha will always have true friends among the Lower Rings. We all do our part."

"And we won't soon forget it." Extracting himself from Ning'er's shoulders, her meathead escort—who Ning'er was very much beginning to suspect was not nearly the meathead he made himself out to be—opened the door to the back room with a flourish. He even sketched a little bow as he held it for her. "After you, 宝贝儿."

Under other circumstances, it might have been kind of hot. He was the sort of guy she'd sometimes flirt with when she was lonely and stuck working the late shift at her bar. Fun vibes, clearly down for a good time, and pretty enough to look at without being intimidatingly handsome. Under present circumstances, it was all Ning'er could do not to kick his shins as she stalked into the room.

He winked at her over the frames of his glasses, grinning as if he could read her mind and found the notion of violence perfectly charming. The door swung shut behind him. "The name's Zi'an, by the way. Ke Zi'an." Gallantly, he took her metal hand and brushed his lips across the backs of her knuckles. "Humble Beishida history student and law-abiding citizen by day. Freelance explosives specialist and ne'er-do-well hand of the Red Yaksha by night—one of several, you may have noticed. A pleasure to make your acquaintance."

Ning'er blinked owlishly at him. Zi'an. So this was the man who, presumably, handled the Red Yaksha's dirty work. She took in the well-muscled shoulders, the shape of his hands, and backed up a step. "Is this how you greet every girl you try to abduct off a balcony?"

A grin of sheer delight spread across Zi'an's features. "You've got a good memory."

"You're a little hard to forget," said Ning'er dryly.

That, if anything, made Zi'an grin wider. "You put up a solid defense." The affable grin remained in place, but his gaze was sharp behind those fancy glasses. "Which, presumably, is why Cheng Yun invited you here."

Ning'er tilted her head, matching him gaze for gaze. "Presumably. He did promise me an introduction to my kidnappers." She stuck her flesh hand out. "Zhong Ning'er."

Zi'an grinned. "Oh, I know. I've heard all the stories from A'rong. Ah, and before I forget." From his trouser pocket, he fished out a slim, translucent chip and dropped it into Ning'er's palm. "Blueprints for the job, current route plans. Plug that into your comm-link and give it a study when you get a chance, will you, my dear? I'm sure it'll be a breeze."

Ning'er, reasonably certain that breaking into a heavily fortified corporate facility would not be a breeze, was about to ask exactly what kind of stories A'rong had been spreading around, when the door opened again. Two young women entered. The first, long and lanky, sported a bright purple pixie cut and deep circles under her eyes. Her stunning companion, built short and plump, filled out a navy-blue A-line dress with a perfection only achievable via bespoke tailoring. The girl's already striking features were accentuated with deep red lipstick and eyeliner that could have sliced a body from head to toe.

"I'm not telling you that it's impossible, Zhenyi," insisted the plumper, more glamorous girl, flawless red mouth pursing around all the consonants. "Just improbable. There's a marked difference, and I'd like for us to be cognizant of the risks before we move forward with—"

The plainer girl interrupted with a heavy sigh. "Feifei, enough. You think I haven't run the risk calculus over and over again?" She ran a hand through her close-cropped hair. A wink of silver fingers caught Ning'er's eye. It took her a moment to recognize them as prosthetics—just the forefinger and the middle finger, not an entire limb, but prosthetics all the same. "I was there the first time, remember? I don't love the risk any more than you do, but the potential rewards—"

"Might even slightly unfuck this fucked-up kingdom?" interrupted Zi'an. He sidled between the women and, in one dramatic gesture, draped his arms over their shoulders. Both rolled their eyes but leaned into Zi'an's touch with the ease of longtime friends, accustomed to casual physical affection. "Certainly. Worth it, in my opinion."

"Everything always is to you," muttered the glamorous girl.

Zi'an batted his eyes at her. His arm dipped down to slide around her waist. "Thank you, Feifei, it means a lot to be truly seen and understood."

"Much to my own misfortune," remarked Feifei without any particular heat.

"You do invite it by rising so consistently to his bait," murmured Purple Pixie Cut—Zhenyi, that was her name—the side of her mouth twitching just a little. "It would seem Cheng Yun has competition, so far as aspiring martyrs go."

The expression Feifei leveled at Zhenyi might have been called a glare coming from a less coolly refined woman. "Excuse me." In a perfunctory motion, she slid free from Zi'an's grasp, ignoring his exaggerated sigh of disappointment. From her purse, she extracted a compact and a lipstick tube. Carefully, she began to touch up her makeup, red mouth forming a little O. "In any case, I'm not here to indulge Zi'an's frivolities. Nor am I going to pretend to approve of this remarkably dangerous scheme that Cheng Yun's cooked up." With dainty, expert movements, she blotted her lips.

"Aw, you know it's not a bona fide A'yun scheme without a little danger in the mix," cajoled Zi'an. "Besides, you're fine with being a part of the Red Yaksha. Not exactly a risk-free occupation."

"We're all hands of the Red Yaksha, but Cheng Yun wears the face," retorted Feifei without missing a beat. "We all endure risk, but none on the same level as his. You'd think he'd be more cautious."

"Ah, but how many revolutions has caution sparked? Anyway, I didn't want to talk about that."

Zhenyi's eyebrows climbed. "You didn't want to talk about our harebrained scheme to breach Lilium security and rescue an imprisoned populist hero?"

Zi'an batted a dismissive hand at her. "We can save the shop talk for after we've all had some proper tea and snacks. I'd much rather talk to Feifei about—"

"You're new here," interrupted Feifei.

Ning'er blinked. The other girl was staring right at her. So, suddenly, was everyone else in the room. "Uh," said Ning'er, looking Feifei's ample-bodied, sharply dressed figure up and down, from the tips of her shiny dark princess ringlets to what looked to be imported Italian pumps on her feet. Girls like Feifei had always made Ning'er feel shabby. Rarely did they mean to. Rarely did they even seem to notice the existence of Fifth or Sixth Ring girls at all, the way Feifei was very clearly noticing Ning'er right now. It was just the way they waltzed through life, the sensibly fashionable and well-fed girls of the Fourth Ring with their perfect hair and nails and eyeliner that magically seemed to stay in place no matter how much everyone else was sweating. Evidently, the power of proximity to the Upper Rings made them immune to hair frizz.

"I'm the thief Cheng Yun found," said Ning'er, tugging self-consciously at her faded red sweater. It was the nicest thing she owned, and it had a gaping hole under one armpit she still hadn't found the time to mend. What else could she be to these people, really, but a thief? "I was recommended by Ge Rong."

"Ge Rong? Curiouser and curiouser. Thought that guy was just Cheng Yun's supply man. Didn't realize that the supplies included thieves-for-hire." Feifei's friend—Zhenyi—peered at Ning'er with heightened interest. Zhenyi, close-shorn hair sticking up at all ends, hands stuck in the pockets of an oversized blazer that had clearly seen better days, was a little less visually intimidating than her friend. Still, her appearance carried subtle markers of a life kinder than Ning'er's: the blazer, despite the faded fabric, was clearly constructed from good, sturdy material, and purple hair dye of such a vibrant quality didn't come cheap. Even Zhenyi's cybernetic fingers, minor as the prosthetics were, had been constructed from high-grade material, and bore customized decorations—in Zhenyi's case, a pair of closely intertwined birds, the feathers on the fenghuang's wings carved along the length of the metal digits—which had to have cost extra cash.

Ning'er looked Zhenyi up and down. "Let me guess. Zi'an's fellow kidnapper?"

Abruptly, Zhenyi smiled. "You're quite slippery."

"And you're quite strong," Ning'er rebutted.

"Glad we're all exchanging the appropriate niceties," said Cheng Yun as the door swung open to admit him. He was dressed smart casual: nice slacks, well-fitted waistcoat, no masks or dramatic red cloaks to be seen. If Ning'er let her gaze slide out of focus, he might have passed for just another well-to-do young man about town. Yet even without the mask of the Red Yaksha, or uniform of the Young Marshal, his presence shifted the energy in the room. Feifei fell quiet, hands clasped and immediately standing at attention, while Zhenyi bowed her head slightly. Even Zi'an straightened a little, those clever eyes of his sharp and bright behind his glasses. All three—whether they realized it or not—had pivoted themselves subtly toward the entrance, facing Cheng Yun as if obeying some secret law of gravity.

It was actually pretty funny until Ning'er noticed that she'd done the very same.

"Cheng Yun!" cried Zi'an, delighted. To Ning'er's alarm, he strode forward to tug Cheng Yun into a hearty hug. Ning'er braced herself for Cheng Yun to balk or shove Zi'an away.

Cheng Yun stiffened, just for a moment. And then, before her eyes, the boy known as the Young Marshal gave a smile of sheer relief and melted into the embrace. His eyes fluttered shut. "Hey, man," he muttered against Zi'an's shoulder. "I'm glad to see you." He drew back after a moment, looking around at the room's other occupants. His expression was startlingly warm. "All of you. It's been too long."

Ning'er followed his gaze around the room. It was a bit like standing on the outside of a bubble looking in. "Where do you all even know each other from?"

"Isn't it obvious?" Zi'an grinned. He spread his hands. "We are, collectively, the Red Yaksha. Welcome to the fold."

Ning'er frowned. "I thought Cheng Yun was the Red Yaksha."

"Oh, he is," said Zhenyi. "Technically. But as Feifei said, he's only the face. The man in the mask from all the stories. But he does have to delegate from time to time. Much to his chagrin." Her eyes glittered with amusement. "One man alone can't wreak all the havoc that's been attributed to the Red Yaksha, much as A'yun wishes otherwise. That's where the rest of us come in. The hands, the feet, the body."

"Okay, rephrase." Ning'er rubbed the bridge of her nose. "Where did you all first meet?"

"Mostly school," supplied Zi'an, who'd evidently decided to take pity on her. "Parties, protests, social justice clubs. The usual suspects."

"Except for me," said Zhenyi. "I'm an old lady, and proud farmer stock, thank you very much."

"I'm a sorry, did you just say that you're a farmer?" Ning'er blurted out before she could stop herself. Without really thinking about it, she gave Zhenyi a once-over.

Zhenyi grinned, tugging at the ends of her purple hair as if reading Ning'er's mind. "Once upon a time, yes, I knew my way around wheat. I left Hebei in search of better things when I was a kid, after seeing one of the Lark's broadcasts."

"That's not all." Feifei snorted. "She's neglecting to mention that along the way, she also became a self-taught biohacker." She gave Zhenyi a nudge in the ribs. "One that got good enough to run with the Lark herself, back in the day."

"And she's only about four years older than the rest of us, tops, so don't let that old lady talk fool you," added Zi'an with a glimmer in his eyes. He winked at Zhenyi.

Zhenyi waved a demurring hand at them both. "What a lot of flatterers I've fallen in with. Still, as the Young Marshal here says, it's been too long since we were all together in one place." She strode forward to take their leader's hand. "You work too much, Cheng Yun."

"On the contrary, I work just enough. But thank you." Cheng Yun squeezed her cybernetic fingers once, affectionately, before letting go. "But I can't afford to burn my cover. Right now, I'm precisely where the ministers need me, which is to say, under their noses." He nodded toward Feifei, bowing his head. "Thank you, by the way. I know . . . helping me keep up the ruse hasn't been easy for you."

Feifei remained a little less gregarious than the rest of the crew, hanging back with her arms folded. At Cheng Yun's thanks, her body language stiffened still further, shoulders climbing up around her neck. "I'm not naive enough to think I've got much of a choice."

Cheng Yun looked at Feifei. Ning'er wasn't sure how to describe his expression, but it took her by surprise. The Young Marshal in his portraits and televised appearances had never looked anything other than certain of himself. This boy, though, big eyed and thoughtful, was something else. "You can always walk away," he said. His voice was soft. "I wouldn't stop you. None of us would. And none of us would think less of you for it either."

Feifei's shoulders slumped at last. "Oh, I know that too. That makes it worse." Her fingers itched toward the purse where she kept her compact, the same way Ning'er sometimes saw smokers' fingers itch toward their cigarettes. "But who else would keep the lot of you in one piece?"

Her attention flitted back toward Ning'er, who fought an instinctive urge to bolt. Being on the receiving end of Feifei's full attention felt very much like being a bug pinned to a corkboard by a scientist. An intimidatingly glamorous, judgmental scientist. "I don't suppose anyone's filled you in on the details of the job you're interviewing for?"

"The broad strokes," said Ning'er.

Zi'an's face lit up. "Oh? Then you know that Cheng Yun here has it in his head to solve a murder." His eyes glittered. "A regicide, to be precise."

"Zi'an," said Cheng Yun. A note of caution clung to his voice.

Zi'an shot an imploringly long-suffering glance at him. "Come on, you may as well tell her. It's pretty goddamn weird to ask someone to prison break a rebel leader and never actually tell them why. Besides, who in their right mind actually thinks the Huiming Emperor died of natural causes? Mysterious illness, my ass."

"Zi'an," repeated Cheng Yun, but this time it was less admonishment, more resigned sigh.

Ning'er frowned. "What does the old emperor's death have to do with the Lark?"

"Everything," said Zhenyi quietly. "I should know. I was there the day we all thought she died."

That got Ning'er's attention. She used to run with the Lark, Feifei had said, but the implication of that hadn't fully registered until this moment.

Zhenyi caught Ning'er's look and offered a thin smile. "Don't look so impressed, kid. Feifei may fancy me some romantic fallen general, but I'm no soldier—not a real one, anyway. If you're wondering how I survived the massacre, that's easy: I took the coward's route. At the first sound of gunfire, I ran like hell. I was a deserter."

"You were a kid," said Zi'an. His voice had gone quiet. "And terrified. You did what you had to to survive."

Zhenyi shrugged. "It doesn't really matter now. But what does matter is how the emperor died—how Huiming died." Her eyes had gone distant. "Half the ministers at court are in the pockets of Lilium. The biggest pharmaceutical company in the kingdom, the one that created the oxyveris drug—or as we commonly call it, Complacency. And one of Huiming's final acts as emperor was to propose new laws limiting the corps' ability to line the pockets of the influential. Is it any wonder a man in his twenties fell suddenly, mysteriously ill? Or that the ministers who were supported by Lilium were the same men who insisted on replacing the emperor with a toddler they can groom to their liking?" Zhenyi folded her hands before her, prosthetics glinting under the studio lights. "No one could prove anything. No one except Bailing."

Air froze in Ning'er's lungs. Corporate chokehold on the court was the worst-kept secret in Beijing. Still, the ministers whose pockets they lined might have been greedy, but they weren't stupid.

"They wouldn't have left a paper trail," Ning'er breathed out at last, disbelieving even now.

"They didn't think they did," corrected Zhenyi. "But Bailing kept closer tabs on Huiming's enemies than most." Her expression darkened. "Lilium is a pharmaceutical company. If anyone knows how to hide poison in a dead body, it's them. But you know what's a good deal harder to obfuscate? Money trails and supply chains. It was never any single shred of evidence that would have been damning on its own—it was what it all added up to—and Bailing collected it all. Phone recordings. Fiscal records. Even scrapped pharmacy reports they thought they'd gotten rid of. Why do you think she was willing to march on the First Ring with such confidence?" Zhenyi's smile was sad. "Why do you think we were all so willing to follow her?"

Ning'er swallowed. It was a lot to take in. The idea that Huming's own ministers had assassinated him was a popular rumor, but the idea that it could be substantiated—truly substantiated—was something else entirely. "Is that why you're all trying to rescue her now? Because you want to solve a homicide?"

"It's not about the murder," Cheng Yun cut in.

"Well, it's a little bit about the murder," Zi'an said dryly.

"It's about exposing the Lilium for who they really are," continued Cheng Yun. His face had taken on a strange cast, eyes wide and almost feral, staring past them all at something that wasn't there. Like he'd seen a ghost. "It's about finally being able to prove what everyone from the First Ring to the Sixth already knows: that we haven't been ruled by our own ministers in a long time. Not when they depend on cash flow from pharmaceutical executives to keep them in power." His mouth tightened. "That's why the Complacency epidemic happened. Why it's still happening. Why kill a good moneymaker?"

Ning'er's skin crawled. It didn't take much for her to feel it: the sense memory of Complacency thrumming through her veins, the terror and exhilaration. The desperate need for something that she saw mirrored in her father's eyes. "You can really prove all that?"

"We could," said Cheng Yun. "But the only person who's documented it all—who knows where the bodies are buried—is He Bailing." One of his fists clenched. "That's why they never killed her, you know. As long as she was alive, there was always a chance they could torture the location of the evidence out of her and have it destroyed."

Ning'er spoke without thinking: "How do you know they haven't already?"

The look Cheng Yun gave her was ghastly. She took a step back. He still had that unfocused expression in his eyes, like he was looking past her at someone or something else, but she still didn't like being the target of a face like that. "Because if they had," said Cheng Yun, "my father wouldn't still be spending every waking hour trying to hunt it down. As long as that information is out there—and they don't know where it is—it's a threat to their power. To his power."

"Okay," said Ning'er.

That glassy, unfocused look cleared from Cheng Yun's face. "Okay?"

"Yeah, okay," said Ning'er. She spread her hands. "A job's a job, right? Maybe you want to earn a quick handful of kuai. Or maybe you want to remake the kingdom. Either way, I get paid, right?"

Privately, Ning'er thought destabilizing the kingdom was probably a bit of a reach, secret evidence or no. But she couldn't lie to herself either: something inside her chest fluttered at the thought of seeing the Lark in the flesh, even just for a moment. The Sixth Ring girl who'd flown beyond the grimy confines of her birth. The Sixth Ring girl who'd nearly given Ning'er something akin to hope.

Besides, she really did need that cash.

"You only get paid if we hire you," Feifei pointed out, not unkindly.

"Fine." Ning'er folded her arms. "What do you want from me? References? A cover letter? Escaping another kidnapping attempt?"

"How about troubleshooting our plan, for starters?" Feifei's voice was cool. "Because here's what you'll be getting into if you're hired, thief. Twenty-four-seven boots-on-the-ground patrol, plus state-of-the-art cybertech sentry posts. Then there's the matter of the reinforced walls around the Lark's holding cell and the grid of laser-triggered alarms you'll have to make your way past. We'll have to account for other currently unknown variables within the lab—if they're willing to hold a teenager for years while faking her death, heaven knows what else they've got cooking in there. And that's not even getting into the kind of prison sentence you'd face for directly targeting a corporate facility with ties to the throne—"

"I do believe this is what your fellow medics refer to as an anxiety spiral," interrupted Zi'an, his voice light. "We've addressed most of those obstacles. Blueprints of the building, the placement of the sentries, even individual biographies of patrolmen on duty. Besides, it'll be on Duanwu. Everyone's going to be busy watching the dragon boat races and the emperor's annual tour of the Rings. The Brocade Guard and most of the major gendarme units are going to be diverted to protecting him. No one's going to be looking into an obscure corporate lab." His eyes narrowed. "We're not going to get caught, not if we're smart about it, and we're plenty smart. This will work. It's just a matter of—"

"Putting our lives and livelihoods on the line," said Feifei. "I know what an anxiety spiral is, Zi'an. That doesn't make the risk any less real. All I want is for everyone here to consider whether the reward is worth it."

"It is," said Zhenyi quietly. She held Feifei's gaze. "People forget that at the end of the day, the Lark—Bailing—is still just a girl. Still just another human being. All politics aside, that girl deserves her freedom. She deserves to live—really live. It's not right what the ministers have done to her, holding on to her like some museum relic all these years."

Feifei's ballerina-proud shoulders slumped a little, the protest gone out of her. "You're right, of course." Resignation hung dankly heavy in her voice. "I'm a medical student, after all. How could I show my face in class again if I turned my back on someone else's right to life?"

Zhenyi shrugged, relenting, and added, perfectly matter-of-fact, "Honestly, without you, Feifei, we'd probably all have been dead ages ago. Well, maybe not all of us. Definitely Zi'an, though. Probably Cheng Yun, too."

"Hey!" protested Zi'an.

"She's not wrong," said Cheng Yun. "Especially considering that she doubles as our fixer."

Ning'er frowned. "Fixer?"

Cheng Yun glanced at her. "Feifei's parents run a network of print shops—comes in handy for keeping alibis, cover stories, and aliases intact."

"Despite Cheng Yun's very best attempts to get his own extremely important alias blown sky-high," supplied Feifei, her voice dust-dry. She tapped him matter-of-factly on the chest with a manicured finger. "You're by far your own most valuable commodity, at least when it comes to the team you've assembled. The Young Marshal means something. It's a powerful position to have. You need to stop taking so many risks with it."

"Don't think of it as risking my alias," suggested Cheng Yun blandly. "Think of it as my steadfast faith in your fixing."

Feifei pinched the bridge of her nose, exhaling slowly. "I just don't see why you have to choose the riskiest, most violent possible solution," she said. "I've told you a million times. As the Young Marshal, with the power and reputation you've already amassed, you're already perfectly situated to change the shape of politics in Beijing. Play your cards right, and you'll outlive the old guard, and you'll certainly outlive your bastard of a father. You don't need to run around making grand gestures and tempting prison sentences." Her voice softened, near imperceptibly. "You don't even really need to be the Red Yaksha, not if you don't want to."

"Doesn't he?" Zi'an cut in. "The Beiyang clique have been in power since 1915. We've endured what, a century and a half now of watching the ministers puppeteer the Hongxian Emperor's descendants while claiming to serve whatever sorry, wide-eyed child is easiest to stick on that joke of a throne. They're too set in their ways. You can't fix a foundation that's rotten all the way to the core, and you certainly can't build on it. Besides, we don't have the time to spare." He spread his hands, striding out to the center of the room. "Look at the state of this city. Hell, look at the state of the whole damn kingdom. Natural disasters the ministers and nobles do fuck-all about, while they tithe the citizens who can least afford the tithe—"

Cheng Yun sighed in a way that suggested that this rant, too, was old hat. "Zi'an."

"You know I'm right!" insisted Zi'an. His cheeks flushed. "It would take what, years? Decades even?" He shook his head. "It'll be too late. You'll be stuck salvaging something that's way past saving. Better we act now, the sooner the better. I know Zhenyi agrees with me—"

"Zhenyi does not agree with you," said Zhenyi archly. She paused. "Well, actually, I do agree. But I don't know that breaking into a heavily guarded lab is a particularly intelligent course of action without an extremely airtight plan. Do we have an airtight plan?"

The others all jumped in at this point—to dissent from or defend Cheng Yun's potentially non-airtight plan or to debate Ning'er's qualifications, Ning'er had no idea anymore. She tuned them out, turning her attention instead to the drive Zi'an had dropped into her palm.

She'd always been good at troubleshooting.

She stuck the drive into her comms. As the schematics popped up on the screen, she began scrolling through them one by one, chewing on the solder line of one cybernetic thumb. It was probably bad for her teeth, gnawing at the metal like that, but it had turned into a thinker's habit.

It wasn't a bad plan, all things considered—it was, in fact, a lot smarter than any Ning'er would have expected a bunch of privileged university kids to come up with. But not a single one of them had cut their teeth on life in the Sixth Ring. That created certain blind spots.

"Hey," she said. "Has anyone had a second look at these schematics?"

No one heard her over the din of the ongoing argument. Or they just didn't care. Why would they? They hadn't even hired her yet. And even if they did, no one ever actually cared what the help had to say.

"Hey," Ning'er repeated. Maybe they didn't want to hear it, but she wasn't about to turn this gambit into an actual suicide mission. There were risks and then there were risks. Corpses didn't collect paychecks.

When no one responded, Ning'er sucked in a breath. She glanced around the room once to scope it out: Feifei and Zi'an appeared to be locked into a debate for the ages, standing close enough to kiss. Each time Zi'an spoke, sharp eyes glinting behind those glasses, Feifei's red mouth pursed so hard it looked like it hurt. Zhenyi looked to be playing referee, hovering near the two of them, murmuring at them both, one hand on Zi'an's elbow, the other on Feifei's shoulder.

Cheng Yun, meanwhile, hovered around the outskirts, occasionally interjecting in mild tones, but mostly leaving his crew to their own devices, like a parent who had given up on all control of their children. For one fleeting moment, he caught eye contact with Ning'er. Their gazes held for barely a split second, but it was enough time, amidst the cacophony, for him to raise his eyebrows at her like a challenge. She didn't doubt that the right word from him, carefully chosen and timed, would shut the rest of them up. He probably knew it too. And yet he made no move to quiet them. Instead, he just gave her that look.

What a pain in the ass this Red Yaksha was turning out to be.

Ning'er took a moment to gather herself. *Breathe in, breathe out. Your breath sustains you. Your breath sustains you even when nothing else does.*

Obedient to the memory, Ning'er drew her breath in through her diaphragm, and then bellowed, at the top of her lungs: "Hey! Assholes! Everyone shut the fuck up unless you want to get yourselves killed!"

It was actually pretty hilarious how quickly the argument simmered down. Ning'er looked up and down the room once more, at a now rapt—and slightly scandalized-looking—audience. Almost sheepishly, she held up her comm-link in one hand, Zi'an's chip in the other. "Feifei's right. Your plan has a problem," she informed them, returning to her normal indoor voice.

Feifei frowned at her, but the expression looked more thoughtful than accusatory. Her gaze darted between Ning'er's face and the chip, frown deepening. "With the risk factor involved, yes," she said slowly. "But everything on that chip should check out. I spot-checked all the data Cheng Yun gathered, and—"

"It's not the data that's the problem," said Ning'er. "And for what it's worth, I don't think it's your fault." She glanced around the room, trying to alleviate lingering traces of awkwardness over her existence being so suddenly remembered. "Any of your faults, really. There are just certain things you don't see."

Cheng Yun was also frowning now. "How—"

"It's because none of you are Sixth Ring." Now it was Ning'er's turn to raise her eyebrows at him. See how much he liked being the subject of judgmental inquiry. "That was your question, right? How I could possibly catch something you, the mighty Red Yaksha, missed?"

He had the good grace to look chastened at that.

"It's this one route you've picked." Ning'er pulled up one of the carefully drawn maps and hit the projector button on her comm-link. A hologram sprang to life. The quality was a little shaky—a cheap device was a cheap device, after all—but clear enough for the rest of them to see what she meant.

Ning'er pointed at the offending route with one metal finger. "You see that? That route's no good."

"No good?" Feifei echoed. Curiosity colored her voice. "It's perfect. What's wrong with it?" She squinted at the route. "It's an abandoned back route out of the main laboratory facilities. No cameras, no standardized security protocols."

"Exactly." Ning'er mimed tapping the hologram for emphasis. "Which means that every last street rat and beggar who's been tossed off their designated corner takes shelter there. The android patrols and gendarme may do their damned best to keep the streets free of undesirables, but the hungriest people tend to find a way. If we take that route, we'll evade the sentries posted on the property, sure. But we'll run straight into a whole other kind of trouble."

Feifei's head tilted. "Wouldn't the kind of folks stuck camping out in an abandoned tunnel love to stick it to a bunch of sentries even more than we do? You'd think they'd support the cause."

"Maybe," said Ning'er. "But not as much as they'd love to collect on the reward money they'd get for snitching. That's food—a good three square meals a day, even—for at least a month."

Feifei's mouth pursed again. When she opened it, her voice was quiet with concession. "I hadn't thought of that."

Ning'er shrugged. "Why would you?" She risked another glance around the room. "It's like I said. None of you have ever had reason to see it. That's not an admonishment, by the way," she added.

Feifei's head tilted, eyes narrowing a little, expression clinical. "Isn't it?"

Ning'er didn't rise to the bait. Instead, she sucked in another breath and tried that trick good public speakers had of catching eyes with everyone present in an audience. She didn't think she quite pulled it off—she wasn't the Lark, after all—but neither did the crew balk at her attention. "I know you guys are trying to hire a thief," she told them. "And you probably had some idea of what that meant: someone to get into tight spaces you can't fit into. Someone who can handle pressure and high stakes." She licked her lips, her mouth dry, pulse a steady thrum behind her ears. "Someone who wouldn't be afraid of doing what you asked of them. I can be all those things. I'll earn my cut, I promise. But I don't come from the same place you all do."

"I don't think that's fair," protested Feifei. "None of us here are Upper Ring except Cheng Yun—"

"And none of you are Sixth Ring, either," Ning'er interrupted. "None of you are the lowest of the low."

"I used to be," remarked Zhenyi without heat. "In a manner of speaking, of course."

Ning'er winced. A tendril of shame curled through her. Stupid. Zhenyi, of all people, would know—maybe worse than Ning'er—how it felt to go hungry. The farmer's daughter, whose life back home would have sustained itself on the whims of flood-water and failing crops. "I didn't mean—" Ning'er began.

"It's all right." And the way Zhenyi said it, she really did make it sound all right, none of the passive aggression Ning'er might have used. "But I think I understand what you're saying." She offered a wry smile. "There's a silver lining to people seeing you as a penniless country bumpkin or a girl from the gutter: some-times it means you see what they can't." Zhenyi gestured at the schematics with a glint of her prosthetic fingers. "Isn't that right?"

Ning'er swallowed. She'd been expecting a reprimand, not a defense. "I . . . yes. Thank you." Gathering herself, she eyed the rest of her audience. "I haven't worked with a crew before," she told them honestly. "Truth be told, I'm not really used to working with anyone. But I need the work, and you, presumably, need your Lark. So if you do hire me—and I know you haven't decided that yet—we're going to have to trust each other. Which means that when I say I see something that the rest of you don't, I'm going to need you to listen. Are we square with that?"

If they said no, she wasn't sure what she'd do next. She was in no position to bargain, really, not with this crew. As silence trickled into the room, doubt settled into her belly almost immediately. Who did she think she was? Why would denizens of the Fourth Ring, or even the Fifth, deign to square with a girl from the Sixth?

Then Cheng Yun spoke. "We're square."

He'd spoken so quietly. Still, Ning'er's head jerked toward him, and their gazes caught dead on.

"We barely know you," Feifei pointed out. She sounded so clinical, so practical, but a hint of real concern hung at the edges of her voice. "Trust is a precious commodity, and it takes time to learn. To ask for it now is . . . not unreasonable, but it's not the easiest thing in the world, either, given what's at stake. You're a stranger to us still." Her head bobbed, just once, almost apologetic. "I hope you can understand that."

Of course. Ning'er's shoulders wanted to slump. Why would they trust her the way she needed them to? Feifei could make all the excuses she wanted, but Ning'er had been a Sixth Ringer all her life. She knew how to read between the lines of what folks said, versus what they actually meant. She knew what Feifei must privately think: that Ning'er was no carefree college girl, no up-and-coming daughter of affluent merchants or bourgeois shopkeepers. Ning'er had never set foot in a university in her life, let alone one of their lecture halls or social justice clubs. She carried none of the ties that bound this crew. Maybe she didn't owe them shit, but they didn't owe her either.

She was ready to say as much when Cheng Yun spoke again. "If you can't trust her . . ." He paused, the first time she'd seen him look truly hesitant. Then he gathered himself. "Trust me, then," he said. A high priest, making an offering to his acolytes, or a prince to his people. "Trust me instead."

One by one, in real time, Ning'er watched their faces change. Each nodded once, quietly, a clear acknowledgment. Feifei was the last, but seeing her peers concede, she joined them, lowering her eyes. And just like that, the tide of the room turned.

Ning'er swallowed a strange bitterness. It should have been a relief, the sight of Cheng Yun's crew falling in line on her behalf. But it wasn't really on her behalf, was it? Not in her own right. She'd caught the way they looked at Cheng Yun, the way all of them—even Feifei, with all her reservations, even Zhenyi, presumably older and wiser than the rest—deferred to his judgment. The Red Yaksha, icon of the people, had found a band of peers who loved him. That much was obvious. She'd put on a mask and cloak and traipse around Beijing, too, if it won her this measure of unconditional love. And right now, their love for Cheng Yun was the one thing buying Ning'er—the hired thief, the gutter girl, the unknown element—the trust of these bright-eyed university students.

Zi'an grinned at her. "Well, lovely thief," he said. "It appears that congratulations are in order. The Red Yaksha has spoken. You're hired."

Ning'er made herself smile at them, accepting the boon for what it was. She had the good sense to be grateful. Even if it was just for crumbs at the table. Crumbs beat starvation. And if Ning'er ran this crew right, she'd be going to bed with a full belly for a very long time.

CHAPTER 5

Children of the Gutter

Ning'er may not have looked like it, but generally speaking, she was the kind of girl who planned her life carefully.

You had to be, to live in the Sixth Ring and survive. In a world build on uncertain foundations, small plans were how girls like Ning'er survived. You took control of what you could. Android raids, vindictive landlords, and shitty tippers at the dive bar where you carved out your rent? All outside of your control. Pinching pennies from day to day, saving what food you could, and of course, obsessively calculating the precise cost of the knockoff prosthetics your friend engineered for you? Well, it was something, at least. Ning'er even had spreadsheets on the console in her studio of the going rates for wares like Ge Rong's.

Ning'er had a plan for the days leading up to her job for Cheng Yun's crew, too. She would stay quiet, keep her distance, and continue, as best she could, life as usual. Sometimes, thieves who worked on crews tried to befriend their colleagues. It was a mistake, in Ning'er's opinion. Unprofessional at best, and a genuine risk at worst if things went wrong on the job. You didn't shit where you ate. Best to keep eyes on the prize, without the inevitable petty politics of the interpersonal interfering with anyone's performance.

Besides, the rest of the crew seemed to have the situation well in hand. As it turned out, Zhenyi, the girl with the phoenixes on her fingers, was quite the admin whiz. She'd kept spreadsheets of supply chains—the ones still in reasonably reliable operation, in any case—along with individual schedules, routes through the city, and estimated wait times at Ring gate checkpoints. Ning'er was impressed, despite herself, but Zhenyu's extreme competence also minimized Ning'er's own motivation to get heavily involved with the whole operation beyond what the crew explicitly requested of her.

So she remained polite but distant. It was all part of the plan. And the plan would have continued to go just fine if not for one Ke Zi'an.

The whole business began innocently enough: with actual work, rather than pleasure. Or so Zi'an had insisted when he'd proposed the idea to the rest of the crew.

"I'm telling you, my blasts won't work the way they should unless we go," he'd been saying when Ning'er walked into the meeting at the café, all of two minutes late and already irritated with the happy hour cleanup shift that had cost her the time. She'd been relieved to find only Zi'an and Feifei present.

The relief, as it turned out, would be short-lived.

Feifei, seated across from Zi'an, arched both brows, arms folded. "Your explosives won't work, unless we go to this . . . dingy dive bar."

If Zi'an was fazed by the flat disbelief in her tone, he didn't show it. "That's right," he told her cheerfully. "It'll be good for you, 宝贝. You can't live your entire life in laboratories or splurging on fine dining. We all have to leave our comfort zone eventually."

Feifei's cheeks colored, though her expression didn't shift. Ning'er was impressed. "We're planning a burglary, not a rager," Feifei informed Zi'an. "Surely you can acquire the supplies you need for your job somewhere else."

"Alas, no can do," Zi'an spread his palms, an exaggeratedly peaceable gesture, gaze imploring over the frames of his glasses. "The only bastard guaranteed to stock the chemicals I need is Pirate Yang, and the only way Pirate Yang will deign to see me is if I meet them on their turf over at Blue Star Brewpub. My hands are tied." He paused. "Possibly literally, if Pirate Yang turns out to be in a poor mood."

"Wait." Ning'er frowned. "You don't mean Blue Star Brewpub in the night life district of the Sixth Ring, do you? A couple blocks around the corner from Yu's Books?"

Zi'an's gaze flitted immediately toward her, sharp and quick as a bullet, before his features settled into the usual grin, gallant and inviting. "Why, Ning'er. This is quite the boon! Are you saying you know Pirate Yang?"

"I know a seedy bar called Blue Star Brewpub," Ning'er offered carefully. She paused. "Technically, I work there."

Zi'an, for his part, seemed delighted by this. "It's settled, then," he crowed. "We'll head there—"

"It is not settled," said Feifei and Ning'er at the same time. Startled, they exchanged glances.

Zi'an didn't quite pout but came remarkably close for a grown man. "Whyever not?"

"It's my workplace!" exclaimed Ning'er.

"And technically," Zi'an put in smoothly, "we are your colleagues. Just from a different job."

Feifei shook her head. "I still think there's got to be a better way to get your hands on your . . . ingredients than visiting a . . ." She trailed off awkwardly, glancing toward Ning'er. "Well, a . . . an establishment with . . . less than sparkling reviews, which I'm sure is no fault of the staff—"

Ning'er waved a forgiving hand. "Oh, it's a dump, there's no need to beat around that particular bush. A seedy dive bar is a seedy dive bar. If it were remotely respectable, they could afford to pay me more, and presumably I wouldn't be risking life and limb attempting a prison break." She leveled a stern look at Zi'an. "Nevertheless. It is my place of work. I can't go mixing jobs like this."

His expression softened almost imperceptibly. "It doesn't have to be like that," he said. "Work your shifts as usual. The rest of us will just be normal patrons, enjoying a Friday night drink among friends while I chat up Pirate Yang. Nothing wrong with having a good time with your buddies and chatting up one of the regulars." He paused. "But if it's a no, well, I suppose we'll figure out something else."

Ning'er hesitated. That was the thing. Zi'an, for all his swagger and rowdiness, always seemed to read her signals for what they were and respected the boundaries she'd set. It surprised her, actually, but some guys were like that: all brash charm on the outside, surprising emotional intelligence on the inside. He still flirted and winked at her, and threw around casual, easy physical affection like candy, but if she said no to dinner, or a teahouse social, or a night out with the rest of the crew, he didn't push, and he didn't generally ask a second time.

And right now, he was leaving a choice—a choice on which his own job hinged—in her hands. Waiting, unblinking behind the gleaming lenses of those ever-present glasses.

She looked away from that too-perceptive gaze. "Shouldn't we wait and ask Cheng Yun? He's the one calling the shots, right?"

"True," allowed Zi'an, "but I'm our detonation expert." He winked at her. "Cheng Yun is many things, control freak among them, but he's no micromanager. He'll let me call the shots on my own work, because he knows that I know it best."

Ning'er sucked in a breath carefully, considering her options. "Is there anyone you can get your supplies from besides this . . . Pirate Yang?"

Zi'an hummed. "Perhaps." Then in more serious tones, "I don't actually know." His gaze hardened. "I'd find a way if I had to, though."

She believed him, was the thing. If one of her patrons really did pay tips with black market money—which, honestly, Ning'er couldn't exactly throw stones at—then meeting at Blue Star Brewpub on Ning'er's shift was probably their best bet at getting their hands on the goods. No telling when another opportunity would come up.

Ning'er had rent due inside the month. She needed this job done sooner rather than later.

She huffed a sigh. "Well, then, I suppose Blue Star Brewpub it is. I'm closing this Friday night, which is also when we get the biggest crowd of regulars, so that's your best bet for catching your friend." She hesitated. "I'll cover you."

Which was really the beginning of the whole disaster.

Ning'er was disappointed, but not surprised, when Ge Rong turned down her invitation to the Blue Star Brewpub. She'd known it was a long shot. Still, her stomach twisted when she saw the carefully blank expression that slid across A'rong's features when she mentioned the word "bar." A'rong hadn't touched a drop of liquor since his art school days, when cocktails of Complacency and shitty baijiu had eventually driven him to drop out, so he still didn't trust himself there.

Which was all very well, but Ning'er never trusted herself much, either. She didn't begrudge A'rong his caution, but it was hard not to begrudge him its luxury.

So, when she went to work, she went alone.

The Blue Star Brewpub was housed in a repurposed warehouse that looked more like a dungeon from the outside, all grim gray industrial blocks. The only spot of brightness against the backdrop of the building was the shiny silver retina scanner where Ning'er scanned herself in. Music pounded out an off-kilter beat in the background. It was some shitty has-been band, but at least the Brewpub kept its speakers lower than most of the other bars in the area. Ning'er didn't relish bar conversations that inevitably devolved into nonconsensual screaming matches, all thanks to some irrepressible bass line. She doubted her new crewmates would, either.

Those crewmates arrived, exactly as Zi'an had planned, about an hour into Ning'er's shift, when the crowd was lively enough to give cover, but not yet at its thickest. Feifei had excused herself from their little escapade, citing an excess of coursework, though Ning'er suspected Feifei was really just trying to avoid a night on the town in one of the seediest parts of the Sixth Ring. Instead, Zi'an had arrived with Zhenyi—and remarkably, Cheng Yun himself—in tow.

Ning'er allowed herself a moment to appreciate the sight before her. Zi'an and Zhenyi made an almost ostentatiously glamorous pair. Zi'an's broad shoulders filled out a wine-red suit jacket, paired with gold-framed glasses with lightly crimson-shaded lenses, a combination that should have looked tacky, but instead somehow made him look charmingly confident in the sheer force of his own casual handsomeness. Zhenyi, floating in on his arm, was resplendent in silver-embroidered violet qipao that matched her hair, mechanical fingers glittering like rings in the low lights of the bar.

Beside the two of them, Cheng Yun should have looked unremarkable in his plain dark trousers and plain white shirt, sleeves cuffed above the forearms, no accessories—no mask or uniform or trappings of either the Red Yaksha or the Young Marshal—in sight. He was the friend in a group that you glanced past, to admire their more visually glamorous companions. And perhaps, had he been anyone other than Cheng Yun, that would have been the case. Yet even plain-clothed, Cheng Yun still drew the eye as he cut through the crowd, quietly shadowing his friends: the proud soldier-straight line of his back, the shadow of those long lashes on the sharp planes of his cheekbones, the way that full mouth of his curved upward at the corner, just a little, watching his friends' antics as Zi'an swanned through the bar with Zhenyi in his wake.

"Pirate Yang," crowed Zi'an, sidling up to a stout, beady-eyed patron in a bowling hat. Ning'er squinted. Bowling Hat had been in a few times, though they always kept to themselves.

"I told you not to call me that," said Bowling Hat in what had to be a habitual monotone. "I'm an experienced businessperson, not some misguided parrot owner with a failed sailing career."

Zi'an pouted, batting his eyes over the glinting golden frames of those ridiculous glasses. "Ah, but Pirate Yang has such a fine ring to it, and like a good pirate, you do procure the best-in-class goods, do you not?"

Ning'er might have imagined it, but she thought she saw the corner of Pirate Yang's mouth twitch. "For an equal exchange of favors? Always."

Zi'an paused, mid charm offensive, head cocking slightly to one side. "And by favors, you mean money, correct?"

Yang batted a dismissive hand at him. "Oh, I have money," they said, a statement Ning'er was instantly and wildly jealous of, as much for the blasé tone as the words themselves. "That's not what I need right now."

Zi'an's eyelashes dipped to half-mast. The charm offensive was back in full force. "Then what, 亲爱的, do you need?"

"Not what you're thinking, so cool your jets," drawled Yang. "This place never bothers to hire decent bouncers. And my personal security detail bailed on me last minute. What can I say? Good help is so hard to find in the Sixth Ring." Their gaze slid up and down Zi'an's physique. "You look like a nice, strong young man." The gaze flitted to Zhenyi, who received a similarly approving little smile. A startling expression, in truth, on such a resting bitch face. "And that's no delicate peach blossom you've got there either. The two of you will do nicely."

"For what, exactly?" asked Zhenyi.

"For filling in as amateur security for the night, of course," said Yang. Another wave of the hand. "Don't look so concerned. You can still enjoy the bar, the mingling, the drinks, even. Hell, hit up the dance floor for all I care. But this is what I ask." They tapped one bony finger against Zi'an's broad chest. "I get you your goods. And in exchange, you and your friends stay here, enjoying our generous hospitality until closing hour. And during that time, you keep an eye out for—and get rid of—any trouble you spot that might interrupt my . . . business." They tapped Zi'an a little harder, forceful enough to push him back slightly. "You dig me, 帅哥?"

Zi'an raised both hands, dramatically peaceable. "I dig, I

dig!" He chuckled, seemingly carefree, but Ning'er didn't miss that increasingly familiar glint in his eyes. "Though this is a suspiciously cheap price you're extracting, Pirate Yang."

"I can make it steeper if you persist with the ridiculous nicknames," said Yang sweetly. "Consider yourself lucky tonight, boy. You'll have the goods by the end of last call, provided that the bar's still in one piece."

Ning'er watched in rapt silence as Zi'an hesitated, murmured something to Zhenyi, then sketched a graceful little bow. "As you wish."

The two of them retreated, along with Cheng Yun, who'd been remarkably silent through the entire process. Ning'er watched them go, anxious for reasons she couldn't entirely place. Quietly, she sidled a bit closer to Yang. "You so sure that was a good idea?"

Yang eyed her sidelong. "Friends of yours?" They snorted. "Oh, don't look so surprised. I saw the way you watched me watching them. You know those guys." They smirked. "Or maybe the cute girl."

Ning'er went faintly red. "Not well."

Yang raised their hands. "Hey, I'm not asking for details. You're the one who was asking questions. I'm just fine keeping to myself."

Ning'er did raise a questioning brow at that. "You and your . . . secret pirate life."

Pirate Yang groaned. "Heavens, and here I thought the whole point of taking business meetings in this dive was not attracting too much curiosity from the help." They considered Ning'er with a calculating gaze. "Look, you don't rat out my business with them to your boss; I won't rat out whatever yours is. We cool?"

"As ice," said Ning'er, a bit surprised. Truth be told, she

doubted her boss would care. The owner of Blue Star lived some-where in a tacky Fourth Ring townhouse, putting on airs of des-perate, wishful proximity to the Upper Rings and telling anyone who would listen that he was an investor. That half his properties were cheap rentals in the Fifth and Sixth Rings, well, that didn't make for good cocktail talk. The bright side was that he rarely visited the actual premises.

Which, honestly, was probably how businesses like Pirate Yang's—and heaven knew how many other patrons—had flour-ished in silence right under their noses. Well, it wasn't like Ning'er was in any position to judge.

"Just tell me they'll be okay," said Ning'er tersely, unable to quite look Yang in the eye.

"Your fancy little friends?" Yang sounded surprised that Ning'er was even bothering to press the issue. "Oh, they'll be just fine." Then, a little more bitterly, "Their sort always are."

Ning'er glanced toward Yang carefully. That kind of state-ment could mean one of two things. A caustic dismissal of a more visibly privileged class, even fellow Lower Ringers. That much, Ning'er could understand. But Ning'er couldn't help but wonder if it wasn't also a veiled warning—or a threat. People were always more comfortable with putting others in danger if they assumed invincibility.

"Oy, barkeep!" A man on Ning'er's half of the bar banged his beer bottle repeatedly on the counter. "Are you earning your tips tonight or what? I said I wanted another Tsingtao!"

And just as quickly as it had come, Ning'er's train of con-templation was gone. She plastered a smile onto her face. "Right away, sir."

It went on that way for a while. Ning'er lost herself in the dull but familiar tempo of taking orders and mixing drinks. A gin and tonic here. A cheap bottle of cider there. More than half an hour in, she was barely even seeing faces anymore, just a dim chorus of ingredients, requests, numbers. The clink of Ning'er's metal hand against a shot glass, a wine glass, a tin of bottom-shelf whiskey.

"Excuse me, miss, I'd like to place an order."

"Sure thing," Ning'er called for the hundredth time that night, tossing a dish rag over her shoulder as she turned, other hand pressing stray, sticky tendrils of hair back from her face. "What will you—" She cut herself off abruptly.

Cheng Yun stood alone at the bar, hands stuck in his pockets. Even here—hell, maybe especially here—in his plain white shirt and cuffed sleeves, amidst the din and jeering of a dive bar, he somehow looked like a curious god, calmly and quietly making his way among mortals for the first time.

"—have," Ning'er finished faintly. She tugged the dish rag from her shoulder and began wiping down the counter for something to do with her hands as much as anything else. "What will you have?"

"You're the barkeep, aren't you? Surprise me."

Ning'er paused, one hand still reaching for a bottle of coffee liqueur that she really, really hoped had been properly refrigerated. At least the cream was still good. "Those are dangerous words."

"Maybe," said Cheng Yun. "But I'm going to need to get used to putting my life in your hands anyway." He shrugged. "May as well start now."

She studied him through narrow eyes. Cheng Yun met her gaze head-on, unfazed. Under the bar's dimly flickering lamps, he didn't look nearly so much like the Young Marshal. You didn't often see Beiyang poster boys half lit in a gloomy blue glow. It was unflattering on just about everyone, but on Cheng Yun, it just made him look like a particularly lovely, washed-out ghost.

For just a moment, staring into those big dark eyes, Ning'er could picture the Lark sitting in his place. She flinched immediately from the thought.

"You have a funny sense of humor, you know that?" she observed at last.

"Generous of you to notice his sense of humor at all," said Zi'an, materializing at Cheng Yun's back. Ning'er started. Zi'an, catching sight of this, grinned, clearly pleased with himself, and winked at her. "Fetch me a White Russian, will you, 宝儿?"

Ning'er pulled a face at him, but this was still her place of work, and he was still a customer. "One overpriced cocktail, coming right up."

"Much appreciated, my dear. Anyway." Zi'an clapped an arm around Cheng Yun's shoulders. "You know all those magazine interviews and puff pieces on the Young Marshal? You know, the ones that go on about how he must be a prodigy to achieve such heights at such a young age? They all want to know his secret sauce, when it's obvious to anyone who spends thirty minutes in his company: he has no work-life balance. It's always either duties to the emperor's throne or rebellion against the emperor's throne with this guy. Working that side hustling, two-job life."

"That makes two of us," deadpanned Ning'er.

Zi'an laughed. "Touché, touché." He whistled as she slid his White Russian down the counter. "Hot damn. You really do that just like a pro."

Ning'er flexed her metal hand. "I get a lot of practice."

"I believe you." His comm-link buzzed. He glanced down and

pulled a face of his own, sighing as he scrunched up his nose. "Zhenyi. It appears that our duty calls."

Cheng Yun frowned, half rising from his seat. "I should—"

Zi'an shoved him back down. "You should not," he said firmly, and with a surprising amount of seriousness. "Stay put, Cheng Yun. It's just a rowdy drunk—hardly a three-man job. Zhenyi and I will go earn our keep as good Lower Ringers do." He grinned, clearly meant to take the sting out of the joke. "You keep your Upper Ring ass safe on this side of the bar and look out for our darling thief here."

Before Cheng Yun could mount further protest, Zi'an sauntered off like a man on a mission.

This time, before Cheng Yun could rise to follow him, Ning'er caught hold of his wrist. "Don't."

His gaze flicked down to their joined hands, then back to her face, eyebrows raised. Face warm, Ning'er dropped it. "No one likes being micromanaged," she said, by way of explanation. She hesitated. "Is it true, by the way? Zi'an's take on your whole personality." Trying to find a way to stave off her own uncertainty around him, she began rummaging around behind the bar. What on earth would a guy like Cheng Yun want in his drink, and how could she achieve it without accidentally poisoning him? "Do you really only care about work and politics and nothing else?"

His answer was quiet and carefully light. "Is that what you think of me?" If she didn't know better, she'd have thought he sounded hurt and was trying to hide it.

She shook her head, more in frustration than denial. Her hands busied themselves with his drink. "You're like this stern, serious guy, so easy to lose behind the larger-than-life icons you play. Doesn't matter if it's the Red Yaksha or the Young Marshal."

A dash of lime spritzed up the tonic water she found. "Between the two of them, there's not really room for anyone else. Least of all a guy who's just . . . plain old Cheng Yun. But right now, you're not dressed up in masks and cloaks, and you're certainly not wearing a uniform. And unless I was very much mistaken, less than five minutes ago, you made an honest-to-goodness joke." She poured a hopefully nontoxic concoction into the cleanest glass she could find and slid it carefully across the bar toward him. "So, you tell me, Cheng Yun. What should I think of you?"

"I think that all depends." He leaned forward, elbows on the bar, chin balanced against crossed fingers. He hadn't yet touched the drink. "On what you want from me."

Well, at least he was asking the easy questions. "Money," said Ning'er promptly.

Cheng Yun sighed. "This from the girl who was hounding me for workaholism ten seconds ago. Is money truly all you care about?"

"Yes." Ning'er's answer was frank and immediate. "Why wouldn't it be? Should I long for some magical better world? For change?" She blew a raspberry. "Pass. Between money and social upheaval, I'll take the option that puts food in my belly, pays my bills, and saves me from homelessness."

He took a long, thoughtful sip from his cocktail before answering. "I'd think you'd want the option that takes homelessness off the table entirely. This cocktail is excellent, by the way."

"Practice. And our last decent bottle of tonic water." She tilted her head, staring openly at him. "You really do believe that's possible, don't you? A perfect world."

"Not a perfect one," he countered. He took another sip, smiling. "But a better one."

She continued to stare. "You really want to know what I think of you?"

"Mmm." He twirled the straw around the drink. "Please."

"I think you're the most dangerous fool I've ever met," said Ning'er. Her blood thrummed hot under her skin. She wished, momentarily, that she was the one drinking instead of him. A drink excused almost anything stupid you could say.

Heaven above, why did this boy make her so damn stupid?

Too late to backpedal now. "It's like I said before. You lack a sense of realism. You claim to want to build a better world for the downtrodden, but most of the downtrodden live here." Ning'er gestured as the gloomy, industrial expanse of the cheap bar. "In the Sixth Ring. You can't build a better world for people who have no interest in participating. Most of the people here, they're like me, hungry and cold and living from one paycheck to the next. You think you'll get them involved using, what, your fancy politics? Dream on."

"He Bailing did it."

The way he said the Lark's given name—that intimate caress of his voice, like he really knew her, like he'd truly loved and lost someone—sparked her blood hotter still. "The Lark was ours," she snapped, her voice rough and possessive. "No one ever wants to talk about where she really came from. Easier, I guess, to make up stories about fallen princesses or rebel students, but the Lark was a Sixth Ring girl. She belonged to the gutter, just like me, my father, and every other patron at this bar tonight. That was why we—why people from the Sixth Ring followed her." Ning'er's throat tightened. "She came from the same garbage place we did, so when she said she'd lead us out, we believed her. That's not something you can fake."

He didn't respond, stirring his straw into the drink and watching her with steady dark eyes. If she'd offended him by laying claim to the Lark, he didn't let on.

She shook her head. "All this nonsense about hope, and a better world, and the things you're willing to risk, when you have everything to lose? I don't get it. That you, literally the first-born son of Minister Cheng, of all people, would give up everything you have, just to—"

"Second-born son," he interrupted.

Ning'er stopped short. "What?"

"Second-born son." He took another swig of his drink.

She watched the knot in his throat bob as he swallowed. "I never hear anything about your older brother."

"That's because he's dead." The words were frankly spoken, heavy with the weight of a scarred-over grief. "My father never talks about it, so neither do the media."

Ning'er tried to find something to do with her hands, which felt abruptly clumsy without some task at hand. The crowd had trickled down to a slow night, which meant she didn't even have a real, work-related excuse to extract herself from a conversation that had pitched itself suddenly toward something dark and cold. "Was it political?" she asked quietly. Media outlets never reported assassinations as assassinations, per se, but everyone knew what it meant when someone—especially someone young and powerful and highly placed—died unexpectedly.

"It was a Complacency overdose, so who's to say? Happened one night at a Second Ring club." He must have caught the awful, pitying look on Ning'er's face, because he offered her a humorless smile in return. "As far as I know, no one set him up. Believe me, I've asked." Cheng Yun rubbed the heel of his palm over his temples, eyes fluttering shut briefly. Even under the bar's awful lighting, Ning'er caught the telltale hint of pink in his cheeks that told her he was less than sober. He was already halfway through his drink. "My brother was brilliant and charming and the apple of our father's eye, but he lived life on the wild side. It could have happened to anyone."

Unbidden, memories of Baba flashed through Ning'er's head. The way he'd been before Complacency. The way he was now. The man he might have become without it. Of all the fucked-up, tragic little things she thought she might share with Cheng Yun, this hadn't been it. "Could it?" she asked. "Have really happened to just anyone?"

Cheng Yun met her gaze, steady and sure and so terribly, quietly sad. Sadness hung strangely on a boy like him, dampening his natural warmth at the edges, dimming that ridiculous glow of optimism he so constantly exuded. "Not all tragedies are vehicles for beautiful life lessons or poignant inner meaning," he said, with a surprising lack of bitterness. "Sometimes, they just happen to you. Sometimes, they just break your heart."

He spoke too softly—and with too much clearly long-held resignation—for the words to be an admonishment, but Ning'er found herself flinching from them all the same. A telltale sting made its way to the back of her throat and behind her eyes. God, would he have shared any of this if he weren't just a little drunk? Why had she poured him so goddamn much alcohol? She opened a mouth, guilt-ridden and dry-tongued, to say something—what exactly? Words of comfort? An argument? A joke to take the edge off the tension?

The unpleasantly familiar sound of breaking glass shattered the moment. As one, Ning'er and Cheng Yun looked up. Zi'an and

Zhenyi were on the near side of the dance floor, closest to Ning'er's half of the bar, struggling with a clearly discontented drunk. The remains of a cheap glass glittered around his stumbling feet as Zi'an wrapped a companionable arm around the man's waist.

"Come along now," said Zhenyi, voice carrying even over the crappy music. She sounded like a remarkably patient schoolmarm. "I think you've had quite enough fun for one evening, wouldn't you agree?"

The man slurred something incomprehensible. Zi'an patted him sympathetically on the back. "We'll take that as a yes. Let's get you home."

Ning'er released a breath, relieved for reasons she didn't entirely understand, as they trundled the man out the door. It wasn't as if grouchy drunks were new here. Maybe it was just the fact that someone Ning'er knew, even just from a job—someone besides herself—had played witness. The whole business made her feel oddly exposed.

"Excuse me," she told Cheng Yun. She grabbed a mop and broom, raising one in each hand and shrugging her shoulders at him. "Duty calls."

The mess wasn't bad, thankfully. Any time Ning'er got stuck with cleanup duty, she counted her blessings when it was just your garden variety spill and not something involving vomit or actual human excrement. She'd taken care of the worst of it, and had returned from freshening up, when Zi'an arrived at her side—a little sweaty and out of breath, presumably from depositing his belligerent drunk safely outside the bar, but looking no worse for wear.

"There you are!" He spoke in the same confident tones he always did, but there was a sheepish undercurrent to his demeanor.

"Say, are you busy at the moment? Zhenyi and I are trying to earn our credit with Pirate Yang over there, but it doesn't seem right that you're stuck cleaning up after us in the process."

"That's surprisingly astute of you," drawled Ning'er, not entirely joking, and actually a little impressed despite herself.

He shrugged. "I may not be Sixth Ring. But then, I'm not Upper Ring, either, am I?"

Ning'er cracked a small smile at that. "I do have a break, as it so happens."

The music had changed, as though the automated DJ had also sensed the shift in mood upon the triumphant return of the bar's amateur bouncers. The generic, off-kilter rock beat shifted, slowing toward something with a more definable rhythm, clearly designed with club-floor dancers in mind.

Zi'an went with it, extending his hand with a flourish. "May I have this dance?"

Yes, she wanted to say. "I usually work through my break," she offered instead, embarrassed at what a killjoy this probably made her sound like. Then again, half the patrons had already gone home, and the usual late-night crowds weren't pouring in—no doubt pinching pennies because of earthquake-related wage cuts. After that initial clamor for drinks earlier in the night, Ning'er had barely seen any other customers besides Cheng Yun's crew. She hadn't even gotten any requests for second rounds. Normally, that would have been shitty news—fewer patrons meant fewer tips—but she'd been glad, for once, not to divide her attention. Not after the way Cheng Yun, red-cheeked with liquor, had talked about the Lark and his brother, and the little ways the pieces of a shattered heart collected themselves inside a body. She hated how easy it was for him to tug her attention toward him, even half drunk, even when he clearly wasn't really trying. She hated that he could almost make her care.

"All work and no play makes Ning'er a dull bird," sang Zi'an. His fingertips waggled, along with those expressive brows of his.

Oh, fuck it. On impulse, Ning'er took the proffered hand. "One dance," she warned him.

One dance was all he needed. Zi'an, ever gallant, spun her into a loose embrace with the kind of grace that came easily to men used to charming. His lead was easy to follow, the sort that made the follower look like a more accomplished dancer than she actually was. Ning'er positively flew across the floor with him, laughing despite herself, while Zhenyi whistled and clapped behind them.

One dance turned to two, then three. Zhenyi joined in after the second, good-naturedly twining her metal fingers through Ning'er's flesh hand. Another couple dances later, Zi'an shouted, "Switch!" Deftly, he spun Ning'er toward Zhenyi with one arm, capturing Zhenyi's own waist with the other. Ning'er stumbled over both their feet, apologies dissolving into helpless laughter as the three of them giggled over the mess they'd made, shoulders knocking together.

Through the throng of bodies, Ning'er caught Cheng Yun watching them all, his expression unreadable. He seemed to have sobered a little, the glass sitting near-empty beside him. That, in turn, sobered her.

Tamping down on adrenaline-fueled giddiness, she extracted herself from his friends and made her way toward him. "Hey. You good?"

He offered a wry smile. "I'm not a total lightweight, if that's what you're worried about. I've had some water. I'll be fine." His sight line flitted toward the figures on the dance floor.

Ning'er followed the look, unable to resist the urge to tease. He looked so wistful, watching his crew goof off like any other college student in the city. Then again, that's what they were. "What, not gonna join in on the fun, boss? What's the matter, two left feet?"

Cheng Yun shook his head, stirring the remains of his drink. It was mostly crushed ice at this point. "You should know," he said carefully, "Zi'an's very gallant, but also something of a ladies' man. He'd absolutely respect your boundaries, but I'll warn you now, if he's hitting on you, he might actually mean it."

Ning'er's gaze tracked Zi'an out on the dance floor. He had one of Zhenyi's hands caught between his palms. The mood lights spilled out across the breadth of his shoulders, the square-cut line of his jaw as he spun her, handsome head thrown back with laughter.

Ning'er's gaze returned to Cheng Yun's. She raised her eyebrows at him. "Am I supposed to find that upsetting?"

The high points of Cheng Yun's cheekbones pinked a shade of red visible even under the mood lights.

"Oh, relax." This was kind of adorable, actually. "Can you blame me for being intrigued? He's a lot hotter than most of the guys I pick up in here after work." Ning'er paused. "Even if he is, technically speaking, a crewmate." She wrinkled her nose. "On one hand, unprofessional. On the other hand, hot."

Cheng Yun didn't quite look scandalized, but his throat made the most remarkable sound. She grinned at the surprise flashing across his features. She liked him better scandalized than sad. She'd hated the way sadness looked on him, how it dimmed his light from inside out, hollowing him with darkness.

Straightening abruptly, she offered her hand to him with a

little bow, mimicking Zi'an as best she could. "Don't worry, boss. I have no plans to have my wicked way with your boy out there. But I would be honored if you'd grace me with a dance."

It was impulsive of her, like so much of what she'd done lately. For a fraught moment, as the proposition left her tongue, she regretted it. Risky enough that she spent so much time arguing politics with the guy responsible for paying her. Worse, probably, to push his buttons this way. Maybe he really did have two left feet. Maybe he hated dancing. Maybe he hated fun.

But, god, she'd do anything to keep him from looking so sad again.

The calluses on his hands startled her. She blinked, as he rose, catlike, from the bar stool. The corner of his mouth tipped upward, ever so slightly, as his eyebrows furrowed. It lent him a rakish look. "You're our host, technically," said Cheng Yun. His tone was neutral, carefully light. "I'd be a poor guest to refuse you."

Before she could entirely process that statement, he'd maneuvered her out to the center of the floor. It was different from the way Zi'an had moved her. He had that same smooth quality to his step, but the hand at her waist was lighter, his fingers barely touching her. Yet still she found herself following him instinctively, his touch somehow capable of command in even the barest slivers of movement. "Where on earth," she demanded as he spun her out, "did the Red Yaksha learn to dance?"

A quick tug reeled her back in. "Which answer do you want to hear?" He made space between them, capturing her spare hand—the metal one—with his other. Some men flinched away from prosthetics on a woman, even ones as nice as Ge Rong's handiwork, their hands hungry solely for human flesh. Others fetishized the metal, crooning fantasies in Ning'er's ear that made her want to deck them.

Cheng Yun did neither. Instead, he used them to pull her along into a complicated spin that left her embarrassingly short of breath.

While she sucked oxygen back into her lungs, he spoke to her. "Shall I tell you that I learned as the Young Marshal, on ballroom floors of the palace with foreign dignitaries, well-schooled by tutors my father paid for, the same way he paid for his place among all the luxurious, glittering wonder of the court?"

His speech was smooth, effortless. He must have been working even harder than she was to keep up the pace of their dance as the lead, yet he might as well have been carrying the conversation from an armchair. Ning'er wasn't sure whether to be annoyed or impressed.

Fleet-footed, he drew her across the dingy floor of the Blue Star Brewpub, maneuvering effortlessly around other dancers, his steps matching hers perfectly. Hell, she was barely keeping up. "Or would you prefer to hear that I learned on the floors of bars and clubs like these, anonymous and drunk on cheap beer, looking for an escape, same as everyone else? Would that make me more palatable?"

He dipped her. His arm, snaking across her back, caught her before she could turn it into a misstep. His head dipped low toward hers, eyes like black coals under those awful mood lights, face pale and drawn in sharp relief. For a strange, terrifying moment, he looked close enough to kiss. It was what all those boys Ning'er picked up after her shift would have done. The moment to seal the deal, to initiate another mindless, heartless night of easy fun.

Cheng Yun didn't kiss her. Instead, his lips dipped just past her jawline, against her ear, like he meant to whisper a secret. "I don't pretend to know everything about you," he said. His murmur was nothing more than a gentle rumble against her skin, barely audible above the music and noise of the bar, but it stopped the breath in her lungs. "I'll ask you, please, not to assume you know everything about me."

Before she could process that—much less articulate an adequate comeback—he'd tugged her back to her feet. Once she had her balance, his hands fell away from hers as he bowed. "Thank you for the dance, Ning'er."

Ning'er glanced around the floor, feeling awkward and exposed. Zi'an was preoccupied relaying some dramatic tale to Zhenyi, who stood laughing at his animated hand gestures, purple head thrown back, shining under the cheap glow of the bar's overhead lamps. It made her look years younger. Ning'er couldn't remember the last time she'd seen two people so clearly and utterly at ease with each other.

Once again, it put Ning'er on the outside. And that was okay, she told herself. It was what it was. "I'm not assuming I know everything about you," she said at last to Cheng Yun. "I'm just trying to know more than I do. It's not personal. I just . . . this is a big job. A dangerous one. I have to know the person I'm working for."

She swallowed hard. "I trust you because A'rong trusts you, and presumably, you trust me because he trusts me too, but at some point, can we really keep relying on him to play middleman?"

Cheng Yun's expression softened, even as his mouth took on a wry little tilt. "Fair. That probably counts as overtime, even for him."

Ning'er couldn't help it. She laughed.

The night should have ended there. Ning'er's shift was almost over. Zi'an and Zhenyi had survived their single altercation doing security duty for Pirate Yang, which meant Zi'an had earned his haul, fair and square. Hell, while they'd been busy with that, Ning'er had even managed to reach some sort of understanding with Cheng Yun. A productive evening all around. It would have been a good note to go home on.

In hindsight, Ning'er really should have known better than to think it could all be that simple.

She wasn't sure how it happened, exactly, or why it had to go and happen in this particularly ill-timed moment. All she knew was that one second, she'd been making a surprisingly graceful exit from Cheng Yun's embrace and the next, someone—decidedly not Cheng Yun—was muscling past her, all rough aggression.

"Pirate Yang!" the person howled. "Pirate Yang, you filthy cheating fuck, get your ass out here!"

Zi'an materialized—once again, seemingly out of nowhere, which he seemed to have a knack for—and raised a pair of placating hands. "Hey now, that's no way to go addressing an honest customer at a respectable establishment." Ning'er winced. As far as de-escalation efforts went, he could have done worse, but this was Zi'an. His shit-eating grin was doing him no favors either.

Their assailant seemed to agree with Ning'er. Barrel-chested, bald, and heavily tattooed, it didn't take much effort for him to crowd into Zi'an's space. "That's no concern of yours."

A second man, with near identical ink, crowded Zi'an from the other side. "That's right," he agreed. "We've got business here."

Zhenyi inserted herself smoothly into the mix. "And so do we."

Cheng Yun started forward. Ning'er's metal hand clamped

down on the crook of his elbow before she could think better of it. "Stay put. I'll handle this."

He turned toward her, eyebrows raised. "What happened to letting Zi'an and Zhenyi handle matters?"

"That was for a common case of dealing with the drunk and disorderly." Ning'er narrowed her eyes at the scene unfolding before her. "This is different." The tattooed men sizing up Zi'an and Zhenyi were clearly unhappy, but they looked stone-cold sober. Matching tats didn't always indicate gang affiliation, but it was a solid bet. That—combined with their apparent grudge against Pirate Yang—told Ning'er that they more than likely came from a savvier criminal element than your average bar brawler. Organized crime types weren't huge at Blue Star Brewpub, but they came by often enough that Ning'er had developed a sense of familiarity. And that familiarity told her that they'd have to tread cautiously here. Especially if Yang had already pissed these guys off.

"I'll be right back," she told Cheng Yun, and hoped to heaven she wasn't tempting fate. Her very best customer service smile in place, she swanned off toward the tattooed men.

"Excuse me." She approached the big bald one first, eyelashes at half-mast. "Can I help you, sir?"

He looked her up and down, appraising. Ning'er bore it with a weary sort of patience. She was used to this part, too—the customers who figured barkeeps were as much a part of the menu as the drinks they served. "Maybe after we deal with Pirate Yang."

"I'm afraid dealing with Pirate Yang is going to have to wait," said Ning'er. "I'm very sorry about that, but we're about to close. I'm sure Yang would be more than . . . delighted by your company during business hours."

The bald man's smaller companion laughed. "Nice try. But

we've already been cheated once by Yang. We won't be cheated twice, you understand."

"Like hell you won't," called Yang. Ning'er turned, startled, as Zi'an's supplier waded into the fray, mouth a long thin line, eyes like flint. "To set the record straight for the hundredth time, I never cheated either of you in the first place, you big stupid lugs, so quit spreading that rumor around. It's hurting business."

"You promised us means to make our own Complacency!" snarled the big man.

"And I delivered," put in Yang smoothly. "I gave you exactly what I said I would: the refined components of the fire blossoms that Complacency is made from, which, mind you, have value in their own right, so you're not being particularly grateful right now. It's not my fault that neither you—nor I, for that matter—know what else goes into that particular recipe."

"You implied—" began the small man, fists clenched.

"And you were stupid enough to believe," said Yang. Their eyes were hard. "Get out of this bar, both of you. Sell the powder I gave you and be happy with the earnings. You'll still turn a profit, and without bringing the wrath of the Beiyang ministers down on all our heads. Quit while you're ahead."

"Yang," Ning'er began, alarmed, but it was too late. The big man had already hurled himself at Pirate Yang.

Zhenyi intercepted him first. Jamming an elbow into his windpipe, she sent him reeling back toward Zi'an, who caught him tight around the waist in a bear hug and bore him to the ground with a crash. One knee pinned to the big man's belly, Zi'an turned his attentions toward the smaller man next, hands up. "There's still time for you to take Pirate Yang's advice, you know," he offered companionably.

In response, the smaller man picked up one of the empty beer bottles on a nearby table. He smashed the end on the table's edge and advanced on Zi'an, who raised his hands higher, eyes narrowed behind his glasses. "No? All right, then." He reached around his back, toward his belt.

They never had a chance to find out what, exactly, Zi'an had been concealing inside his belt. Something whistled through the air. The small man stumbled, once. Then his eyes rolled into the back of his head as he slumped unceremoniously to the barroom floor.

Zhenyi flipped the little dart gun between her hands a couple times. It was a pretty little thing, sparkly and silver and, Ning'er was quickly realizing, perfectly disguised as a decorative finger. "And yet again," Zhenyi observed, remarkably calmly, "even when they're not around, Ge Rong and Feifei save the day."

The bigger of their two assailants chose this moment to lurch upward against Zi'an's knee, snarling and trying to find his feet. Without so much as sighting her target, Zhenyi raised the dart gun and shot him, too. He slumped back to the floor.

She looked around at her rapt audience. "Relax. They're just pumped full of some garden variety paralytic that Feifei cooked up a while ago." She waved the dart gun in front of her face. "A'rong very kindly took the liberty of repurposing one of my prosthetics."

Zi'an, looking faintly shellshocked, but no worse for wear, rose cautiously to his feet. "To absent friends, then." In more serious tones, "Thank you, Zhenyi. Really." His gaze slid past her, toward Pirate Yang, and narrowed. "You knew they'd come for you tonight, didn't you?"

Yang blinked owlishly. "What, these two goons? You think I tie bells around the necks of every petty criminal element in the Sixth Ring?"

"Honestly, it wouldn't surprise me." Zi'an folded his arms. "But you're still alive, and the bar hasn't crumbled down around our ears. So how about those components, huh?"

Yang chuckled. "Under all the flirtation and swagger, you really are pure business, Zi'an. I like that about you." From beneath the bar, they extracted a plain black briefcase. "As promised," they said, passing it carefully into Zi'an's outstretched hands. "Never let it be said that I let an honest business partner down."

"Perish the thought," drawled Zi'an. He peeked under the lid of the briefcase. Evidently satisfied, he nodded once and clicked it closed. "I won't say it was a pleasure doing business with you, Pirate Yang, because . . . well, you know." He nodded vaguely in the direction of the unconscious bodies on the floor. "But I'm grateful for your wares, nonetheless. I trust you'll handle cleanup?"

Yang batted a hand at him. "Get out of here before curfew fucks you." They glanced toward Ning'er. "You too, barkeep. Looks like your boyfriend's already picked up the tab for all those drinks you served your friends."

"My—" Ning'er began indignantly.

"You're welcome," Cheng Yun interrupted smoothly.

"Gah!" Ning'er jumped. Immediately embarrassed, she tried to cover by grabbing the doorknob behind her, leaning against it in what she hoped was a casual pose. Not easy, given the way the knob jutted into the small of her back. Actually, that was pretty painful. Wincing, she edged herself sideways. "How long have you been standing there?"

"Long enough to ensure that everyone on this crew is still alive," said Cheng Yun dryly. "And paid for. I assume you don't want all those drinks you made to come out of your paycheck."

"Oh." Of course. Well, that was nice of him. "Right. Thank you?"

"It's nothing." And to a guy like Cheng Yun, Ning'er supposed it really was nothing. He looked past her, toward Zi'an and Zhenyi. "You guys go on ahead—take care of those and make sure they're stored safely. I'll walk our thief here home."

"Your thief can get herself home, thank you very much," Ning'er protested. "Really, I've walked home alone past three a.m. more times than you know. Sometimes across rooftops, even. As thieves do."

"Good, that makes two of us," said Cheng Yun, with the confidence that could only belong to a boy who moonlighted as the Red Yaksha. "So it should make the route easier." He offered her his arm with a gallantry Ning'er suspected he'd learned from Zi'an. "Shall we?"

Ning'er wanted to be annoyed. Or resigned. She definitely didn't want to be charmed. Still, when she took his arm, the firm and solid anchor of it, a bit of that giddy warmth from the dance floor seeped its way under her skin.

She really did, in moments like these, understand why the rest of his crew followed him the way they did. Why they loved him. All the loneliest, most embittered parts of the girl her father had abandoned—the one that lived at Ning'er's core—ached with understanding.

The Outer Rings after dark were, generally, no one's idea of a good time. The neighborhood around Blue Star Brewpub at this hour, though, was quiet, at least. Stepping out into the dark on the arm of the Red Yaksha, Ning'er felt a bit like a girl in a fairy tale. Or a ghost story. Hard to say which when it was still only just unfolding.

The small hours past midnight transformed the little streets around the nightlife district into their own world entirely. The

only source of light in the dark came from the yexiao carts, ped-
dling late-night snacks to drunk and weary denizens: bowls of beef
noodle soup and fresh kebabs sizzling on their sticks, hot porridge
spooned out into cartons. The carts charted out Ning'er's path
home like lanterns guiding travelers through an underworld, their
glow flickering against the inky black of a moonless night, trailed
by the long shadows of hungry patrons.

"It's freeing, isn't it?" remarked Cheng Yun abruptly.

Ning'er glanced up at him. "What do you mean?" She'd
released his arm, but he remained at her side, the bulk of him
still a solid anchor against the eerie after-hours world. He walked
straight-backed, hands in his pockets, gaze fixed resolutely ahead,
yet just as he had on the dance floor, somehow kept perfect pace
with her stride. Not an easy feat for a boy a solid six inches taller
than she was.

"Liminal space," said Cheng Yun. Then he paused and shook
his head. "Heavens, that sounded pretentious, didn't it? I just
meant, the way it feels to be just another person on some lonely
street, hours after midnight, but well before dawn. Completely
anonymous, completely untethered by expectation. Don't you
find it freeing?"

The words struck Ning'er with unexpected force. Of course.
Where else would either the Young Marshal or the Red Yaksha
find true anonymity, except after three a.m. in some unchartered
neighborhood in the bowels of the Sixth Ring? Where else would
he have the space just to be a boy called Cheng Yun and not a
figurehead at all?

It was a world apart from Ning'er's life. But she thought she
understood, at least a little.

"That's why I started stealing," she admitted. "That feeling you just described." It wasn't a confession she'd intended, but making it felt right. As they walked, she flexed the metal fingers of her prosthetic hand, opening and closing the fist. "At first, I told myself I was just scaling buildings and breaking into places to test myself. Riding a Complacency high, seeing if I could be as strong as I was before my father sold my limbs, and then make myself stronger still. After I proved I could, I told myself it was for the money. For the cash I could rake in, selling all the beautiful things that rich people left unattended."

She swallowed, risking a glance at Cheng Yun. He was still walking beside her, still staring straight ahead into the darkness without a word. Just listening to what she had to say. "Both were true," she told him. "And neither were true. I just wanted to feel like I had some power over my own damn life for once. And I could take that power by taking things from the people who had it. They never knew it was me. It didn't matter that it was me, which is maybe the only time in my life that being a Sixth Ring girl hasn't mattered at least a little." She chewed on her bottom lip, remembering the looks from the taitai at the café where she'd first met Cheng Yun's crew, before Zi'an had stepped in to rescue her. She hated needing a rescue. "A thief can be anyone. I could have been anyone, and it wouldn't have made a difference. At the end of the night, I had what used to be theirs. And, I don't know, it finally made me feel . . . it made me feel . . ."

"Free," said Cheng Yun softly. A single word, spoken into that dark space between the yexiao carts, the sleepy murmur of these neglected streets.

Ning'er wanted to object. Objection had become habitual, a jerk of the knee. Instead, she simply said, "Yeah. Free." She shook her head. "But lonely."

She could practically hear the question beneath his silence as his footsteps drifted subtly closer toward hers. "I don't have many people in my life," she told him. "I . . . it's hard to hang on to people outside of family out here, and mine left me a long time ago. So I learned to walk alone. Usually, it doesn't bother me." She shrugged. "Usually. But I'm only human."

"I don't think that's true."

Her temper flared. She sighed, reeling it in with some effort. "What, are you going to tell me how my own life is? I'm tired, Cheng Yun, I really am—"

"I should have been more specific," Cheng Yun interrupted. "I apologize. I just meant that . . . well. You do have family. You have Ge Rong."

She paused, caught by surprise. "That's different. He's not my blood."

"So?" Cheng Yun stopped walking. Slowly, he turned and looked at her—really looked. She took a step back, swept on some invisible current that accompanied the full force of that dark, unblinking gaze. He gave a harsh little chuckle. "If blood alone defines family, we're all in trouble."

Her heart fluttered as she looked up at him. The younger son of Minister Cheng, heir to a dead boy's unfulfilled legacy. Blood wouldn't be a boon to him, would it? Blood would be a curse.

"You have a family, too," she pointed out. "Not one by blood. But Zi'an, Feifei, Zhenyi . . . even Ge Rong. I've seen the way they look at you."

"They look at me the way good soldiers look at a leader they respect," said Cheng Yun. "Believe me, I've been in the gendarme long enough to know. The way Ge Rong sees you is different. He wouldn't have bent over backward to get you into my crew otherwise. He really does love you, you know, even if you make him crazy sometimes. As well as he'd love any sibling." Cheng Yun's voice, usually so certain, so perfect, faltered, just for a moment, and Ning'er thought again of the brother the Young Marshal used to have. The lost apple of Minister Cheng's eye. The small, senseless tragedies that would break your heart without rhyme or reason.

Would the elder Cheng boy have loved his little brother, had he lived? Or would he have simply been another obstacle in the Red Yaksha's crusade against tyranny, more family turned enemy, a tragedy of a different sort? A more bitter, complicated way to break a heart?

No one would ever know, least of all Cheng Yun. No wonder Cheng Yun, playing the Red Yaksha, had sought out the love of denizens from the darkest underbelly of Beijing. No wonder they gave it to him so freely. Ning'er couldn't honestly say who'd be worse starved for affection: the hungry orphans of the Lower Rings or the second son of an Upper Ring family, haunted by a ghost who'd left him alone in their father's big empty house.

Her shoulder knocked into his. As she stumbled, his hand snaked out to steady her elbow. "Thanks," said Ning'er gruffly. "Truly." She wasn't talking about his hand at her elbow. And from the way a smile flashed over his lips, he knew it too. Why was her throat tight? He really was just a boy, like so many others she'd taken home for cheap comforts in the absence of steadier company. Just another misguided, big-hearted boy.

They were nearing her apartment now. She hazarded a glance at him from beneath her lashes. Studying Cheng Yun in this moment, the stark play of shadows over those fine features, the slight quiver of the full mouth and soft edges to those blazing dark eyes, Ning'er thought she understood him a little better.

"Come up for a cup of tea," she offered. "It'll sober you up."

That was bullshit, and they both knew it. He'd sobered hours ago. But he smiled a bit and inclined his head just the same. "All right."

She regretted the impulse behind the invitation, just a little, when she flicked the lights of her studio on. More a closet than a studio, really, and one she barely had the time to clean properly, despite its bare-bones furnishings. She took the sorry sight in with a single sweeping glance: one bed, one monitor, and truly god-awful lighting. She could imagine how it would look to a Second Ring boy. "Before you say anything, I know the place looks like garbage," she began. "I got a discount from the asshole landlord for taking a smaller room with only one window and next to no sun, but Ge Rong helped me install bioluminescent lights to make up for it, so it's really not so bad, plus the monitor actually supports some half-decent gaming systems, which is cool—"

"It looks like my dad's place," Cheng Yun interrupted.

Ning'er couldn't have possibly heard that right. "Excuse me?"

"Sorry, I should have specified. Not the current house. The place he grew up in. When he was a kid." Cheng Yun ducked his head a little as he followed Ning'er into the studio. He had about half a foot on her; the low plaster ceilings of her little broom closet suited her just fine, but he had to be careful not to whack his head. "He used to tell stories."

Ning'er snorted. "So it's not all bullshit after all? Those stories that Minister Cheng's exam scores saved him from a life of destitution in the Lower Rings," she clarified.

"The Sixth Ring, to be precise." Cheng Yun's gaze on hers was steady, almost defiant. "Does that surprise you?"

"Honestly? Well, yeah." Ning'er had grown up on tales of Minister Cheng's bootstrapping, but that didn't mean she could square with it. She could see him in her head so easily: that dimple-grinned, honey-voiced man on all the TV screens, the one who seemed to have the entire court wrapped around his little finger. The idea of a man like that spending a day of his life anywhere but the lap of luxury simply didn't click.

Cheng Yun gave a dark little chuckle. "You'd be shocked at the things my father was willing to do in exchange for a life in the Upper Rings. Or maybe not. I wouldn't know, would I? I grew up in the Upper Rings. I never had to second-guess my lot in life, the same way he did." Cheng Yun shook his head slowly, his face thoughtful. A little sad, maybe. "A'ye can put on all the airs he likes, but once upon a time, he was—to borrow your pejorative— as much a child of the gutter as you."

Like the Lark had been. "How did he get out?" Ning'er hated how hungry she sounded, asking something like that about Minister Cheng, of all people. "Was it really because of the civil service exams?"

Cheng Yun sat down on one of the two stools by her bed, arranging his long limbs awkwardly around the creaking joints of the furniture. "Easy answer? Yes. My father was always a good test taker when he put his mind to it." The corner of his mouth tilted upward. "The more complicated one, though? I suppose you could call it friends in high places. A'ye always just called it a scholarship."

Ning'er frowned. "Scholarship?"

Cheng Yun sighed. "The Beiyang ministers have always made a grand show of being a meritocracy because technically, anyone can sit the exams, and anyone who scores well enough can enter their ranks." He shook his head. "But they'd need tutors, exam guides, or at least a working library or study room. And kids like my dad needed money to pay their way for all those things. And who better to offer their charity than a wealthy corporation?" He smiled unpleasantly. "And guess which corporation provides the most generous scholarships to hungry kids from the Lower Rings vying for positions at court?"

Ning'er closed her eyes. "Lilium Corp."

"Got it in one." Cheng Yun gave a raspy little chuckle. "A'ye grew up convinced that the only way to keep himself comfortable and his family safe was to toe the line. When the Lilium executives ask him to jump, he'd ask how high. He did all the right things: voted for the laws they wanted, pushed for the appointments they favored. Even married my mother because they wanted him to keep up appearances. Not that she bothered sticking around once she gave him a couple sons. The heir and the spare." He paused. "Though A'wei never did like me calling myself the spare. Said it was cruel to diminish myself that way, and that making a habit of cruelty, especially toward yourself, never boded well for how you'd treat others." Another pause. "My fathered adored A'wei. Everyone did."

"A'wei," Ning'er began softly.

"My brother. Cheng Wei." He said his brother's name hurriedly, quietly, like someone accustomed to bulldozing his way over the memory. Your own grief, in so many ways, just another obstacle to efficiency. "He always . . . Cheng Wei and A'ye, they understood each other. Better than I understood either of them, maybe, but I think that's because A'wei understood everyone he ever met. They had this way about them, when the two of them were in the same room." Cheng Yun's voice had gone dreamy, distant. "It never mattered how rotten of a mood our father was in. A'wei always knew how to make him laugh." He paused, then looked Ning'er in the eye. "Please try to understand. My father's not a bad man."

"Uh," said Ning'er awkwardly. What exactly was she supposed to say to that? Minister Cheng was, well, very much a bad man. Even if he wasn't, by all appearances, a pretty shitty dad, there was the matter of the crackdowns he ordered, the way he kept neighborhoods like Ning'er's running thick with android patrols programmed to care more about money than people. And for what? To pay a debt to Lilium Corp? To keep his precious position at the imperial court while Complacency executives pulled on his puppet strings like he was just another child emperor they could manipulate at will?

Ning'er looked at Cheng Yun, opened her mouth, and closed it again. How stupid, the way a pair of big earnest, long-lashed eyes could freeze your tongue.

Cheng Yun, to his credit, seemed to guess what Ning'er was thinking. The corner of his mouth tipped up self-deprecatingly. "I should rephrase," he said. "My father wasn't . . .well, he used to be different."

"When your brother was alive," said Ning'er quietly.

Cheng Yun inclined his head. "My father still did awful things," he said bluntly. "But he seemed . . . I thought . . ." He trailed off, shaking his head. "People are not the sum of the worst things we've ever done," he said at last. "And for a while, back when A'wei was around, A'ye seemed like the sort of man who understood that, who wanted to be . . . who could be better than he was. Does that make sense?"

Ning'er swallowed a sudden and ridiculous lump in her

throat. It did make sense, most of all to her. It made more sense than she wanted it to. "I had . . . have . . . a baba like that too," she told him. "One who used to be a different person, and then . . . then wasn't."

Cheng Yun's gaze softened on her. Ning'er looked away, blinking rapidly. She'd learned to bear the force of the Young Marshal's regard—his intensity, his dedication, his convictions, but she thought his kindness, concentrated on her, might undo the fragile thing growing between them entirely. She cleared her throat. "When did things change? For you and your father, I mean."

She'd expected him to say something about his brother's death. Instead, his answer was prompt and unexpected. "When I met He Bailing."

Of course. Ning'er closed her eyes. "The Lark."

"The Lark," Cheng Yun agreed. Ning'er's eyes fluttered open. She didn't even know if Cheng Yun did it on purpose, speaking that name like a prayer, no matter how many times he said it, like taking a god's or a lover's name in vain. "I was in the youth branch of the gendarme—A'ye got me started early. And there was a time when I'd have done anything to help him. I thought that even—even after A'wei died, maybe if I worked hard enough, did well enough, forged myself into the perfect soldier, maybe that would be enough. Maybe I could make A'ye happy, too." Some unknowable sentiment flickered through those dark, expressive eyes. "After a few years, I think both my father and I gave up on that particular notion."

He didn't tell Ning'er how he'd come to his conclusions, which left her a nasty amount of room to guess at the answer.

Her metal fingers tightened into a fist. "I'll put the kettle on," she said quietly. "Keep going."

Cheng Yun shook his head, freeing himself of the memory. "Anyway, I—freshly thirteen—had been tasked with keeping the peace at one of the Lark's rallies." His mouth twitched. "My orders were pretty clear. I wasn't supposed to be paying attention to whatever Bailing was saying, and I certainly wasn't supposed to be considering the possibility that any of it might be true."

Ning'er set the teacups between them on the rickety stool and began to pour. "So that was how you were radicalized. By being incredibly bad at following instructions."

His laugh was sudden and bright. "That's one way of putting it, isn't it? I guess that's the difference between my father and me. He always did as he was told." He sobered again. "And for a boy who wanted out of the Sixth Ring, I guess it paid off. At a cost, as in all things."

A shudder ran through Ning'er, like the first shock of Complacency that had ever hit her system. How it had felt to fly across the rooftops of Fourth and Third and Second Ring buildings and wonder how it might feel simply never to return to the Sixth. She hated that she might understand, just a little, how Cheng Yun's father had felt as a young man.

Sipping her tea, she studied Cheng Yun—so out of place in her shitty apartment—for a long moment. She tried to picture Cheng Yun and his family—his doomed socialite brother, his minister father—as Sixth Ring men. The picture wouldn't come together in her head. Upper Ringers simply had an air about them that she couldn't imagine the Cheng family without.

Then again, Ning'er was a thief. Only so many stones could be cast from behind the walls of a glass house.

A loud buzz from the clock above her monitor startled them both. "Shit," muttered Ning'er.

Cheng Yun blinked owlishly at her over his tea. "What's the matter?"

"Curfew." Ning'er rubbed the spot between her eyes. How could she be so stupid? "I set the alarm every night to remind me of when the damned android patrols are gonna be out and about in the neighborhood. I, uh, don't usually have to worry about house guests." She colored slightly. "At least, not Upper Ring house guests."

His cheeks went pink. "For what it's worth, I wasn't expecting to get stuck in the Sixth Ring after curfew, either."

"I'm sorry," said Ning'er, and really meant it. "I should have thought of what it would mean, inviting you up here so late. You should stay the night. You can take the bed; the floor's honestly not so bad; I've slept in worse—"

"Ning'er," said Cheng Yun, in very patiently amused tones. "With respect, I'm not going to banish you to the floor of your own apartment."

"I invited you in!" Ning'er protested.

His head inclined. "And I accepted your invitation. Don't put that on yourself. I'll sleep on the floor."

Ning'er's cheeks warmed. "You're a guest, though. And my boss. Technically."

He raised his eyebrows at her. "Which means you should acquiesce when I request the floor, should you not?"

She opened her mouth, then closed it again, silently outraged at the entire situation. There was, of course, a completely reasonable compromise here. An odd heat had filled the scant space between them in her little shoebox of a flat, which left her about 90 percent certain that they were, at this point, playing Awkward Sleeping Arrangements Chicken. She looked at Cheng Yun, with his soft eyes and the faintest trace of color high on his cheeks. She looked at the floor. Finally, she looked at her bed. Internally, she cursed.

Ning'er stood abruptly, her mind made up. "This is stupid," she announced. She grabbed a spare blanket—threadbare, but enough in a pinch—from the cubby beneath the bed and tossed it atop the mattress. "Neither of us should have to sleep on the floor when the bed can fit two people adequately." Very carefully, she avoided eye contract. "It'll be a little cramped, but it's better than no bed at all."

She couldn't bring herself to turn around and face him. Instead, she busied her hands with smoothing out the extra blanket, as if it was a totally sensible and normal thing to invite your boss to sleep in your bed after the curfew alarm rang. Just a casual courtesy, and not something that could be read into in a weird way.

Heaven above, the last thing she needed was for him to read into it in a weird way. Or worse, think that she was reading into it in a weird way.

"Are you sure?" he asked at last. She still hadn't turned around, so she couldn't see the look on his face, but she heard a little hitch in his voice as he spoke. Fucking fantastic. "I wouldn't want to—I mean—"

"Look," she blurted out, turning to face him at last, "I promise not to grope you in my sleep so long as you don't grope me. Deal?"

He stared at her, pink cheeked. She stared back at him, no doubt even redder, despite her best efforts. She regretted the words as soon as they left her tongue. Frantic, and trying not to look frantic, she searched his face. That full mouth was slightly parted, his eyes wide. Horribly, it occurred to Ning'er that she didn't actually know anything about the Young Marshal's sexual or romantic history. She'd always assumed that the angel-faced darling of the gendarme would have his pick of other hot young things to tumble as he entered adolescence, yet here he was in her apartment, blushing like a virgin on his wedding night at the faintest allusion to sex.

Then again, Ning'er—who had decidedly tumbled her share of lovers from age fifteen onward—wasn't exactly looking especially suave herself in this moment. Maybe she'd misread him this entire time. Maybe he found her so repulsive that even the mention of sharing a bed had traumatized him, and now he was going to fire her on top of everything else. Maybe the cheap floor would cave in beneath them and they'd die in the untimely demise of her apartment building, sparing them from further interaction.

Then, quite abruptly, he shook his head and miraculously laughed again. It was a small one this time, really more of a chuckle, and seemed to surprise him as much as it surprised her. Still, the tension between them loosened, just a little. "All right," he said. "Mutually assured lack of groping. You have yourself a deal."

Ning'er blinked and swallowed. "Right, then," she said, gathering herself. Clearing her throat, she gestured to the bed with an awkward little flourish, like she was a maître d' showing a customer through a restaurant door, or something equally terrible. "Shall we?"

Amazing, she thought glumly, *that I ever got laid in my entire life.*

It took them a moment to settle comfortably beside each other on the mattress. Ning'er held herself a little too still as his weight shifted into place at her back. He'd wrapped himself in the spare blanket, turning to face the opposite direction, and given her a modest couple inches of space between their spines. Chaste and careful, a world of difference from all those boys she'd brought home. They'd been all winding limbs and eager mouths, as desperate and hungry to consume her as she had been to consume them. Nothing like the boy curled neatly at her side now, trying to give her the lion's share of the narrow mattress.

She wasn't used to being offered space, not when there was so little to share in the first place.

Still, a small bed was a small bed. Across those two inches between them, she could still feel the warmth of him. Every sigh and shift of his body, the rolling creak of the mattress springs, ghosted across the periphery of her awareness.

Had Cheng Yun ever brought companions home to his own bed? Against her will, Ning'er's mind wandered to the bedroom in his father's Second Ring mansion, no doubt three times the size of her entire apartment. Once again, she thought of the lovers that might have been available to the famously beautiful Young Marshal: girls with perfect faces and ample, well-fed figures like Feifei, or lithely built, broad-shouldered young men like Zi'an. Scions of Upper Ring families with expensively maintained wardrobes, skin care, haircuts, and coffers of money and opportunity to offer.

"Ning'er?" Cheng Yun's voice was soft, slightly muffled in her spare pillow, but it startled her all the same. She thought he'd drifted off already.

"What's up?"

"Have you done this before?" Was that embarrassment she heard in his voice? Was Cheng Yun, Young Marshal and Red Yaksha, the boy who wore two masks and lived to tell the tale, actually embarrassed? "Shared a bed with someone else, I mean."

She rolled over to face him, too surprised by the frankness

of the question to avoid it. "Sure," she said. "I'm guessing you haven't?"

She couldn't tell if he was blushing in the dark, but she'd have put her money on it. "I haven't really . . . made the time. To meet people."

Ning'er felt the corners of her mouth twitch. "Heaven above. So, Zi'an was right about you. You really are married to the mask." She hummed thoughtfully. "Not for a lack of girls throwing themselves at you, I'll bet. And boys. People in general, really."

His embarrassed silence told her everything she needed to know. Her grin widened of its own accord. "Well, gee, boss." Emboldened, she knocked her knee lightly against his under the covers. "Why didn't you ever take any of them up on it? No one pretty enough for your standards?"

"It wasn't that," he said softly. "I had some . . . good opportunities, I guess. My father would have encouraged it. It's good for the family image, I guess, being associated with old money. It just never seemed right to me."

That piqued Ning'er's attention. "Because of your father?"

He shook his head minutely, rustling the pillow. "Because of me." He paused. "Anyone close to me would think they were getting the Young Marshal, or maybe the Red Yaksha, but none of them would have gotten both, much less plain me." He offered a sardonic, fleeting smile.

Ning'er winced. "Fair. Rough break, though."

He laughed quietly. "You get used to it."

"You shouldn't have to."

His eyebrows climbed. Ning'er's heart gave a jolt, as she realized, belatedly, how that must have sounded. Great. All she needed was for Cheng Yun to think she was propositioning him. She most

definitively wasn't. Sure, he was stunningly beautiful and photo-
genic and had been a marvelous dancer. Sure, he was here in her
bed, knocking his shins against hers under the covers, wide-eyed
and softspoken beside her here in the dark. Sure, maybe in another
time, in another place, if she'd seen a boy like him leaning across
the bar, perhaps she would have offered him a sly little smile, told
him with a wink that his drink was on her, and—

"Thank you," said Cheng Yun abruptly.

Ning'er propped her head up on her own pillow. They were
nearly nose to nose, but it was harder to read his expression in the
dark. "For?"

"Letting me stay here with you. Letting me . . . share space
with you." He ducked his head against the pillow. "It's new for me,
being around someone this way. I like it. Being with you."

Ning'er swallowed. He hadn't looked away from her. Even
between the layers of blankets, his warmth was tangible, the
weight of him in her bed, close as any lover she'd ever had. They
were at a fork in the road. She could sense it in the electricity
filling the scant air between them, could swear he sensed it too.
Did she know which way she wanted to turn? Hell, did he? She
stared at the spill of his hair on her pillow, his slightly parted lips,
and those goddamn eyes of his, soft and dark and enormous. Want
tugged at her, intangible and hungry and replete with a strange,
desperate, and deeply ill-advised yearning.

Then, with an effort, she knocked her foot against his again,
casual and friendly, insulated by the bedcovers. "Thank me when
we rescue the Lark," said Ning'er. She yawned, careful and delib-
erate. "By paying me."

She swore she heard him laugh, quiet and startled and perhaps just a little delighted, as she finally drifted off toward sleep.

CHAPTER 6

A Wrench in the Machinery

Cheng Yun was gone when she woke up.

She didn't notice immediately. The last she remembered was falling asleep with him warm against her back, the steady beat of his pulse somewhere against her shoulder. Her legs had been a little cramped, partially entangled with his in the narrow bed, but it wasn't anything she couldn't get used to.

Her first clue that she was alone in bed was the luxurious stretch in her knees when she rolled over. Her eyes opened. The bed was warm where he'd been. She sat up on her elbows, groggy eyed. No trace of Cheng Yun anywhere in the apartment.

Well, at least in that respect, he wasn't so different from her actual one-night stands from Blue Star Brewpub.

As if in answer, her comm-link beeped at her from beside the bed. Ning'er fumbled around until she switched it on. The text from Cheng Yun blinked at her from the screen in blocky letters: More protests. Emergency work detail calls. I'll contact you when it's safe. At the very end: P.S. Thank you again. Stay safe. Things are going to get bad for a while.

Protests. Ning'er's heart hammered against her ribcage. She'd thought the worst of them were over. Apparently, she'd thought wrong.

Her comm-link buzzed again, loud and insistent. Ning'er scrambled to pick up. "Cheng Yun?"

"Who the fuck are you talking about?" demanded a stony voice at the other end of the line. Ning'er winced. She didn't often speak directly to the Blue Star Brewpub's manager, but it was impossible to mistake his voice. No one else in her life sounded that pissed off that frequently. "Never mind, I don't care. I'm calling to tell you that we're letting you go."

Ning'er's insides turned to ice. "What? Why?"

"Why the hell do you think? The bar's gone, girlie."

"What do you mean, gone?"

"I mean gone, gone. The fucking rioters have trashed the place."

This couldn't be happening. Ning'er ran a hand through her hair, clutching at the ends. "What about repairs? Insurance?"

Raucous laughter greeted this suggestion. "Who do you think I am, the emperor? I'm not made of money, kiddo. We gotta cut our losses while we can."

"Then pay me severance," Ning'er blurted out. "I need that last paycheck."

"And I already told you, I'm not made of money."

"But you owe—"

"I don't owe shit for work that hasn't been done, and now that I don't have a bar and you don't have a workplace, that work's not going to be done, is it?"

"Please." The edges of Ning'er's vision were starting to blur. "My rent—"

"Is not my problem. Goodbye, Zhong Ning'er." And with that, the line went dead.

"Fuck," said Ning'er to the empty dial tone. She double-checked the yellowing wall calendar above her monitor. Sure enough, three angry red circles marked the date: her rent payment, due a solid two weeks before Duanwu. Even with a paycheck from Blue Star Brewpub, she'd come up short. Now, without even that meager sum of money to rely on, she'd be worse than short on rent. She'd have to start rationing her food after a week if she didn't do something drastic. Which left her with three options:

One. Start preparing for eviction. Undesirable, for obvious reasons.

Two. Ask Cheng Yun for a handout. Even less desirable.

Three. Sell her prosthetics again.

"Fuck," Ning'er repeated, and slouched over to her monitor. It didn't take her long to ferret out what she was looking for. In certain industries, everyone knew everyone. She copied the information to her comm-link before she could think better of making the call.

"Hello?"

Ning'er closed her eyes for a long moment. "My name is Zhong Ning'er. I work—I used to work for the Blue Star Brewpub. We met last night."

A huff of recognition on the other end of the line. "Well, I'll be damned," said Pirate Yang. "Well, I don't ask how you found my contact information. If you're desperate enough to go looking, that means you've got something you want to buy . . . or something worth selling."

Ning'er's metal fingers tightened on the comm-link. "The second one. Can we meet?"

"Depends on what you're selling."

Ning'er barely kept her breath from hitching. Sorry, Ge Rong. "A couple of prosthetics, perfect replicas of the latest Chrysalis model. One arm. One leg. Both used, but in fine condition."

"Ah." There was no sense of judgment layered into Yang's voice. Which honestly made the whole situation feel worse. "All right. You've got one hour. Meet me by the remains of your old workplace. Be there on time, or not at all."

The call clicked off before Ning'er could say yes or no. Her breath hitched. In the absence of Yang's tinny voice on the other end of the speaker, the sounds of the street drifted up toward Ning'er's apartment window. The neighborhood had never exactly been quiet, and shouting wasn't unusual. And yet. Ning'er's ears strained. There was an undercurrent to the yelling outside—a sense of collective fear—that made her blood run cold. It sounded a little too much like the yelling on all those old tapes of the Lark's last demonstration.

Maybe that, more than anything else, was what made up Ning'er's mind. She was glad she left when she did. Crowds were starting to gather in the streets, some angry, others panicked and fearful, all of them talking of the earthquakes, the farmlands, the supply lines, and oh, the rioters, what if the rioters made their way here? To this neighborhood? To this particular home?

Ning'er didn't have space in her head to worry about her apartment getting looted on top of everything else. Focus, Ning'er. Concentrate on the task at hand. Worry later. Thank the heavens her work—or, she thought with a pang, what used to be her work—wasn't far.

The sight of Blue Star Brewpub's remains greeted Ning'er with an unexpected pang. For a moment, she stood swaying a little on the sidewalk, struck, and unsure how to process feeling so struck. It wasn't like she'd harbored great sentimental attachment to the place that had chronically underpaid her.

Still, it had survived wild drunken nights, bar fights, and

android raids. Ning'er never expected to see it look like this: its windows and overhead lights smashed and permanently dimmed, the door kicked in, cheap furniture broken beyond recognition. The neon-bright sign—once a tacky, glittering thing, the characters lit up in bright red over cheesy tourist trap holograms of the royal city—hung halfway off its hinges above the ruined doorway, its lights and colors buzzing and flickering weakly in the wind.

"Heavens, what a wreck." Ning'er had barely noticed Yang sidling up beside her until the smuggler was a scant few feet away. It felt odd, seeing Yang by daylight. The cover of darkness had granted them a sense of mystique, an untouchable little creature of the night. Now, Yang looked like what they'd probably been along: a person only maybe five to ten years older than Ning'er, but painted over in exhaustion, from the hunch of their back to the shadows growing under their eyes, stark against their golden skin. Their hair, unwashed, sat in a greasy circle under that same old bowler hat, their hands shoved into the pockets of a black windbreaker.

Ning'er swallowed and made herself give Yang a nod. "So, are we gonna do business or what?"

Yang chuckled. "I like the enthusiasm, barkeep. Those Fourth Ring university students who dropped in the other night, they were friends of yours, right?"

"Friends is a strong word," said Ning'er cautiously. "Colleagues, more like. From another side hustle."

"Side hustle, eh?" Yang's eyebrows climbed.

Ning'er narrowed her eyes at Yang. "A necessity I'm sure you're familiar with, Pirate Yang."

Yang held their hands up. "Relax, I wasn't judging. Besides, if you're running with Ke fucking Zi'an of all people to make a few kuai here and there, I can't fault you for being twitchy." They sighed, gaze darting from side to side. Ning'er followed their gaze and winced. Whoever had torn Blue Star Brewpub apart had clearly moved on—the sounds of ruckus were blocks away, leaving Ning'er and Pirate Yang a temporary cocoon of quiet, but who was to say how long that would last?

Coming to an apparently similar conclusion, Yang jerked their head toward another street corner. "Well, come on, then, Zi'an's girl."

"I'm not Zi'an's girl," Ning'er protested, even as she followed along.

"Whose, then?" Cursory curiosity colored Yang's voice. "The girl with the purple hair? Not someone I figured for your type, but hot enough, I suppose."

"No, I—"

"Don't tell me it was the beautiful one." Yang glanced back toward Ning'er, evidently impressed. "Long lashes, perfect skin, looks just like—"

"Not him either!" snapped Ning'er hurriedly. "Now do you have a buyer for me or not?"

"Patience, 亲." Yang tugged Ning'er into a—well, it was a pretty dank alleyway, but no one jumped out of the shadows to grab Ning'er or stick her with a paralytic, so there was that. "I've got a buyer for you, all right, but not for those Chrysalis knockoffs."

Ning'er blinked in surprise. "I don't own anything else of value."

"Oh, but you do." Yang's gaze drifted subtly downward.

"My prosthetics—"

"I'm not talking about your artificial limbs," said Yang. "My buyer wants the remaining organic ones."

That stopped Ning'er dead in her tracks. She was a child again, suddenly, her hand in her father's, his eyes glassy with a Complacency high. They'd walked into a back-alley lab on the edge of a Fifth Ring neighborhood. Her father had walked back out, carrying a daughter with one leg, one arm, and an envelope of kuai.

Ning'er wasn't the only Sixth Ringer to have traded literal flesh and blood in exchange for cash. No one was exactly certain what buyers wanted with organic limbs, but in times of true desperation, if you found the right black-market contact, an arm or a leg could pay your rent. Voluntary amputees were a dime a dozen in the Fifth and Sixth, and prior to the Red Yaksha's hack on Chrysalis Corp, few of them had the luxury of working prosthetics. Rumors swirled throughout the Lower Rings about where those missing limbs went—perhaps to corporate labs in need of cheap organic material to experiment on, perhaps to something more sinister. One year, half the Sixth Ring had been convinced that the emperor had some princely cousin who secretly indulged in cannibalism. Ning'er had heard it all, but she'd never had hard evidence for any of it.

It was a useless question, but Ning'er found herself asking anyway: "Who's the buyer?"

"Ah, barkeep," said Yang, almost pityingly. "You know better than to ask for something as dangerous as names in this business. Here's the deal: I have a contact who will buy your remaining arm and leg for six thousand kuai. That should cover your next handful of missing paychecks, at least. Take it or leave it."

Oxygen slowed to a halt inside Ning'er's chest, which tightened. An hour ago, she'd been broke and wondering how she'd make rent. Six thousand kuai would cover rent, and then some. It was a good deal. More than. And yet.

"You really don't know anything?" Ning'er pressed.

Yang heaved a tremendous sigh. "That curiosity will get you killed, 宝贝儿. But if you really want to know more—"

"I do."

Yang studied Ning'er for a long moment. "Like I said, I don't know their names. I make a point not to. But it's a lab. And you didn't hear it from me, but the shell company that owns it is a Lilium Corp subsidiary."

Ning'er frowned. "That's it? Just a shady lab owned by oxyveris peddlers? That's all you know?"

"What do I look like, an online search engine?" Yang sighed again. "Look, if you want to sell, here are the contact drop coordinates." Quick as a flash, they had their comm-link out, fingers whisking across the screen. In response, Ning'er's comm-link lit up and buzzed. Coordinates obtained. "Ask the buyer your own questions if you must."

Ning'er hung on to her comm-link, staring at the information blinking back at her: the encoded spot where she could, should she choose, arrive for the first voluntary amputation of her life, and pocket money that would keep her alive, fed, and sheltered for another couple months. Maybe three or four, if she stretched it.

But it would also mean relearning how to do everything again. How to walk. How to run. How to climb and fly and steal. She only had a couple weeks before Duanwu. It wasn't enough time.

And how exactly do you plan to feed yourself for two weeks without a paycheck, whispered the traitorous voice in her head. You've got to look out for yourself first, don't you?

"Thank you," Ning'er said at last. She met Pirate Yang's eyes. "I know this was a risk for you. I won't forget that you took it."

Yang blinked, then shrugged. "No risk, no reward," they

pointed out. "Besides, I did put your buddy Zi'an through his paces to earn his loot, heaven knows what he's going to do with it. Still, he saved me what may have been a more thorough beating than I could afford." Their gaze gleamed, full of assessment. "I appreciate a good enforcer as well as anyone. I guess I figured I could reward him and his pretty purple girl both by helping you out. Besides." They winked. "Maybe you'll be in a position to help me make some money one day, hmm?"

"Doubtful," said Ning'er honestly. She shoved her hands into her pockets. "We're Sixth Ring folks, after all."

Yang smiled. It was an unexpected flash of an expression, just barely ghosting over their lips, but it softened those calculating eyes, for just a moment. "Sure, barkeep. And Sixth Ring folks gotta have each other's backs. Or who the hell else will?"

Before Ning'er could quite process that, Yang jerked their head again. "Leave now. Before the troublemakers make their way back around here."

Sure enough, the distant sounds of shouting and tussling were growing louder. Ning'er glanced at Yang. "What about you? Will you—"

"Honestly, 宝贝儿, what do you take me for?" Yang made a dismissive gesture that would have bordered on rude, had it not been for the faint grin resting on their face. "I'll survive. I always do. It's what Sixth Ring folks do. Now get."

Ning'er got.

Making her way back home was considerably harder than making her way out had been. Already busy on an ordinary day, the main streets had begun to teem with crowds, running either to or from the riots, depending on the shape of their panic. Ning'er had barely rounded the corner back to her building when a stranger's body slammed into her at full force.

Ning'er broke her fall instinctively, splaying her arms out to avoid the worst of the impact. Scrapes ripped across the flesh of her human arm as her metal arm sparked against the concrete. "The fuck!" she yelled at the retreating back. "Watch where you're going!"

The stranger spun on his heel. "You watch it!" he yelled back. "Don't you know what's going on?"

"Yeah, yeah, everyone and their mother is taking to the streets, but that doesn't—"

The stranger barked a laugh. "Oh, that's the least of it."

Ning'er sat up with a wince. Around them, the crowd had multiplied, seemingly exponentially, panic palpable as they scattered across the streets, clearly in search of cover. "What's worse than a riot in the Sixth fucking Ring?"

"What the hell else?" demanded the stranger. He was a young man, maybe in his twenties or thirties, wearing the same haggard, tired look Ning'er had come to associate with all her neighbors. He looked, for a moment, like he meant to keep walking and leave her to her own ignorance. Then hesitation flickered across his features. "It's the gendarme. There was a bloodbath in the marketplace. They've been dispatched to all the neighborhoods."

Ning'er's heart rate climbed. "Not their androids?" Usually, a few enforcement androids were plenty for basic crowd control. The gendarme were more than happy to simply dispatch a few robots to take care of business, and call it a day.

The man shook his head. "The riots were getting serious— the higher-ups wanted to make an example of the protesters." He shuddered. "They want to scare us. You can't just delegate that kind of fear to a cheap line of Chrysalis-built robots. They needed to see it through in person. Things are only going to get worse from here. My advice? Go back inside."

Ning'er winced as she pulled herself to her feet. "Thanks," she said, and meant it. It was good advice. In times of crisis, the court only had one response, and it was the kind that shattered bones and bled people out.

"I have a sister around your age," the man said, rough voiced. "Go inside." And he was gone, buoyed by the rest of the crowd.

Ning'er was already halfway down her street when a tendril of dread snaked around her heart. "Wait." She grabbed one passing woman by the elbow. "Which gate was it? Which gate was the one where the big marketplace riot broke out?"

The woman snatched her elbow from Ning'er's grip. "The East, you impertinent little fool! And you'd best listen to that nice young man—get inside, like the rest of us, before they arrive."

Ning'er didn't need to be told who they were. Swallowing hard, she pushed past the woman. "I'm sorry. I can't."

"Your funeral!" the woman hollered after her.

Ning'er ignored the pronouncement as best she could, even as the crowd thickened around her, growing louder with mounting panic. She fumbled for her comm-link and dialed a number. "Come on," she muttered under her breath, ducking around a corner as she tried to avoid the worst of the throng. "Pick up, pick up, pick up—"

"Hello?"

Ning'er nearly wept in relief. "Ge Rong."

"Ning'er, there's a complete cacophony on your end of the line, I can't—"

"The gendarme are here!" she interrupted. She swallowed.

"Your workshop, the one right at the edge of the East Gate, next to that place where they sell the jianbing—"

"Shit." Ge Rong's voice was tight. "Where are you right now?"

"Where the hell do you think I am? I'm heading toward the workshop!"

His voice sharpened. "Ning'er. Turn back."

She didn't. "A'rong, we're completely fucked if the gendarme break into your workshop. Your prosthetics? The circuitry maps? They're all there."

"Which is why I'm going to take responsibility for securing it. You go home and stay put."

"A'rong!" yelled Ning'er furiously. "Goddammit, let me help you!"

"You are," he said. "By staying safe. Go home, Ning'er, please."

She wanted to fling her phone into the pavement. Instead, she breathed in and out, slowly, a couple times as she reined in her temper. Old Man Yu would have been proud.

"I'll call you when it's safe," said A'rong. "We'll meet soon." He paused. "The rest of the crew, too. I think this just sped up our timeline."

Ning'er sucked another breath back in. "How do you figure?"

She could hear noise in the background on his end. Angry voices, a screeching car. Someone screaming. A'rong's voice tightened. "No time right now. Gotta go. More when we catch up. Promise."

"I—" She swallowed. "Be careful, too, okay, dumbass?"

"Always. Bye." The call clicked off before she could get another word in.

Wading her way through the crowd back into her studio didn't take long—Ning'er didn't cut an especially imposing figure, and she was used to dodging around people who didn't pay her any notice. The wait after, on the other hand, was agonizing.

Hunkered down inside with the single window blocked off to discourage intruders, there was no way to know what was happening. Every few minutes, she'd refresh her monitor for news updates, to no avail. She couldn't tell if the cacophony outside signaled the arrival of the gendarme or just more aimless panic. The uncertainty slowed time to a crawl. Periodically, Ning'er scrolled through her comm-link, looking for a news alert, a message from Ge Rong, anything. Every time it turned up blank, an extra hour seemed to insert itself into the grim-lit digital clock on the wall.

When it finally rang, Ning'er's heart nearly skittered right out of her chest. "Hello?" she yelled, fumbling for the correct buttons to swipe. "A'rong, is that you? Are you all right?"

The voice on the other end was muffled. "He can't answer his comm-link right now."

Ning'er frowned, trying to place the voice. "Zhenyi?"

"Yeah." The other girl sounded apologetic. "Sorry if I startled you. Just . . . things are kind of chaotic at the workshop right now."

"Is that where you all are?" Gingerly, Ning'er began to pace the room, still avoiding that window. "If you secured the shop from the gendarme raid, we should be okay for now, at least. Where's A'rong?"

Zhenyi sucked in a breath. "With Zi'an. Trying to locate Cheng Yun."

An inexplicable tremor ran through Ning'er's entire body. "He's at work." She faltered. "On duty with—"

"With the gendarme, yeah." Zhenyi's tone was grim. "Which means he's in the thick of the riots. Probably. Depending on whether they're willing to put the Young Marshal directly in harm's way. He has some value to the Beiyang bigwigs as a figure-head, but that might be outweighed by his use as a soldier. An officer is still an officer, even if he is the son of Minister Cheng."

Ning'er tilted her head back against the wall and shut her eyes. If she was honest with herself, she couldn't say what would feel worse about Cheng Yun being deployed to the riots: the danger to him, or the danger he'd pose to her neighbors. He had such an oddly tran-quil underlying warmth to him in close proximity that she'd almost forgotten what he really was, or at least, what he was to the rest of the kingdom: the angel-faced hammer upon the Lower Rings.

An accusatory, traitorous little voice grew big in her head. *Is that really all it takes to forget where you come from, Zhong Ning'er? A fine-featured boy with big sad eyes who twirls you around a dance floor like a princess and tells you about his poor little rich boy life? Such a simple scam. What a cheap mark you've turned out to be.*

Ning'er shook herself. What was done was done. How she felt about the possibility of Cheng Yun on the front lines didn't par-ticularly matter. What mattered was making sure he didn't blow his cover, die in a riot, or otherwise compromise the job before Ning'er got paid. "What do you know so far?" she asked Zhenyi.

"Probably about as much as you do," said Zhenyi grimly. "He's not picking up calls, and we don't have a way to track him. We're mostly relying on information from the networks that Cheng Yun built on behalf of the Red Yaksha, but no one's reported anything on his whereabouts. Except . . ."

"Except?" Ning'er prompted impatiently, when Zhenyi trailed off.

The other girl hesitated, just for a few seconds, before care-fully adding, "There was one thing. One of our guys claims to have intercepted encoded communications from a couple low-ranking officers in Cheng Yun's unit. What they've decoded so far doesn't say a whole lot, but there was a mention of the Young Marshal near the same coordinates where their unit got deployed to . . ." Here she paused, then added delicately, "Keep the peace."

Ning'er's grip tightened on her phone. "That's not everything, is it?"

"Ning'er—" Zhenyi's tone was calm, cajoling. Ning'er hated it immediately.

"Don't patronize me. Not you, Zhenyi, please." Ning'er swallowed. "You've been a soldier before, right? You've seen shit. You know staying quiet doesn't make something less real."

A pause on the other end of the line. "The gendarme isn't the only thing setting up camp at those coordinates. There's talk of another insurgent. Someone who may have gotten wind of the same intel we did and is headed there."

Ning'er frowned. "One of yours? Did you or Cheng Yun authorize—"

"No. Not one of ours. An independent." Zhenyi sucked in a breath. "We think an assassin. Someone trying to land a blow against the gendarme by taking out the Young Marshal."

Was it possible for a comm-link to actually shatter under her grip? Ning'er was probably about to find out. "What are the coordinates?"

"Ning'er." Now, Zhenyi's tone shifted toward caution. "We don't know anything for sure. Do you know how many sightings of the Young Marshal get posted online by lovestruck tweens? For all we know, this is one of those and our rogue comrade wannabe is about to feel quite silly. We shouldn't assume anything is true without evidence."

"I agree," said Ning'er smoothly. She'd gotten up at some point and started walking out the door. When had that happened? "Which is why I propose that we find that evidence ourselves. If we manage to intercept an assassin, well, all the better."

"You cannot simply waltz into the middle of a gendarme encampment during a riot! We don't have time to forge papers to get you past any of the checkpoints, and the place will be crawling with soldiers. You can't just—"

"Can't I?" Ning'er flashed a quick little smile at her window, even though Zhenyi couldn't see it. "You hired a thief, remember? You wanted someone who could fit into spaces where they don't belong and go where they're not supposed to. I never did give you a trial run. The way I see it, this is the perfect opportunity."

Zhenyi went silent again for a long moment—so long, in fact, that Ning'er worried for a few seconds that the other girl had actually hung up on her.

"Protect him." Zhenyi's voice, usually so smooth and calm, sounded uncharacteristically rough over the crackle of the phone's speaker. "If it's him. If someone's really found him and wants to hurt him. I—just try. Please. Don't let him martyr himself like some soft-hearted idiot. We—the rest of us—we need him more than he knows."

Something twisted inside Ning'er's chest. "I know." She swallowed hard and steeled herself. "I'll do what I can."

"You too." The addition was abrupt, matter-of-fact. "You can't go dying on us either, you know. We need you alive if we're going to rescue He Bailing from her cage. I hear good thieves are a tough find these days."

Ning'er's smile softened. It was just work, she reminded herself sternly. It was still all just work. But it didn't hurt to remember, from time to time, that the girl on the other end of the line was the one person who'd actually known the Lark. The one person who maybe, just maybe, had seen her, not just as a figurehead, but for the girl she'd been.

Ning'er was no He Bailing. But for a few seconds, it was easy to believe, in some foolish corner of her heart, that perhaps Zhenyi cared about Ning'er the girl, too, and not just Ning'er the thief.

The seconds passed, and Ning'er swallowed hard on the sentiment. "You're not wrong," she said at last. Guess I better prove I'm worth my cost. Send me the coordinates."

She stared at the screen for a long moment after she hung up, overcome by déjà vu as she watched a new set of coordinates appear beside the address Pirate Yang had slipped her barely two hours ago. She could still walk away from all of this, if she chose to. She could give up the job and her limbs, and survive to sleep safe just a little longer.

Unbidden, the memory of Cheng Yun curled against her spine ghosted across her mind's eye. The sight of those sad eyes of his. *I like this,* he'd said. *Being with you.* He'd looked at her like she was a marvel he didn't entirely understand. *Thank you,* he'd told her.

Thank me by paying me, she'd said. She'd meant it too.

She heaved a sigh at her comm-link before pocketing it and striding out the door. Her decision on Pirate Yang's offer would simply have to wait. "Goddammit, Cheng Yun," Ning'er muttered as she flew down the stairs and once more into danger. "Your pretty little ass better not have gotten itself murdered yet, or I'll rain hell itself down on your ghost."

CHAPTER 7

The Promise

In the years since Ning'er had first embarked upon her thrill-seeking hobby turned high-risk side hustle, she'd undergone her fair share of trials to get her work done. She's scaled trellises to lift dainty jewelry boxes from high-flying, balconied bedrooms at luxurious high-rises. She'd climbed undetected through skylights and secret back-room windows to pinch family heirlooms from absent-minded businessmen's ill-hidden lockboxes. She'd even done the classic air vent crawl, a rite of passage for any burglar worth her salt.

She hadn't been sure whether to assume breaking into a gendarme encampment would be easier or harder than any of those. As it turned out, the two experiences weren't even really comparable.

She found Cheng Yun's unit wedged up against one of the walls by the east gate of the Sixth Ring, just as the coordinates had promised. The encampment had a ghastly look about it, as though it was one of those hand-painted war posters from the late nineteenth century, when the dynasty's first emperor had first risen to power. A checkpoint had been hastily set up with a couple armed guards waving plasma rifles at anyone who ventured too close, while the rest of the encampment had been sectioned off with makeshift barricades of metal and barbed wire. Behind those barricades, gendarme officers—dressed in uniforms stained with mud, blood, or both—paced nervously back and forth, hands wandering constantly toward the weapons at their belts. Theirs was a young-looking unit, clean-shaven and weary-eyed, and probably not a single member past their midtwenties. There was something darkly romantic about that juxtaposition: the filth and chaos, all managed by what amounted to a gang of kids stuffed into uniforms. If not for the modern trappings of cybernetics and plasma, the whole mess could have been a scene torn right out of the history books.

There was no slick skyscraper wall to scale here, no balcony to climb, no air vent to crawl through. All she had were a bunch of weary, distracted soldiers, and the matter of those silly little barricades.

She had the encampment cased within about seven minutes. After debating a few different options, she picked what she always did: the simplest. Which, in this case, was avoiding both barricades and checkpoint entirely.

"You there!" barked one of the young officers.

Ning'er sighed exaggeratedly and turned her head. Mentally, she ran a quick catalog of the situation: here she was, a young woman dressed in civilian clothes, walking with a very purposeful stride through the back of the encampment, right between two of the lackluster barricades. Quite notably, at the opposite end from the designated checkpoint.

"You really need to mark your entrances more carefully, soldier," said Ning'er in irritable tones.

The officer faltered. He looked even younger than Ning'er, the last traces of baby fat still clinging to his lightly freckled cheeks, which didn't boast even a hint of stubble. His hair, thick and unruly, threatened to escape from beneath his standard issue officers' cap, which looked more like a prop he'd stolen from an older brother's wardrobe than something that actually belonged on his own head. "You," he began, and faltered again, looking awkward when Ning'er didn't break eye contact. "The checkpoint is on the other side of the premises, miss," he said at last, gruffly averting his gaze.

"Yes, I know where the checkpoint is, thank you," said Ning'er primly. "That is quite literally what I just said, wasn't it?" She knocked her metal fist demonstratively against the cheap barbed wire barricade beside her. The officer's eyes grew wide at the sound of metal clinking against metal, then flickered toward Ge Rong's painstaking handiwork.

Inwardly, Ning'er smiled. She had him right where she wanted him. "I'm looking for my boyfriend," she said lazily, twirling a lock of hair around that expensive metal finger. "He told me he'd meet me here."

The officer's eyes widened further, before he looked away again. A hint of color rose in his freckled cheeks. "Your boyfriend, ah, he's gendarme man, is he?"

"No, he's a garbage collector," said Ning'er. She puffed her chest out and looked down her nose at the officer, pouting the way she'd seen Second Ring taitai do when they weren't getting their way. "Yes, of course he's gendarme. He chased me for years when we were in school, you know, and I promised I'd go steady with him if he made it through that fancy training program of yours, and lo and behold, turns out lust is one hell of a motivator. Big surprise, huh? Not that I mind. I've always wanted to be a soldier's girl. Love the uniforms—real smart looking, you know? And I hear the higher ranks make good money, so my baba will like him once we're ready to settle down." She batted her eyes at the increasingly bright red boy before her. "Anyway, can I see him?"

"Um," he stammered. "I'm only supposed to let authorized persons through the checkpoint, since the riots are still ongoing—"

"Oh, please." Ning'er gave an exaggerated roll of her eyes and pouted harder. "Are your higher-ups really scared of some stupid Sixth Ring beggars stirring up a fuss? I don't exactly see a raging battlefield out here." That much had the benefit of being true. The rioters had either moved on or were losing steam entirely. A few scuffles periodically broke out among the straggling crowds on the other side of the barricades, but no real threat of violence looked set to break any time soon. "You're not scared, are you?"

"No, of course not," protested the boy hastily. "But I'll get in trouble with—"

"You know what, fine," huffed Ning'er. She dug her comm-link out. "I'll just call him and tell him some idiot wouldn't let me through even though I explained the situation, not my problem if he takes his temper out on—"

"No, don't!" yelped the boy. His gaze darted from side to side before he relented. "Look, you can come through, just . . . well, just don't tell anyone I ran into you, all right?"

Ning'er winked at him, even as her heart leapt with relief. "You're a gem, kiddo. I'll give my boyfriend a kiss for you." Before he could process that, she sauntered off into the encampment, hips swaying. That whole performance wasn't, in all likelihood, a ruse that would have worked on someone savvier and more experienced than a nervous-eyed boy who was clearly at the bottom of the pecking order. Still, fortune favored the bold—and occasionally, the downright insolent. Ning'er had spent enough time lurking around the outskirts of the Upper Rings to learn a thing or two about how its denizens thought about the world around them. Sometimes you needed to force your way into a place: by scaling a wall or climbing through a vent or breaking a window. But sometimes, if you simply walked in with purpose and just enough entitlement, people didn't bother to question you. Who else would dare do such a thing, except someone who belonged there?

Of course, prosthetics that, at their authentic and legal price, should have been affordable exclusively to the Upper Ring elite, sometimes made a handy prop as well. Ning'er made a mental note to thank Ge Rong for his services, and the many, many ways his gifts continued to come in handy. Well, she'd thank him if she survived this little jaunt.

Locating Cheng Yun himself proved a tad more difficult than simply waltzing into his unit's encampment. Thankfully, she wasn't the only figure drifting through the makeshift barracks out of uniform. She spotted a couple officers, clearly off duty and finally settling into their own exhaustion, stripped down to civilian clothing: well-made basics like well-stitched joggers and soft cotton sweaters. Boring, but practical, and clearly made by a tailor who could afford to charge a pretty penny for solid craftsmanship and high-quality material. It wasn't just the clothing that gave them away, either; they couldn't quite shake that air to them: the proud set of their shoulders, perpetually tense with vigilance, and that careful, soldierly gait to their stride. A handful of other young people in civilian clothes—these similar in style to, but far cheaper than, what the off-duty officers were wearing—also scurried to and fro, looking frantic and miserable, heads bowed, staring at their own feet rather than daring eye contact. Some carried bags of supplies—rifles, plasma ammunition, an array of other weapons—while others lingered around the tents, quietly tidying up and answering barked orders.

The help, then, Ning'er surmised. Probably Lower Ringers looking to earn a handful of kuai kissing gendarme ass. Ning'er could hardly blame them. After all, she thought with a grim smile, technically, she worked for the Young Marshal, too. You did what you had to, to make rent. Maybe now more so than ever. Hell, Ning'er could probably hide her arm and blend in with that band of sullen-faced encampment workers, if the need arose. That was the other thing about anyone who earned their daily coin outside of the Sixth Ring: it rarely occurred to them to pay attention to the help, except to blame them when shit went sideways.

Still, Ning'er did her best to keep out of sight of the other officers—the last thing she needed was someone a little more senior and a little savvier than the poor young man who'd first accosted her to call her into question a second time. Instead, she watched them all carefully from the shadows, hands in her pockets, eyes keen. A face like Cheng Yun's would stand out anywhere he went. Yet not a single uniform she saw came attached to the striking young man with the beatific face.

She was so caught up in her mounting frustration that she didn't fully register the gunshot when she heard it.

Her ears rang. Around her, the weary faces shifted from exhaustion toward alarmed vigilance. Uniformed bodies sprang into action. Shouts began to crescendo, a few startled yells at first, but soon, the telltale sounds of panicked young soldiers were filling the area.

As usual, no one paid Ning'er—the outsider to it all, maybe a girlfriend, maybe an amusement, maybe simply a maid—any mind. That was good. It bought Ning'er time to breathe. And time to breathe meant time to think.

She inhaled. Where had that first gunshot come from?

Exhale. Think, Ning'er, think. Remember. These fancy Upper Ring officers and their Lower Ring lapdogs may have their expensive, soldierly training. But you have something better. You, Zhong Ning'er, have the ears of a thief. The ears of a girl who, long before she started burgling Upper Ring high-rises, learned to listen for so many other things. Yours are ears that learned from birth to listen for the sounds of an android patrol two minutes before curfew, or a mugging outside after your shift at the bar ends, criminal and victim alike desperate for a pay day, or even—and here, Ning'er couldn't help but smile to herself, sharp and humorless—*the boots of gendarme officers on a raid.*

Inhale. Now, figure it out, canny, clever-eared Zhong Ning'er: where the fuck did that gunshot come from?

Exhale. Ah. Ning'er's gaze drifted toward one of the tents in the far corner of the camp. Placed near the gap between barricades. The same spot Ning'er had strolled in herself.

Ning'er glanced around, biting her lip. Charted her path, quick as her eye could judge the distance. And then, like any good thief, she ran like hell toward her prize.

The first thing she heard as she neared was the sound of someone crying. That nearly stopped her in her tracks right there. Her hand paused on the flap of the tent. The person inside— the person inside the tent where Ning'er could swear she'd heard the gunshot that sent the barracks into pandemonium—sobbed, breath hitching on a hysterical little whimper.

Ning'er's blood ran cold. She opened the tent flap.

It took her another moment to fully register the scene laid out before her. A girl, maybe around Ning'er's age, sat crouched at the far end of the tent, eyes red and swollen from crying, a knife gleaming in one of her hands. The other hand clutched her thigh, which sported an ugly burn from what was clearly a plasma gun wound, though Ning'er couldn't guess at the severity. Surrounding her was an entire cadre of officers, their rifles trained on her. The only person without a gun stood between the girl and his fellow officers, back to Ning'er, arms splayed. A gesture of peace.

"You need to step aside, sir," said one of the gendarme in a tight voice. A female soldier, also probably close to Ning'er's age, her hair pulled back in a rigid chignon, the hands on her weapon boasting a steadiness that must have been drilled into her since she could toddle. Her voice trembled only a little. "You're only prolonging the inevitable."

"I'm sorry, sergeant," said the unarmed officer. Ning'er froze. She knew that voice. Surprisingly soft, typically quiet, yet capable of filling an entire room. "But I'm not budging until the rest of you stand down. You've made it very clear that you don't intend to handle this situation responsibly without me quite literally in the way, so in the way I shall remain."

"Sir, please." Another officer, a boy, this time, big and broad. His hands weren't quite as steady as the girl's, the deadly end of the plasma rifle shaking as he spoke. "That kid's not gonna thank you for doing . . . whatever it is that you're doing."

"Well, no, after you shot her, I expect not," drawled Cheng Yun. "Too little too late, wouldn't you say?"

"I'm right here, you know." The cornered girl spoke up for the first time. Her voice was raw and thick. An aborted sob hitched in her throat. "For a room full of imperial dogs who are scared shitless of some kid your own age, you sure like to pretend I'm not."

"Shut up," the big-shouldered officer spat at the girl. "You came here thinking you'd assassinate the Young Marshal, and now you're presuming to—"

"Chao!" Cheng Yun, his soft voice gone whiplike, turned around at last. Ning'er's breath caught as he glared pure fire at the bigger boy. "That's enough."

"Sir," protested Chao. "This girl came here to kill you—"

"Yes, I'm aware," said Cheng Yun dryly. "And, in fairness to her, it wasn't without reason." He glanced over his shoulder at the girl with the knife. "Isn't that right—Ruofei, wasn't it?"

The girl—Ruofei, apparently—ducked her head, shoulders trembling. "I just wanted to do something," she mumbled. "Something that would help my neighborhood."

"So you chose murder," observed the officer with the chignon, her eyes narrowed. "Pray tell, kid, how is sneaking into a gendarme encampment at the height of a riot with a poisoned knife in tow something that would help your neighborhood?"

Cheng Yun's would-be murderer glared, red-eyed, at the other girl. "How could you understand?" she spat. "All my life, you gendarme have talked a big talk about protecting us, but I've never even understood what you were protecting us from. All I've ever seen you do is hurt and frighten us. A bunch of Upper Ring officers, brainwashing desperate children of Lower Ring families to fill out your ranks and police our own."

Ruofei's eyes blazed. "Have you ever watched your friends and family beaten by boys from your own neighborhood? The same kids you dressed in uniforms and turned against their people because you convinced them that the only way to fill their bellies was to eat their own? Have you been beaten within inches of your life for the great crime of being caught out five minutes past curfew? Have you had your most sentimental belongings rifled through and torn apart in the name of a search for some nonsense contraband or another? Because I have. And worse. Many times."

She barked a laugh, hysterical at the edges. "And whose name do you invoke to justify your cruelty? A child's. So yeah, I poisoned my knife and came to kill the best of you." Ruofei spat at Cheng Yun's feet. "I'm not sorry. I wish I'd finished the job."

For several long, agonizing seconds, the tent fell deathly quiet. Even the chaos outside seemed to fade to a gentle din as the Young Marshal and the girl who'd declared her wish for his death stared each other down.

Then Cheng Yun put his hands in his pockets and bowed his head. "Well? No one's stopping you from finishing it now."

Ruofei's eyes went wide. Hatred still colored her expression, but there was something to that look in her eyes. Hope, almost. Guarded and wary and half-feral, but a hint of hope all the same. Her hands rose in surrender. She opened her mouth, starting forward toward Cheng Yun. The knife wavered between her raised fingers, trembling.

She never got a chance to speak.

"She's going to stab him!" roared Chao. "Sir, watch out!"

Pandemonium erupted. Ning'er dove as a flurry of plasma rifles went off. The canvas floor of the tent cushioned her fall, but she felt pebbles scrape up against her elbows as she pulled herself low for cover. One of the blasts hit the strip of lights at the edge of the tent, plunging them all into flickering darkness. Scant, haphazard illumination fluttered in and out of existence through the sudden pitch-black.

Swearing, Ning'er crawled forward on her elbows, squinting through the occasional flash of light cutting storm-bright across the tent. Praying that none of the panicked gendarme would step on her, or worse, shoot her, she scooted forward as quickly as she could. Every once in a while, a flash of brightness beamed across something in her path. An officer shouting frantic orders to the others. Another beating a retreat for the exit. Another moaning on the floor, clutching a wet, dark stain on his uniform.

Someone grabbed Ning'er's wrist. "What are you doing here?" hissed a voice in the shell of her ear.

His voice was hoarse, an edge of something feral to it, but she'd know it anywhere. She snatched her hand free from Cheng Yun's grip. "Saving you from getting knifed or shot, apparently."

Cheng Yun's breath hitched hot against her ear. "Ning'er, you need to go."

"Not without you."

"Please!" Something about the way his voice shifted—the raw, pleading, broken sound of it—made Ning'er look at him at last.

She almost wished she hadn't. It took several flickers of those dying lights to parse what she was seeing: the girl Ruofei lay cradled in Cheng Yun's arms, her eyes wide and unseeing, her torso soaked with blood from the plasma rifle blasts that had struck her dead-on. The knife lay uselessly beside her, clattered on the floor of the tent a few inches from one lifeless hand.

Cheng Yun's head bent over her, hair covering his eyes, kneeling on that bloody floor as if in prayer.

But this was no temple. Ning'er reached her own trembling hands over the dead girl's corpse to clasp Cheng Yun's shoulders. "Cheng Yun. There's nothing you can do for her now. And I need to get you back before something worse happens."

He looked up at her. His face was deathly pale beneath those ghastly flashing lights, those liquid dark eyes of his enormous. "I can't just walk away like this," he hissed. "My unit—"

"Is in chaos right now. That works out for us," added Ning'er brusquely. "Zhenyi only barely got report of the one assassin in time. Who the hell knows who else might be making an attempt on the Young Marshal's life? For all you know, it's one of your own officers. You're not the only person in Beijing who can wear two faces, you know. Which means the only place we can be sure of your safety is with the rest of the crew you handpicked. You're just going to have to be one more MIA soldier for a little while."

She could see the gears turning behind his gaze, even now. The calculations running through his mind, and the slow, awful realization of the truth behind every word she'd said. With each flash of light, she saw a shift in his face. A slow deadening of those big dark eyes.

She wasn't sure exactly when it all finally clicked for him. All she knew was that she saw it when it happened, that resigned little nod of his head. It was the only signal she needed. She twisted her wrist, grabbed his hand, and hauled him across the floor of the tent, half dragging him behind her as they stumbled through the flashing darkness. Blindly, her fingers found the edge of one of the tent flaps. Now or never.

"When we get outside," she panted in his ear, "run for the space between the barbed-wire barricades. As fast as you can."

She tore the tent flap aside. They ran.

The world faded around her. For long moments—she couldn't tell if they were seconds or hours—her awareness trickled down into only the smallest, most immediate sensations. The blur of blue sky and gray concrete of the outer edge of the Sixth Ring neighborhood. The jolt of the uneven, rocky surface of the ground against the desperate sprint of her feet. Cheng Yun's sweat-slick fingers scraping against her palm.

Then Cheng Yun fell.

It shocked Ning'er back into herself. She almost followed him to the ground, tugged off balance by the dead weight. She caught herself with one palm, wincing at the spark of concrete against Ge Rong's painstakingly constructed casing. "Come on, A'yun," she panted, trying to tug him back to his feet. "We gotta get back up."

He didn't get back up. The world slowed as Ning'er paused and looked at him. Really looked at him. He was pale—more than pale, really, ghost-white—and breathing heavily, sweat-slick hair plastered against a clammy forehead. Balanced awkwardly on his knees and splayed, wobbling fingers, he had his free hand clutched tight against his ribs.

Ning'er squatted beside him, even as her blood ran cold with a silent dread. "What's the matter?" She tried to make her voice gentle, but it came out rougher than she meant to, raw with her own abrupt anxiety. "You have a rib out?"

Silently, he shook his head. Slowly, he removed that trembling hand from his side. His palm was smeared lightly with blood.

At first, Ning'er was relieved. It didn't look like a deep wound, the blood minimal. Then she looked at the sweat pouring down his face, the labored rise and fall of his chest, and reckoned with a far worse possibility than any flesh wound. "Cheng Yun," she said slowly. "Tell me she didn't get you with that knife."

"Grazed, I think," he managed. His voice was faint and reedy. His eyelashes fluttered. The elbow keeping him upright collapsed.

"Cheng Yun!" Ning'er caught him before his head could hit the ground.

He chuckled thinly, a weak little rumble against her arms. "Guess Ruofei wasn't bluffing about coating her blade with poison."

Ning'er's mind raced. An antidote, then. They had to find an antidote. "Any chance you know what kind?"

"Beats me. Whatever it is packs a punch, though." He coughed violently, his entire body shaking against Ning'er's.

She held him closer instinctually. As if that would slow the shaking. As if the force in her own body could somehow slow the poison coursing slowly but surely through his. "That's okay," she told him. Why was her voice so high-pitched? "That's okay," she repeated. "That's what we have Feifei on hand for, right? She'll know what to do, she's got university training, going to be a real doctor soon, she'll be able to figure out an antidote."

"Ning'er." His voice was quiet, and surprisingly calm. Almost amused, in a resigned sort of way. "You're babbling."

Ning'er sucked in a breath and bit her tongue on an instinctive, panic-fueled denial. "You're right," she said instead. "Okay." She fumbled for her comm-link. "I'm going to call the others. We're going to get you out of here. And we're . . . you're . . . going to be all right. You'll see."

He didn't respond. Maybe he couldn't. Or maybe he was just saving his strength. But his chest still rose and fell. Ning'er focused on that as she dialed Zi'an.

He answered immediately this time. "Ning'er!" he thundered. "Where the hell have you been? The last I heard of you was some cockamamie story from Zhenyi about you waltzing off into a gendarme encampment to foil an assassination attempt on Cheng Yun."

"Yeah, well." Ning'er rubbed the back of her head. "If we want my foiling attempt to be successful, I'm going to need transport—preferably with Feifei in tow—at my coordinates. Before Cheng Yun's gendarme buddies or a second assassin find us first, if you please."

Zi'an went quiet. "You found Cheng Yun."

"Technically, yes." Ning'er couldn't quite keep the tremor out of her voice. "Zi'an, he's in bad shape. Please hurry."

Zi'an exhaled slowly. "I'm on it. Hang in there. Both of you. Just hang in a little while longer."

After Feifei and the rest of the crew arrived, Ning'er lost track of time for a little while. There had been a great deal of terse orders being barked, Feifei's perfect red mouth pulling thin as she checked Cheng Yun's vitals, and Zi'an helping Zhenyi load Cheng Yun into the back of the car he'd commandeered. Between them all, Ning'er found herself aimless, hanging back as the others tended to their friend.

A temporary safehouse in the Fourth Ring had been scoped out. It was owned by another pair of university-age students Ning'er couldn't name—though she thought she'd seen their faces around the café where they'd all taken to meeting. Apparently, one was a classmate of Feifei's, and the other was a contact who worked with Zi'an on other jobs. Neither asked questions.

The street around the safehouse had largely cleared by the time they arrived back on the block. Only a few telltale scraps of the chaos the gendarme had wrought remained: a few broken barricades, overturned trash bins, a discarded protest sign here or there. A few citizens still milled about, all frantic murmuring and tense bodies, the ghost of violence still lurking in the air. The streets had returned to tentative life, but it was a different life than the one that had come before: an edge of anxiety to the shouts of shopkeepers selling wares, the pedestrians hailing cabs or asking for directions to a train stop.

Feifei hadn't said a word edgewise to Ning'er the entire time. If she knew what had poisoned him—or whether she had an antidote—Ning'er had no idea. With Zi'an's help, Feifei had managed to bundle Cheng Yun upstairs. Ning'er could only assume with the way she hovered over him, murmuring to herself and checking his wound, that the medic didn't consider all hope lost for her patient.

So Ning'er waited. Sitting alone on the bottom floor like a useless idiot, she waited.

It didn't take long for the screams to start. It was a raw-throated wail, faint, but chillingly audible through the walls, even from downstairs. Ning'er's heart slammed into her throat. A few minutes later, a rush of footsteps pounded down the stairs. Zhenyi, paper white, sweat beading her forehead beneath a riot of purple hair, clamped a fist around Ning'er's arm. "Come upstairs."

Ning'er let herself be led up the steps. The screams were louder now. Her prosthetic hand went tight around Zhenyi's prosthetic fingers. Metal scraped against metal in an ugly screech. "Heaven help us. Is that him? Is that Cheng Yun?"

The other girl was silent. Ning'er wanted to throw up.

"It's not as bad as it sounds," offered Zhenyi at last. She freed her hand from Ning'er's death grasp with a firm but gentle jerk of her wrist and began to drum her fingers against the banister, a nervous tic, as she stared down at the unresponsive grains in the wood. "You know those rumors about Lilium experimenting with developing new substances, right? Narcotics, both uppers and downers, but also . . . well. Peddle your wares anywhere near the glittering halls of the imperial court, and you can always find a buyer for a good poison. And if that poison doubles as a torture drug, all the better. Ever heard of Devil's Mark?"

Ning'er had. Her fists curled. If Complacency pushed your body into unnatural levels of strength and focus, Devil's Mark did the exact opposite—it built a hell out of your own head. Ning'er wasn't surprised that they'd been sibling drugs created by the same pharmaceuticals company, two halves of the same terrible coin, born in the same labs. Dose a man with a small, concentrated amount of Devil's Mark, and it would heighten every negative sensation in the human body: worry, fear, even physical pain. Dose a man with a larger amount, and he'd be dead within days. It was cruel, agonizing way to go. If you used Devil's Mark to torture someone, maybe it was just business. A bad day at the office. But if you used Devil's Mark to poison, well. That was personal. Ning'er had heard rumors of the Brocade Guard—the emperor's hand-selected personal guard, chosen from the most promising ranks of the gendarme—using Devil's Mark to interrogate uncooperative suspects, but darker rumors had spoken of something else: personal vendettas carried out against the Beiyang government's most dangerous enemies, putting Devil's Mark to work coaxing out slow and agonizing deaths.

How the hell had a desperate Sixth Ring girl gotten her hands on such a thing?

Ning'er fought back the bile rising in her throat. "How much Devil's Mark was coating that girl's knife?"

The door to Cheng Yun's sickroom opened, admitting an exhausted-looking Feifei. "Thankfully not enough to ensure the victim's death," said the medic, stripping off a pair of plastic gloves. She was elegantly clothed as ever, in a deep purple peplum top that curved perfectly over her frame, but the cloth was sturdy and practical, easy to wash: clearly meant for work. Her face, though, was tight and drawn, free of the carefully applied makeup she usually wore. It made her no less beautiful, but it did make her look younger and more tired. She paused, closed her eyes for a moment, as she leaned against the wall. "Let's just hope your rescue didn't blow his cover."

Any sympathy Ning'er had nursed in her heart for the other girl vanished. Incandescent rage burst to life in its place. "His cover?" she said, disbelieving. "His fucking cover? That's what you care about? That's what you consider the worst-case scenario, losing his stupid cover with the fucking gendarme?"

Feifei's mouth went tight. "It's what you should care about. You don't get paid if we get made, after all."

That stung. Ning'er tried to cover her hurt. "Who cares what I care about? I thought you were in training to become a doctor. What kind of medical student cares more about her patient's political schemes than whether he lives or dies?"

Feifei's eyes flashed with anger of their own. "How dare you. You've known him for all of twelve seconds. The rest of us—"

"Feifei. Ning'er." Zhenyi's voice was soft, but sharpened its edges on both their names, as it cut through the mounting argument. "That's enough. The last thing Cheng Yun needs right now is for us to quarrel among ourselves." She bowed her head toward Feifei. "What does the prognosis look like?"

Feifei sighed, slumping further against the wall. It made her look strangely fragile. "I thought we'd lose him, at first," she said. Her voice had also turned small. "Devil's Mark isn't the quickest acting poison on the market, but you don't need much in your system to feel its effects. When we first arrived, I thought he was already dead. The way he looked . . ." The professional mask slipped, just for an instant, before she swallowed and continued. "He was barely breathing. I lost his heartbeat, twice. And once I—we finally managed to get him stable—"

"That's when the screaming started," finished Zhenyi quietly.

The screams, in fact, had quieted a little at last. Ning'er could still hear something going on behind the doors of Cheng Yun's sickroom—some shuffling, maybe, and what sounded like an occasional awful, gasping sob—but anything was better than that raw-throated howl of agony.

Zi'an emerged a moment later. "Ning'er." Zi'an's face, usually so full of good cheer and flirtation, looked as drawn and pale as Feifei's. "Thank heavens you're still here. He says he needs to speak to you."

"Cheng Yun?" Ning'er's fists tightened. Her entire body felt like an exposed nerve, raw with anxious energy. "Can he even speak at all?"

"He's trying." Zi'an rubbed a hand over his face, in what looked like a halfhearted attempt to shake the nerves of the past several hours. "He's . . . insistent."

"I'll go," decided Ning'er. She'd have to face the sight of him eventually, whatever condition he was in.

"Ning'er." Zhenyi caught her elbow again. "Just . . . be careful. He's more fragile than he seems."

"Even when he's not pumped full of drugs," muttered Feifei. "Damn him." She nodded to Ning'er, schooling her own features. "If he—if anything happens, I'll be just outside the door. Try not to linger. He needs his rest. So, hurry."

Ning'er didn't need to be told twice. She practically bulldozed her way into the sickroom, stomach churning and pulse wild. People talked about adrenaline dumps all the time. No one ever talked about wondering whether it was physically possible to vomit up your own heart.

Well, if she did, Feifei would save her. Maybe.

The sight that greeted Ning'er in Cheng Yun's sickroom froze her in her tracks. The figure splayed on the cot looked nothing like the one that had left her bed that morning. His skin was waxy and pale, his hair damp with sweat and plastered to a clammy forehead. He was mumbling to himself, eyes closed. Even pitched low, she could hear the rasp in his voice.

Ning'er stepped forward, and paused, feeling for all the world like a helpless fool. Why had he asked for her? What could she possibly do for him, in this state?

His eyes opened. "You're here," he rasped. His pupils were bright with fever. "Thank you."

Ning'er didn't say anything, unable to stop staring at the broken thing lying on Cheng Yun's cot.

"Oh, don't give me that look," the thing croaked. "I'm not so badly off."

"You should see yourself before talking big like that." Still cautious, Ning'er drifted a few steps closer. He looked worse the nearer she came. The waxy complexion was practically gray, the blown pupils making those big dark eyes enormous in a hollow face.

She wanted to flinch away. Instead, she took a seat at the bedside. Someone had left a cool, damp towel beside the pillows. Swallowing, she picked it up. Hesitantly, she pressed it gently against Cheng Yun's brow. Her teeth clenched as she emitted an involuntary hiss of sympathy. His skin was still hot to the touch.

He watched her movements. Each breath he took seemed to drag itself unwillingly from his chest. "My brother died this way," he said, in what might have been conversant tones if he could breathe normally. "A'wei, he—" His eyes went even wider, then squeezed shut as a shudder ran through his entire body. Another whimper escaped him.

The sound of it unfroze something inside of Ning'er. Her metal hand still pressing the cloth against his brow, her free hand found its way to Cheng Yun's. He clutched her fingers so hard she thought, for one wild moment, that he might break them, but she didn't let go. She wouldn't let him go. Not in this moment. Not like this.

"It was my fault," mumbled Cheng Yun. "I didn't tell you that part. It was my fault. I killed my brother." He sobbed, a small, awful little sound. "I killed A'wei."

"It wasn't," said Ning'er. She squeezed his fingers. "No rhyme or reason to some tragedies, remember? You didn't do that. Life did."

Cheng Yun's chest heaved. "Our baba said it was my fault. He said—"

Without thinking, Ning'er dropped her forehead against his, the washcloth damp between their skin. "Fuck whatever your father said. He's not here. You are. You're the one who has to decide, right now, to live. To . . . to free the Lark and build your brave new world, right? So the two of you can fuck over those regicidal Beiyang ministers once and for all."

He rasped a laugh. "I didn't think you cared about brave new worlds or the Lark. I thought you cared about a paycheck."

With a jolt, Ning'er remembered her meeting with Pirate Yang earlier that day. The offer for quick money, an alternate solution to her debts. All it would cost her were a few more pieces of her body. Hell, had that really happened just that morning?

"I do care about my paycheck," Ning'er told Cheng Yun, but the words sounded hollow, even to her own ears. "But I'm not the one living your life, either, am I?"

When she lifted her head, at last, from his, he was staring at her with the strangest expression. Maybe it was a foolish, romantic notion, but she could also swear a hint of pink had crept back into those pallid cheeks.

"I remember now," he said, hoarsely, "why I asked for you."

Ning'er frowned. "To break the Lark out? Yeah, I got that bit loud and clear—"

"No." He looked and sounded suddenly more lucid than he had during this entire encounter. "Why I asked for you, when the others all thought I was going to give up the ghost."

Ning'er tried not to feel too relived that he was talking about his own death in hypothetical past tense. She was no doctor, but from the sickly complexion and the sweat still beading his brow, she doubted they were out of the woods with their fearless leader just yet. "Surely that was just for my charming bedside manner."

He huffed another weak laugh. "That. And a favor."

What kind of favor did a man need on his deathbed?

He seemed to read the question in her face, even through the haze of his fever. "When the time comes—whether it's today, tomorrow, or a hundred years from now, I need you to sell me out."

Ning'er had been holding his hand the entire time. She dropped it abruptly. Whatever she might have expected Cheng Yun to say, it hadn't been that.

He closed his eyes for a moment, as if to gather himself. "The Red Yaksha and the Young Marshal are, right now, opposed figures in the public imagination. When—if—I die, I need you to tell them the truth about who they are—who I—really am." His eyes slitted open with an effort. "You'll make good money on the information. I have proof. Identity papers. Documentation. Confessions. It's worth something. Don't take anything less than the highest bid. The more money, the greater the guarantee of spread."

"I'm not going to betray you for money," Ning'er began, half-indignant, but he cut her off before the argument could progress.

"You have to. It's the only way to ensure that the people will have the truth that we've . . . that I've been denying them all this time."

"You need to stop talking," said Ning'er. A faint sense of panic stirred in her gut. He was delirious. He didn't know what he was saying. "You're not making any sense, and you're so sick still—"

"Please don't patronize me." His voice sharpened, despite the rasp in his throat. "Think about it. Just for a moment. What will it do to the court to have the Young Marshal revealed as the Red Yaksha, undercover among their ranks all along?"

He must have seen the answer bloom in Ning'er's expression because when they locked eyes again, he pulled that ghastly, sweat-beaded face of his into the most savage smile she'd ever seen.

"It would discredit them," said Ning'er. "Badly."

"It would crumble them," said Cheng Yun.

Ning'er didn't think she'd ever seen someone so close to death's edge look so thrilled at the idea of his own demise. "Well," she said. "It's a pity, then, that Feifei saved your ass."

She took his hand again, more firmly this time. "So you're going to live, at least for now. Which means that we survive another day without me betraying your trust for money. Sorry to disappoint, A'yun."

He might not have heard her. His eyes had fluttered shut again, and when she gave his fingers a squeeze, he didn't respond. Still, his chest rose and fell, his pulse thready but present when she checked for it.

She glanced over her shoulder, toward the sick room door. Feifei would be along presently, in all likelihood, to make sure that Ning'er's proclamation that Cheng Yun would live did, in fact, come true. There wasn't much Ning'er herself could do for Cheng Yun now, and she suspected he wouldn't be up to talking much more. What little he'd spoken had clearly already drained him beyond what was wise. There was nothing else for her in this room. Her time would be better spent seeing if any of the others needed her help. Even Zi'an or Zhenyi could surely provide her with some menial chore to do. Anything to keep her occupied, and far from Cheng Yun's fever-bright, beseeching eyes.

Her mind wandered, unbidden, back to Pirate Yang's offer. An odd, inexplicable guilt filled her belly as she pulled the coordinates for the buyer up on her comm-link. She stared at those numbers for a long moment. "Shit," she said. "Shit, shit, shit."

She dialed a different number, fingers moving thief-swift, before she could change her mind.

"Barkeep." Pirate Yang sounded surprised to hear from her, and a little suspicious. "You figure out when you're going to sell yet?"

Ning'er didn't speak. Her throat tightened.

"Hello? You lost your voice, too, on top of everything else?"

"No," Ning'er managed at last. "I've just . . . I've decided not to sell."

"Why the hell not? That money would set you up with rent, food—"

"I need my body the way it is," Ning'er interrupted bluntly. She looked down at her feet, curling her flesh-and-bone toes inside one boot, then the metal ones inside of the other. "I . . . there's something I promised to do, you see. And if I sell my remaining limbs now, I don't know if I could recover in time—or at all—to get it done."

A pause on the other end of the line. "It's Zi'an, isn't it? Whatever he's bought those explosives for. He's got you doing something for him."

Ning'er closed her eyes. "Something like that."

Pirate Yang huffed a little laugh of surprise. "Your life, your bank account, barkeep. But don't come crying to me if his gig comes to naught and leaves you missing your remaining limbs, and no payday to compensate, either."

"I won't," said Ning'er. "Thanks, Yang. Really."

As she hung up, her gaze flitted back to Cheng Yun's still, gray face. The rise and fall of his chest. Without thinking about it, she settled herself a little closer to him, scooting the seat up to the bed. He'd been so certain of her readiness to betray him, even after death. And she supposed she couldn't blame him. So why did his certainty sting so much?

"You absolute dumbass," she muttered. Her head bent over his. Was she speaking to herself or to the boy before her, unconscious and battling the demons in his own heart? It probably wouldn't matter much, either way. "What a mess you've made of me."

Just a little longer, she decided, fingers twined through his. Just a little longer, she'd stay here with him.

CHAPTER 8

The Point of No Return

Cheng Yun recovered, in the end.

It took about three days. Ning'er wasn't there for it all. Her research for the job—studying the blueprints of the lab, looking for backup exits and unseen entrances—kept her hands full and her mind distracted. For three days, she heard about the worst of the whole ordeal through an exhausted Zhenyi: the fever spikes that took forty-eight hours to break, the chills, the nightmares and delirious hallucinations. He cried out, sometimes: for his dead brother, for the Lark, and once, even for his father.

Feifei steadied them all amidst the worst of it. She pleaded off school for a week so she could see Cheng Yun through the violent throes of recovery. Sending him home to his father—and the attention of the court physicians—would have been out of the question. His cover may have survived the incident—after all, a tent full of his own officers had seen the attempt on their commander's life, and quick thinking on Feifei's part had gotten a message back to his superiors that Cheng Yun had sought private medical attention for the sake of discretion—but they couldn't risk what he might let slip in the height of his delirium.

When he finally emerged from his sickbed—pale and drawn and purple-shadowed beneath both eyes, but alive, lucid, and free from fever—Cheng Yun, true to form, returned to work immediately. They'd all argued against it—Feifei most vociferously—but he insisted on a need to keep up appearances.

"Did he learn literally nothing?" Ning'er griped during a logistics meeting when she found out. Cheng Yun himself was, notably, absent. "How much longer, exactly, is this charade of his supposed to last?"

She tried not to think about the final request he'd made of her, when he'd found himself on death's door. *I need you to sell me out, Ning'er. I need you to betray me, so the people of this country can have the truth, at last.*

"Hopefully just until we free the Lark," said Zi'an in grim tones. He'd been noticeably subdued since they'd nearly lost Cheng Yun, but he still had a bright-eyed, feral optimism about him that left Ning'er equal parts envious and strangely comforted. "Remember, Ning'er: the Lark is our game changer."

The thing was, Ning'er was actually sort of starting to believe him. He and Zhenyi had plotted their vision meticulously. Their break-in route to the Lark's prison was about as secure as anyone could ensure. Their getaway options were sound. And perhaps most important, one of the Red Yaksha's contacts worked for a local news outlet and was on deck to release the Lark's story as soon as she was free.

"And then what?" Ning'er asked once. "You think things will be better if, what, the little baby emperor's slightly older cousin takes the throne instead? You think he's some great guy who will just fix everything?"

"No," Cheng Yun had said bluntly. "But at least people will know the truth. They'll know that this whole system has been a sham all along, crafted by Lilium Corp and their ilk." He smiled. "Truth, in the right hands, is a formidable weapon."

Remembering—and planning—was easier said than done. Morale had hit an all-time low. Meanwhile, the protests continued, and with them, the crackdowns and the gendarme. It meant that streets shut down on the whims of the security task forces, and city curfews within the Lower Rings were enacted seemingly arbitrarily. Every other week, the crew seemed to be planning meetings around this road closure, that canceled train schedule, this curfew adjustment, that transit shutdown announcement.

"I know we have more important things to plan," griped Zhenyi one day, dry as dust, "but just once, I'd love to be able to travel between Rings without running into five different barricades, to say nothing of the abject fear of being sprayed in the face with tear gas for the crime of buying a carton of eggs at the wrong place and wrong time."

Cheng Yun himself was barely available, caught up as he was with the gendarme. He never spoke of what he did during those long, awful work details, but his face told the stories he never would. For all that Feifei had pronounced him recovered—or as recovered as anyone could be, at any rate—the ravages of his illness lurked in the hollows under his eyes, a new gauntness under those already high cheekbones. He was still beautiful, but everything about him seemed more fragile now.

The fragility was only further pronounced whenever he did sweep into a meeting. He lurked at the corners, he gave no flowery speeches, and his rare, quiet, sun-bright smiles became rarer still. Nevertheless, the gravity of the room inevitably centered on him. No matter how little he spoke and how much the others did, gazes drifted sidelong toward him, and telltale lulls in conversation seemed to await his input. Even body language—the direction in which Feifei pivoted the toes of her expensive heels, the drift of Zhenyi's hip, or the way Zi'an chose to lean on the furniture—pointed unconsciously toward Cheng Yun.

Even without accounting for the matter of Cheng Yun and the Great Gendarme Problem, as Feifei pointedly called it, within the remaining members of the crew, scheduling conflicts abounded. University continued at a mercilessly breakneck pace, leaving little spare time for revolutionary extracurriculars. Whenever Feifei wasn't tied up with exams, Zi'an seemed to have essays due.

It was a little surreal, the way a heist became just one more action item to contend with. But for Ning'er, whose potential eviction loomed ever closer, and her bank account—and belly—ever emptier, it was one she couldn't afford to treat lightly.

It wasn't the first time she'd skipped meals to save cash when her coffers ran dry, but she could hardly break into a heavily fortified Lilium-owned laboratory on an empty stomach.

"I know we're planning to hit the lab on Duanwu, but I can't afford to wait that long," Ning'er finally told Zi'an bluntly one day. She'd been dizzy with hunger and half convinced she'd pass out midway through their meeting. "If I'm going to keep working with you guys, I need an advance."

Zi'an raised his eyebrows at her, cocking his head to one side. With Cheng Yun so frequently absent, he had become something of a default second-in-command. "Something you're not telling us?"

Ning'er's face grew hot. There was no shame in this, she reminded herself sternly. They were all Lower Ringers, after all. None of them lived in a world where they could trick themselves into believing that money grew on trees. "Blue Star Brewpub got trashed." Ning'er swallowed and bit the inside of her cheek before continuing. "Tough luck on my part. I thought maybe I could scrounge something up, and there was . . . well, there was a chance to sell a few things of mine, a few days back, to make ends meet, but it . . . it didn't wind up working out." She looked at her feet, wishing she could will her face to stop burning. "I won't be able to make rent this month without an advance. At least a small one."

Zi'an didn't say anything for a moment. Ning'er continued to study her shoes, inexplicably ashamed, and ashamed of feeling ashamed on top of that.

Then his hand clapped her shoulder, warm and large and so sudden that she was startled into meeting his eyes again. She couldn't quite read the expression on his face. He'd narrowed his eyes, which glinted at her, backlit by the last hint of late afternoon sunlight sneaking through the café windows. It made him look like a man gone just a little mad. For the first time, Ning'er could see why Pirate Yang was wary of Zi'an, for all his easy charm and swagger—and why Cheng Yun had recruited a boy like this. There was something to be said for having a wild card on your side when it came to tempting fate. And Cheng Yun and his people, well, they were practically offering fate a lap dance.

Yet Zi'an's voice was curiously flat when he observed, "So, you didn't get in bed with Pirate Yang's contacts after all."

Ning'er blinked up at him, then narrowed her own eyes. "You knew?"

Zi'an looked away. "I guessed." The corner of his mouth lifted, dimpling a cheek. "I know Pirate Yang—have for years. And I like to think that—that all of us here in Cheng Yun's crew, really—are starting to know you. I figured you'd get in touch with them if you couldn't find other income. What I don't understand is why you didn't take whatever deal they offered. Why bother talking to them at all, if—"

"I wouldn't have been able to work for you guys anymore," Ning'er blurted out before she could think better of it. It wasn't information she owed Zi'an—or really, any of them—but once she said it, her chest felt a little lighter. "Or at least, I don't know if I'd have been able to . . . recover, in time." She forced herself to look Zi'an in the eye, this time, when she said, "They offered to help me sell my remaining limbs. The last time I lost organic limbs, it took me a year to adjust, and I was practically living on Complacency just to survive." She swallowed hard. "After I got clean, I had to adjust to prosthetics. That took even longer. I'm guessing you want me to break into the lab where they're keeping the Lark before we all go gray. So I told Yang no."

A million calculations dated through Zi'an's widening eyes. "Who was the buyer?"

Of all potential responses, that certainly hadn't been foremost on Ning'er's mind. "What?"

"The buyer," Zi'an repeated impatiently. "Who were they?"

Ning'er blinked at him. "I don't know. Does it matter? All I had were coordinates—"

"Then what were those?" Zi'an's hands went tight on Ning'er's shoulders. Urgency sat strangely on a boy like Zi'an. Ning'er had grown so accustomed to the version of Zi'an he wore most frequently in public, or even among his friends: easygoing, playfully flirtatious, maybe a little mischievous, but always in the name of a good time and a good cause. She'd rarely heard him sound so urgent about anything.

It threw her off her own game. Her fingers, normally so painstakingly steady, almost fumbled her comm-link as she thumbed through Yang's messages. "Here," she said awkwardly. "I don't know why you'd care, but—"

Her phone was out of her hands and between Zi'an's before he could complete the thought. A hiss whistled between his teeth. "I knew it."

"Knew what?" demanded Ning'er. "What the hell is going on, Zi'an?"

Zi'an thrust her comm-link back into her hands. In the same motion, he grabbed his own comm-link, pulling up a mockup of the laboratory blueprints. "Anything look familiar to you?"

It took Ning'er an embarrassing several seconds of squinting and scanning to spot what Zi'an meant. "Fuck."

"Not necessarily," said Zi'an. He had that wild glint in his eye again, the one that made him look like a mad bomber. "This could be good for us."

"Good?" Ning'er glared at him. "Yang just tried to hand me coordinates to sell my remaining organic limbs to a buyer based out of the same lab that kidnapped the Lark. In what universe is that good?"

Zi'an grinned, showing teeth. "The one where it tells us a little something about exactly what business Minister Cheng's lab deals in." He shook his head, chuckling darkly to himself. "Up until now, we've only known two significant things about that laboratory: that its ownership is registered to Lilium, and that the Lark is locked up somewhere inside. Now at least we know what they're buying—or at least some of it."

Bile threatened to rise from Ning'er's belly. She ignored it. "But why? Stem cell research? Cloning? What's the value in ordinary body parts? We're not even talking high-value internal organs here, or souped-up prosthetics—just plain old arms and legs, flesh and blood, nothing remarkable about them."

Zi'an frowned. His hands, and the blueprints, went into his

pockets as he stared at one of the foggy panes. "I don't know," he mused. "But it's a data point we should bring to the others—Cheng Yun, especially. He may know something about Lilium's inner workings that the rest of us don't, thanks to his family's affiliation." He paused, looking a little guilty. "He's also the one who would have to approve an advance. I'm sorry, Ning'er. I'd give it to you if I had the authority, but I'm just filling in. I could maybe spot you some cash from my own—"

"Let her have the advance."

They both turned. Ning'er's heart dropped. Cheng Yun leaned against the doorway to the café. It must have rained earlier; his hair was damp, curling at the ends as it clung to his too-pale forehead. The dying sunlight, increasingly obscured by grim gray clouds through the windows of the café, only emphasized the darkness of the purple shadows under his eyes.

"You can have the money," said Cheng Yun, addressing Ning'er. "It won't do to have you turned out of your home before we get our work done."

"How long have you been standing there?" Zi'an demanded. "I didn't hear you come in."

Cheng Yun offered them both a thin, ghastly smile. "I didn't want to be heard." He opened his palms toward them. Ning'er was reminded, with a pang, that this boy was also the Red Yaksha. The phantom of the Sixth Ring, unseen and unheard. "Sorry."

"Well, if you were lurking about long enough to hear everything we just said, you've saved us time," Ning'er found herself saying. Both boys looked at her, surprised. She made herself meet Zi'an's gaze, then, with a little more effort, Cheng Yun's. "We would have needed to ask you at some point about what you know."

"Ning'er," Zi'an began, his voice taking on a more placating edge.

Ning'er rounded on Zi'an. "You said it yourself. His family owes everything to Lilium."

"We do," said Cheng Yun, his voice briefly and unexpectedly rough. He composed himself after a moment. "But simply being indebted to a corporate manufacturer won't give you any direct answers about what happens behind closed doors. If they're collecting human body parts for experimentation, they certainly haven't brought up the details between dinner party courses at my father's manor."

"You don't sound shocked," Zi'an observed.

"That's because I'm not," said Cheng Yun. "Like I said, I may not know Lilium well, but I've grown up watching the kind of man their executives turned my father into." The ghoulish little smile grew, pulling at the edges of his increasingly sharp-boned face. It looked painful. "Trafficking human body parts is precisely the sort of business they'd be involved in. I suppose that one way or another, we'll find out to what end."

Zi'an frowned. "I don't know that I like this," he said abruptly. "We don't know what's waiting for us in that lab, but Ning'er has a point. If the same lab is buying actual human body parts from black-market dealers—"

"That's not our mission," said Cheng Yun in clipped tones. He turned his back on them. "The Lark is. This changes nothing." He glanced over his shoulder just once, lashes low, as he caught Ning'er's gaze. He rubbed a hand over his face, expression finally crumpling into the exhaustion he constantly tried to mask these days. "But our thief will have her advance. I'll make certain of it, Ning'er, don't worry. Now, if you'll excuse me, I have business to attend to."

The door clicked shut behind him neatly, quiet and polite, but Ning'er winced as though he'd slammed it. "He's different now," she told Zi'an. She blinked rapidly. "He's been different."

"Near death experiences will do that to people," said Zi'an grimly. He stared resolutely at the door Cheng Yun had just closed on them. "I've known Cheng Yun a long time. But for all the outrageous risks he takes, I don't think he's ever come this close to tasting death itself. Not since . . . well, perhaps not since his brother died."

Ning'er rubbed at her eyes, angry with herself. *Get a grip, Ning'er.* "What do we do, Zi'an? If a crew can't depend on their leader, a job falls apart every time."

Zi'an sighed. "What we can. We support him, as we always have. We follow his lead and try to help as unobtrusively as possible when we see him struggle. But mostly? Mostly, we do our jobs." He clapped her on the shoulder. He probably meant it as a comfort, but all Ning'er felt was the weight of his hand and the words from his tongue.

My job is to betray him, she thought, utterly miserable, and closed her eyes, too weary for once to protest the notion.

Plotting a heist on a tight deadline was, as it turned out, deeply stressful. Ning'er kind of hated that figuring out the actual route through the lab was technically her job.

She'd met with the crew in the back room of that little Fourth Ring café three times now to discuss her progress, and every time, her worries heightened. The job was doable—at least, if Ning'er's painstaking calculations were correct, it was doable—but it was also, without a doubt, the most dangerous gig she'd ever taken on. Even if they successfully outwitted the no doubt very well-paid, very well-trained guards, scaled the walls without anyone tumbling to an untimely demise, and successfully disabled the first layer of the security system, there was still the matter of what Ning'er had taken to referring to obliquely as the Obstacle Course of Death. Perhaps the smug old Lilium executive who owned the place fancied himself a scholar of the Western classics. Old Man Yu had once shared a book of Greek mythology with Ning'er, a battered copy from the used bookshelf at the back end of his shop. Ning'er hadn't thought of the old book in years, but she certainly found herself thinking about it now—in particular, the tale of Daedalus and the labyrinth he'd built to contain the Minotaur.

The Lilium executive was no Daedalus and what he'd built to protect his prize at the heart of the lab was no labyrinth, but it came awfully close. He'd created a veritable jungle of laser trip wires between the first layer of security and the entrance proper. Touch one, and all that work they'd put into evading the guards and disabling that first safeguard would be for naught. You'd have to be a competitive gymnast or a circus acrobat to get through it without alerting the main security system.

Or you'd have to be Zhong Ning'er.

"Can you get through it?" Zi'an had asked as Ning'er pored over the blueprints, charting their route under the anxiously watchful eyes of the crew. Their unblinking stares weren't exactly making her job any easier, but she doubted that snapping at them all to go away and leave her alone would make anyone feel any better.

Instead, Ning'er hummed, tilting her head from side to side. "On a good night, yes. On anything other than a good night . . ." She trailed off. "Well. Anything can happen."

"How comforting," drawled Feifei.

Ning'er glared. The sting of their argument during Cheng
Yun's tango with Devil's Mark was still relatively fresh. Then again,
Feifei had also been the one to rescue their boss from death's
doorstep. Ning'er forced herself to exhale slowly, letting go of
instinctive defensiveness. "I'll make it work. Now, as for getting
the rest of the crew through, I have some thoughts on—"

"Wouldn't it make more sense for you to go it alone?" Feifei
interrupted.

That poured salt on the sting, far more than Ning'er expected.
"Wow," she said. "I figured I might be expendable to you, doc, but
that's cold, even by your standards."

"Not how I meant it." A flicker of regret tugged at the corners
of Feifei's mouth. "It's just that none of us are equipped with your
skill set. Wouldn't we be a hindrance if you brought us along?"

In truth, Ning'er had thought so too, in the beginning. She'd
spent her entire thieving career as a solo act and hadn't loved
being assigned crewmates. Before she'd begun to chart their
break-in—truly chart it, accounting for obstacles and potential
pitfalls—she'd still mostly considered the crew Cheng Yun's
creatures. Nice to have around, but ultimately unnecessary to
the real work.

But then she'd studied the blueprints and run smack dab into
the cold plate glass of reality.

"I don't need all of you present on site, but I do need a support
team," Ning'er said bluntly. "Even if I get through that monstros-
ity of trip wires, that means jack shit without, say, a stealthy demolitions expert who can get me through potential blockades with
minimal noise and debris." She ignored Zi'an's proudly knowing
grin, turning her attention to Zhenyi. "Zi'an and I will also need
someone to run point on us from a safe distance. You're the best

option for that, Zhenyi. You're both the most seasoned strategist and the most experienced in dealing with Beiyang authorities under pressure." Ning'er swallowed. "Of this crew, if there's anyone I'd trust in my ear to steer me out of trouble in the belly of an off-books Lilium lab, it would be you."

Zhenyi nodded, eyes softening. "I'll bring you home. I'd like the chance to do that with my friends this time. What about Cheng Yun?"

"What about Cheng Yun?" Ning'er repeated, a little irritably, trying to pretend that her heart hadn't just leapt into her throat at the inevitable question. Apparently, simply wishing not to address a problem didn't make it magically disappear. Her gaze twitched toward Zi'an's. Mouth thin, he gave her a little bow of the head. Her heart sank. Zi'an might be nominally their ringleader without Cheng Yun around, but he was letting her run the show on this one. Which meant the fucker was also leaving her with the unenviable task of figuring out how to tell a roomful of the Red Yaksha's closest collaborators that their beloved icon was in no kind of shape to be involved in a high stakes heist.

"He is the face of this whole operation," said Ning'er at last, as matter-of-factly as she could manage. "The Red Yaksha. There's no need to risk his neck." She hardened her voice. "Presumably, that's what he pays us for."

"Which is also why," said a clear, quiet voice by the doorway, "I'll be coming along, thank you very much."

Ning'er's eyes fluttered shut in resigned silence as the others exclaimed over the walking corpse of a boy who'd just materialized in their presence. There were a lot of things the Red Yaksha did that Ning'er grudgingly admired, but finding a way to move softly enough to avoid alerting her mostly just pissed her off. The guy's reputation as a phantom clearly rested on some solid stealth skills, but her sense of self-preservation—and ego—didn't love the reminder. Especially right now.

"With due respect," said Ning'er with forced courtesy, "I don't need to be micromanaged, and you're still recovering from a near death experience. Or don't you remember being stabbed?"

"Stabbed is a strong word." Cheng Yun gave her a grim little smile, his expression cheeky. "Scratched, really."

"But poisoned, all the same," Zi'an pointed out. "Ning'er is right. You recruited us to get our hands dirty. To be the hands of the Red Yaksha, where the face can't appear."

"Maybe the face of the Red Yaksha doesn't belong there," said Cheng Yun, "but the Young Marshal does. It's Lilium-owned, after all." He bowed his head. His hair, noticeably in need of a trim, slipped over his eyes, hiding them from view. "You and Ning'er were right, the day when you said I have the strongest ties to them, out of all of us. I may not have been inside this particular lab, but I know my way around a Lilium property. He hesitated. "Which means that if something feels off—something that might put the rest of us in danger—I'll know."

"So you'll make yourself the canary in the coal mine," Ning'er blurted out.

The corner of his mouth tipped upward. "In a sense, sure."

"Those canaries die," Feifei pointed out. The corners of her mouth, in contrast to Cheng Yun's, pulled sharply downward. "The Lark's rescue is many things—mostly foolish—but a suicide mission was never supposed to be one of them."

The smile that had been budding in Cheng Yun's face vanished. "It's only a metaphor, Feifei," he told her gently, but those shadow-rimmed eyes were steely. "I don't have a death wish, but

my brother died from oxyveris." For the first time, the faintest
note of desperation clawed its way into his otherwise steady voice.
"There are certain things that I . . . that I need to understand."

Ning'er didn't believe the whole death-wish denial for a second. Not after the bloody promise he'd tried to extract from her.
Cheng Yun was far too willing to wager his own life in games of
chance.

There are certain things that I need to understand.

Heaven above. Gooseflesh prickled along Ning'er's skin. And
to think that she had once believed that she was the one with a
monopoly on family drama.

"It should be Ning'er's call." Zhenyi's voice piped up unexpectedly, cutting through the strange tension that had filled the
room. Her gaze on Cheng Yun's face was solemn, and otherwise
entirely unreadable. "With due respect, Cheng Yun, this is what
you wanted to hire a thief for—to chart a viable break-in route,
steal the Lark, and make the tough calls on the best way to get it
all done with minimal risk. You ought to get your money's worth.
Let Ning'er do her job."

Cheng Yun's gaze swiveled slowly from Zhenyi toward Ning'er,
as if seeing his hired thief for the first time. Ning'er withstood his
scrutiny in wary silence as his head canted to the side. "You'll still
get paid, one way or another," he told her at last.

His reassurance slapped her across the face with unexpected
force. The kindness in his voice stung worse than any vitriol. She
swallowed hard. "Not if we all die," she told him.

Cheng Yun smiled at her. "So keep us alive." He spread his
hands. "Make your call, thief of ours."

"Easier said than done," Ning'er shot back. "On both counts."
She massaged her temples as the crew awaited her decision with

collectively bated breath. Logically, she knew what the safe call would be. A cat burglar and a good demolitions expert could handle a break-in on their own, probably—especially now that they'd cased the place as best they could.

And yet.

There are certain things that I need to understand, Cheng Yun had said.

The coordinates Pirate Yang had texted her clung insistently to Ning'er's mind. The buyer who would have taken the rest of Ning'er's limbs off her body for the right price. The way her blood had run cold when she saw the way those coordinates matched up precisely to the blueprints for the lab where the Lark was being held.

That lab was owned by the people who'd killed Cheng Yun's brother. Ning'er couldn't fault him for wanting to face his demons.

"That creepy silent walk you do to sneak up on us all the time," she said. "Do you think you can pull it off during a high stakes break-in?"

For the first time, a hint of Cheng Yun's old smile flickered across his features. "What kind of vigilante would I be if I couldn't?"

Ning'er looked at the rest of them. "We could use the extra set of hands," she said. "Who knows? Maybe all that expensive military training will wind up coming in handy if we get cornered into a tight spot."

Zi'an was the first to respond, lifting his shoulders in a calculatedly casual shrug. "Sounds fair enough to me."

That seemed to set the tone. Zhenyi gave a slow, careful nod of agreement. Feifei looked more hesitant but sighed. "It's not as though Cheng Yun's ever been much good at following doctor's orders," she grumbled. Her gaze hung on to Ning'er's for a moment. "Look after him, will you? He's important to us." She hesitated, then added, looking away, "He's our friend."

Something softened inside Ning'er. "I know."

"It's settled then," said Cheng Yun, in a voice that brooked no argument. He gazed carefully around the café at them all. "Let's figure out this labyrinth of Ning'er's, shall we?"

CHAPTER 9

The Maze Within the Maze

Duanwu crept up faster than any of them could have imagined. Weird, the way that could happen. It never felt real, in your head, no matter how meticulously you planned it or how many calendars you marked. But that late May day rolled around all the same, fateful and inevitable.

A nip clung to the late spring air when Ning'er arrived at the designated coordinates, earpiece already tucked in place. She tapped it a few times. "Arrival confirmed. How are we doing on time?"

Zhenyi answered, voice crackling over the static. "Three minutes out. Thanks for being so punctual."

Ning'er bit her tongue on a retort about always being punctual. Instead, she shivered beneath the thin quick-dry fabric of her black jumpsuit. Nerves, she told herself. Just nerves. And nerves were normal when you were risking this much. Glancing at the perimeter of the lab, she wished she could laugh at herself. The building didn't look like anything special, not compared to the ostentatious mansions and luxury apartments she'd been burgling. There were no elaborate enclosed gardens to cut through, no great ivy trellises or wide latticed windows. The place didn't even look that big—three stories from the outside, modest dimensions, nondescript, black-paneled exterior. You could have missed it, tucked away in a largely abandoned corner of the city as it was, on the outskirts of the Fifth Ring.

But Ning'er was a professional. And she'd done her homework. Looks could be deceiving.

"You guys all good to go?" she asked the boys. She waited for their nods. They'd flanked her in silence—Zi'an arriving ahead of Cheng Yun, who completed their little triumvirate, paler than ever in the black Ning'er had put them all in. It made the boys look like great dark crows, swooping in to join Ning'er on the precipice of something she wasn't sure any of them were really ready for.

Then again, you never really felt ready for a job until you actually did the damn thing.

"Good," said Ning'er, when she'd gotten affirmatives from them both. "Medical and bioengineering support team on standby?"

"Affirmative," Feifei confirmed over the earpiece.

"Please try not to break any of Ge Rong's new toys," said Zhenyi dryly. "You wouldn't believe the chunk of money the raw materials took out of the budget."

Which, Ning'er supposed, was Zhenyi-speak for 'affirmative.' "We'll do our best." She laced her fingers in front of her, cracking her knuckles and rolling her neck out. "All right, we all know the drill, but just to review: the doors to the main entrance are bolted, which means we go around them. I go in first. I'll scope everything out before the rest of you follow. I scale my way up to the main floor, get in through the east window, and . . . make my way through Lilium's labyrinth." She tried to sound casual about that last bit and probably didn't entirely succeed. "When I manage to get past that old jumble of trip wires"—*when*, not *if*, she was careful to say—"I should be able to turn it off from the inside and let the rest of you through. From there, the path through the main hall to the basement level where the Lark is imprisoned should be pretty straightforward, but that doesn't mean we get to let our guard down." She bit her lip. "Overconfidence will kill even the best of thieves. What makes the basement level dangerous isn't trip-wire labyrinths or tricky locks or even armed guards. It's the unknown—the parts that weren't in the blueprints."

She glanced toward that eerily nondescript building again, hugging her elbows. "And from what I've gathered, everything important happens on the basement levels." She grimaced. "The parts we can't see from the outside."

The earpiece crackled. "Be careful of the Lark," said Feifei. "We don't know—not for sure—what kind of condition she will be in. Don't try to move her by yourself. Let the boys help. She's a human being, not a suitcase of money. I need you all there when we unlock that cage to deal with . . . whatever happens. I can't emphasize too much how important that is."

Normally, Ning'er would have bristled at being told how to do her job. This time she recognized Feifei's guidance for what it was: sound medical advice, tempered with the giver's caution. Ning'er nodded, even though Feifei couldn't see her, and made careful eye contact with Zi'an, then, a little more reluctantly, with Cheng Yun. "Feifei is right," Ning'er told the boys. "The Lark is the biggest unknown of them all. I'll need you both at my side if—when we reach her."

If either of the boys were shocked at the way Feifei had spoken of the Lark—their would-be savior, their golden ticket to a better kingdom, free of Beiyang rule—neither of their faces showed it. A little pale, a little tight-mouthed, maybe, but no one looked ready to back down after coming this far.

Ning'er allowed herself a small smile and tapped her earpiece. "We stick to the plan unless I signal otherwise." She tapped her earpiece again. "I give the word; you go where I tell you. Clear?"

She waited for their nods of affirmation, which came one by one, with surprisingly little reluctance. Flexing the fingers of her metal hand, she tried to shake off some unnamable discomfort. It felt a little weird, in retrospect, to be the one barking orders for once. Ning'er tried, very hard, not to look at Cheng Yun in particular longer than she had to. This was her job. He trusted her with it, even if things were weird between them now. If anything, he was probably pleased that his hired thief was showing a bit of initiative. Yet she couldn't quite shake the feeling that by taking command, she'd usurped him somehow.

Unbidden, his feverish ramblings rang through her mind: *You will betray me, Ning'er. I need you to. I need you to sell me out. Can you do that for me, Ning'er?*

It hadn't been so long since Devil's Mark had almost snuffed his life out. Since he'd told Ning'er that one day she would betray him, his fever-rasped voice so thick with sudden lucidity, such certainty. She could see it like a painting before her: those big dark eyes, pupils dilated, bright and knowing and desperate as he'd given her his instructions on how to wrong him in the worst way imaginable. All for his beloved greater good.

It hadn't been very long at all.

Ning'er swallowed the memory. Deliberately, she turned without looking at the slight, dark figure bringing up the rear of the crew. No matter. He'd lived. And he was here now.

It wasn't so different, initially, from the average break-in at some fancy manor home. Zhenyi had done a good job of timing their meeting to duck the usual guard patrols, and the late-night janitorial staff had long since packed it in. That alone got rid of most potential witnesses—and the main source of Ning'er's pre-heist anxiety.

The lab boasted a high wall, just like most Upper Ring homes. And just like their homes, you only had to look long enough to find the flaws: edges to the bricks, jutting out just far enough to get a grip with your well-booted toes, your careful and callused fingers. And better still, a bit higher up: a sturdy metal trellis and a few broad windowsills. No real plants—who could be bothered to grow a living thing in a place as desolate as this?—but a decorative vine wound its way along the iron, dangling several feet over Ning'er's head. Ning'er gave her metal arm an experimental tap against the brick. She grinned. How lucky, the way artificial things were often so much stronger than the organic. This would do. This would do quite nicely indeed.

No barrier had ever kept Ning'er out for long. She was no stranger to heights. She'd been scared of them, once, but it had been quashed by everything else she'd gained from them: Exhilaration. Joy. Freedom.

Still, a ghost of the old fear flitted through her as she tested her grips on the side of the wall. Some panicked hindbrain instinct probably, triggered by everything that had gone into this night. Maybe the stakes of the job. Maybe the knowledge of what was inside.

Ning'er forced it all down and began her climb.

Amazing, how quickly fear crumbled in the face of the familiar. Her fingers found purchase on the brick. And slowly, surely, she ascended. There was one harrowing moment where her shoe slipped on an edge. Her heart plummeted through the pit of her stomach as her fingers scrabbled for grip. A shout of distress stuck in her throat.

She made herself swallow it. She'd done this before. She'd fallen. She'd made mistakes. But she'd never broken, not permanently.

Her hands caught ahold of the artificial vine. Its edges seared what would definitely be a new set of blisters across her palm. Gritting her teeth, she kicked her feet back against the wall, scrambling until she connected, again, with that ledge of brick.

The way up the trellis was easier. She twined her feet through the vine, the same way she would around a piece of rope, as she inched her way up, twining and retwining the artificial length of braided coils over her booted feet.

And just like a million times before, in a million other break-ins, she was at the top of her climb and through the window. A dark—and seemingly empty—hallway spread out before her. Ning'er knew better than to believe what she saw. She'd studied the blueprints too well for that. Looks really were deceiving, and Lilium had long thrived on illusion. Now began the hard part.

Ning'er tapped her earpiece, trying not to let her hands shake. "Zhenyi?"

"Copy."

Ning'er breathed out slowly. Then in again. "I've reached the labyrinth," she told the other girl.

A pause from Zhenyi. Then, her voice crackling through the earpiece, carefully neutral: "You have the device in place?"

Ning'er sighed and raised her metal hand. "Really, now. What do you take me for, an amateur?"

"Just checking. If you can still sass, presumably you can still work Ge Rong's gadgets. Get ready."

Ge Rong, for all the crap she gave him, really was something of a miracle man. If a thing could be engineered, his hands could build it. But even A'rong couldn't shut off the maze of laser trip wires remotely.

What he could do, however, was the next best thing. Ning'er

gave one of her artificial fingers a squeeze. At the end of her pointer finger—right where the nail would be on a flesh hand— was a tiny silver clip. Ning'er jabbed it with her thumb.

For a moment, nothing happened. Then that lonely, empty hallway burst into light. Ning'er shielded her eyes with her organic hand, squinting for a moment under the glare. It didn't take her eyes long to adjust, though a part of her wished it had. Long lines of red light had sprung to life, crisscrossing the hallway in constant motion.

Ning'er rolled out her wrists, cracking her neck from side to side. "Now or never, right?"

No one on the other end of the earpiece answered. Their silence left only the thud of Ning'er's own heartbeat drumming in her ears. "Thanks for the pep talk, guys," she muttered.

"You'll be fine." It took Ning'er a moment to place Cheng Yun's voice. A little raspy, but surprisingly businesslike. Then, with a slight edge that Ning'er might have pegged as playful if she didn't know better: "After all, you broke into a gendarme encampment and back out with the Young Marshal in tow. What's some trip wire compared to that?"

A lot, actually, the dolefully logical part of Ning'er wanted to say. The encampment had been easy to sneak into because it was guarded by people. People could be fooled or reasoned with or manipulated. Lasers, less so.

Something about the way he said it, though—the wry, quiet confidence in her skill—buoyed her heart despite the rapid thrum of its anxious beat. There was a lot to be said for someone else's confidence, especially the Red Yaksha's. "See you on the other side, then," she told the others. And before she could talk herself into it, she dove into a roll.

Time blurred. Ning'er's world shifted, blacking out every-thing around her until all she perceived were lines of red dancing through the dark. Her mind narrowed, focus homing in on the exquisite simplicity of the task at hand: make it to the other end of the room without getting caught. A flash of red arced overhead. Ning'er slid beneath, belly flat against the floor.

Immediately, a second line of red slid toward her, this time low across the tiles. Ning'er planted both palms on the tile, and with a grimace, kicked her legs through. Momentum carried her narrowly over. She landed on three limbs, her metal hand scraping along one of the tiles to keep her balance as two lasers swooped toward her. She barely ducked one, and took a Hail Mary leap after the other, rolling into a ball just in time to slide under a third.

Her earpiece crackled. "You good so far?" Zhenyi didn't sound worried, which should have been more comforting than it was.

"Oh, you know," Ning'er panted, "just a bit of a rough night at the office. Fuck!" She hopped over another telltale flash of light. Gravity pulled her into a somersault that just barely brought her out of range of the next.

"Coordinates on your earpiece indicate you're more than halfway through," said the other girl, cool as Hebei on the brink of winter. "Steady does it, Ning'er."

Ning'er huffed a wry little chuckle. "Roger that."

The second half of the maze was easier to get through than the first. Ning'er wasn't sure how much of that was physiological or psychological—her muscles warmed up from those first few jumps and tumbles, her brain adapting to the onslaught of deadly red light—and how much was real. Not that it mattered. She'd take easy if she could get it.

As if to penalize her for her hubris, three lasers flashed to life in rapid succession, arcing toward her like thrown knives. Ning'er bit her tongue on a yell, sliding under the first with splayed legs. She wasted no time finding her feet, but the trip wires continued to flash into motion. Teeth clenched, Ning'er kicked up one foot behind her to evade the backward path of the second laser, arms flung up instinctively to counterbalance. A mistake. The third nearly skimmed her fingertips before she retracted them, pulling her arms tight against her sides.

And then they froze. Ning'er paused, panting, still balanced T-shaped on one leg, arms glued against her ribs for dear life. Straight ahead, the control panel at the other end of the hallway— the one with the master lock that would let the others in—gleamed at her, mockingly innocent.

Right on cue, Ning'er's leg—the organic one, of course it had to be the organic one she'd landed on—buckled beneath her. Because organic limbs succumbed to stupid stuff like muscle fatigue and exhaustion.

Well, shit.

"Breathe, Ning'er." Cheng Yun's voice was clipped and calm. He didn't sound anything like Old Man Yu had, but the unemotional steadiness of his voice—the implied certainty—slammed her out of mounting panic and back into her own body. "You know what to do."

She did, in fact. Or rather, her body did. Her limbs moved on their own, buoyed by years of muscle memory, reawakening without the fog of fear to clamp them tight. The leg outstretched behind her fanned its way up and over the trip wire. Just as Ning'er's balance faltered, she dove one more time, sliding herself forward beneath the last of those lasers before they could collide with her body.

Tucking herself into a ball, she shut her eyes, rolled, and prayed.

She tucked her head automatically as her back connected—slightly too hard—with solid ground. "Ouch!" Her body tensed again, a probable new bruise throbbing along her spine as her ears strained, anticipating the inevitable scream of an alarm. Surely, she'd fucked this one up. Surely, one of those lasers had ghosted across her skin during that roll, and any minute, the guards would come running. Surely—

"You need to let the boys in, Ning'er."

That was Feifei, speaking up at last—and sounding, to Ning'er's surprise, amused. Confused, Ning'er blinked her eyes open. And stared.

The control panel—and the master key switch—stared back at her.

"If your jaw is hanging open, kindly close it and hurry up," continued Feifei. "Zhenyi may be too polite to rush you, but mission control or not, I don't mind reminding the rest of you that we're on a schedule here. Sorry, Zhenyi."

"No need to apologize." Zhenyi sounded like she was trying not to laugh, in fact. "Ning'er, are you quite all right?"

Ning'er pulled herself to her feet, wincing as she worked out the kinks in her spine. No doubt about it—her back was going to turn all kinds of pretty colors by morning. If they survived that long. "Never better." She limped, slightly bow-legged, over to the control panel. "Ready, boys?"

"As ever," said Zi'an, a little breathlessly. "We're at the main doors, on the first floor. And before you ask, yes, I've got my explosives on hand—and a silencer—in case we run into trouble." He chuckled. "No feats of acrobatic wall scaling for us, I'm afraid. So let's hope this works."

"Let's hope indeed," said Ning'er. "Otherwise the two of you are going to have to get real flexible and real unafraid of heights very quickly." Her fist hit the button at the center of the panel. "Showtime."

It was a little surreal how ordinary the whole thing felt. Neither Zi'an nor Cheng Yun said anything when they arrived to meet Ning'er. True to plan, they'd climbed up the stairs from the first floor, like normal people just strolling into this creepy secret lab. They were both still in their black attire and a little pale from nerves, but aside from that, they might have been average office workers, stuck on overtime.

For the first time, Ning'er took the lab in—really took it in. Blueprints were all very well, but they couldn't do the building true justice. You didn't really know the feel of a place until you stepped inside. So far, not even the most lavish of Upper Ring manors had ever quite replicated that feeling—that creeping sense that the building you'd set foot in had a soul of its own. Negotiating with that soul was, in a sense, what all good burglars did.

Ning'er narrowed her eyes as she looked around. The question was, what did this particular building want from her? The facility was as nondescript on the inside as it was from the outside—at least on this floor. It looked less like a top-secret lab and more like an old school that had seen better days. The plain, industrial paint on the walls was peeling at the corners, and the ugly black-and-gray tiling was scuffed and fading. Rows and rows of black-painted, neatly numbered doors could have belonged to an office building or cheap apartment complex. The place was nothing special. A cakewalk to navigate.

The lower levels would tell a different story. No sense getting ahead of themselves. Still, the temptation of overconfidence toyed at the edges of her awareness. As she and the boys made their descent silently down the winding staircase to the belly of the lab, Ning'er couldn't help but suspect that this had all gone just a little too smoothly. A part of her—a big, admittedly foolish part—wanted to believe that a second shoe wouldn't drop.

All thoughts of smooth sailing vanished as soon as they hit the basement floor. A chill skittered down her spine like cockroaches through an alley. This was another world entirely. The main room was crowded with aisles of test tubes, carefully capped, but glimmering with some thick red substance Ning'er couldn't identify and didn't especially care to. It cast an alien glow across the entire premises. Even sealed off from them, that dim red light gave Ning'er a gut-churning sense of unease. Something about the way it washed over everyone's features, like it was already painting them in blood, felt like an ill-timed prophecy.

Ning'er swallowed her discomfort. Creepy test tubes or not, now was no time to back down. She took an experimental step forward.

The alarm that blared through her eardrums nearly knocked her off her feet. She spun in place, disoriented and fighting for her bearings. Her hip smacked into one of the tables, nearly knocking a row of capsules over. Swearing beneath the scream of the alarm, she caught an errant capsule before it could hit the floor.

"What the hell?" Zi'an yelled over the alarm.

"Be quiet before you bring a brigade of guards down on us," snapped Ning'er. Carefully, she returned the container to its original place. It had been made from ordinary glass, sealed tightly at the top. It leaked no hint of that odd red substance on her skin, but she found herself wiping her palm on her jumpsuit all the

same. Her mind raced. *Come on brain, fix this, goddammit.* "All
the security trip wires were accounted for, which means this is
something else."

"You hear that alarm?"

"An alarm isn't always a trip wire. Sometimes it's a signal.
Sometimes, it—" Dread, a stone, dropped to the pit of her belly.
"Shit."

"What?" asked Zi'an, hands over his ears. His face was nearly
white against the black of his clothing.

"It signals that someone's credentials have cleared," said
Ning'er. "It signals that . . . someone . . . someone with ID is about
to enter the building."

Right on cue, the screeching alarm paused. Ning'er's heart
thrummed a steady patter of fear into the silence that followed.
Fear was unnecessary, she thought. Out of place. This wasn't the
end of the world. There were plenty of people who'd staff a lab of
this size. Interns. Technicians. Janitors, even. An alarm signaling
the arrival of a legitimate visitor didn't mean the visitor was an
actual threat.

Then an automated voice crackled over the laboratory loudspeaker: "Guest credentials accepted. Approaching premises."

For one awful, frozen moment in time, no one said anything
at all.

Then, subvocalized from Zi'an, resigned and replete with a
dank sort of amusement: "Well, shit."

"Never mind that," snapped Ning'er. She'd gone into full crisis management mode, even as her heart rattled inside her chest.
"If we just lie low, we can continue—"

The loudspeaker crackled back to life. The new voice coming online wasn't the automated machine's, though. It was too

human, familiar. It spoke through the static, stern with suspicion: "Security system. Please check vitals on Subject 4A-502: He Bailing."

Cheng Yun stumbled at the sound of his father's voice. A crash. Ning'er and Zi'an spun as one. A'yun stood slightly apart from them, near an upended lab table, surrounded by broken glass and a growing puddle of red. His eyes were enormous in the dark, tinted near-gold by the crimson glimmering around his boots.

"Shit." Ning'er had never actually heard Cheng Yun swear before, not even during the worst throes of Devil's Mark poisoning. "I didn't mean to . . ."

To what? To make this worse than it was? To, against all odds, be the one who fucked this whole thing up? Ning'er could have kicked herself. No, this wasn't on Cheng Yun, not entirely. It was her fault. She'd made the call. She'd decided against her better judgment to add a third man to their perfectly adequate team, and now all three of them were fucked.

Cheng Yun had fallen silent, for once seemingly lost for the right words. The pause curdled around all three crew members, ripe with desperate hope. Ning'er exhaled into the taut silence. *Please, please please,* she begged silently, to whatever obscure deity controls the fate of ill-conceived heists, *cut us some slack—*

The alarm began to blare again. The automated voice crackled online once more. "Esteemed guest, please be advised. Intruders detected on the basement level. Recommended security protocol: authorize guard patrol deployment to basement level."

"No," said Ning'er aloud, furious and terrified and desperate all at once. "You've got to be kidding—"

Minister Cheng's voice again, cool, almost casual, interrupted, "Authorized."

"Authorization accepted," said the machine. "Guard Unit 237891, please deploy."

Ning'er shoved aside an instinctive wave of panic. Panic wasn't productive. Instead, her mind raced through the map in her brain. "We have to abort." The concession tasted like sawdust in her mouth. Nothing. This had all been for nothing.

Still, at the very least, she could get the boys—and herself—out of the lab alive.

"You know the bailout plan." She jerked her head toward the stairs. "We run, back out the way you guys came in, no detours. The Lark will have to wait."

Struggle etched its way across Zi'an's face, just for a moment. Then melted away into shock. "Cheng Yun!"

Ning'er spun on her heel, but it was too late. Cheng Yun's earpiece lay abandoned on the floor between them. He was already halfway down the opposite corridor—the one that led to the Lark's cage. The swiftness of his gait shouldn't have surprised her. The Red Yaksha and Young Marshal were both fleet-footed.

Zi'an's face was stark white. Before he could start after Cheng Yun, Ning'er's hand shot out, practically of its own accord, and snagged the crook of his arm, metal fingers snagging on the threads of the black sweater. "No."

"What do you mean, no?" Zi'an rounded on her. "We have to go after him!"

"You," Ning'er emphasized, "need to get the hell out of here."

Zi'an's eyes narrowed behind his glasses. "Me. What about you? What are you doing?"

"I'd like to echo the question," said Zhenyi's voice, crackling over the earpiece.

Ning'er squeezed her eyes shut. "Something stupid," she told them, and raised a hand to her earpiece.

"Ning'er, what—" Zhenyi's voice, starting to crescendo with alarm, was cut off as Ning'er switched the earpiece off and tugged it free.

Grabbing a wide-eyed Zi'an's hand, she dropped it into his palm. "Return this to Ge Rong when you see him again and tell him that we—that I'm sorry." She tried to smile. "I'll find the rest of you if—when we're out. Now go."

Just over her shoulder, Cheng Yun was disappearing down the hallway, pelting toward his true north. *Idiot,* Ning'er wanted to scream after him. What exactly did he think he was going to do with some relic of the past, some near-dead girl, with his own father's guards already in hot pursuit?

He already cut such a distant figure. In just a moment, he'd round the corner, and it would be like he'd never existed at all. In just a moment, he'd be gone.

She could let him go. Technically, he was just a job. Just a pay day. The smart thing to do would be to let him go.

"Fuck," snarled Ning'er.

And then, before she could change her mind, she pelted down the same corridor. Toward the Lark's cage. Toward Cheng Yun's true north. Toward both of their deaths, probably.

Ning'er ran anyway, her gaze fixed on the dark spot of Cheng Yun's hair in the distance. Her lungs burned. She ignored them. Whether she was chasing Cheng Yun or He Bailing, she didn't really know. She had an awful feeling that if she tried to answer honestly, her feet would give out at last under the weight of truths she didn't have the energy to parse. All she could focus on was that distant cut of Cheng Yun's figure, disappearing into the shadows, and her utterly stupid, stubborn refusal to let him go.

So instead, she did what thieves did best: she went after her prize.

CHAPTER 10

Swan Song of the Lark

The basement wasn't like the rest of the building. These corridors weren't lined in plain black doors. Instead, full plate glass displays glowed with that same strange red liquid. It shone too brightly to be blood, but blood was all Ning'er could think of as she tore down the hall.

A slow but steady crescendo of shouts and booted footsteps had begun to build up behind them. The security detail, no doubt. Swearing under her breath, Ning'er picked up her pace. She didn't even know yet if they'd been spotted, and she didn't dare yell out a warning to Cheng Yun.

One thing was certain. They wouldn't be able to rely on speed alone to get themselves out of this mess. A human body wasn't built to sprint forever.

Which left the matter of outwitting the guards to Ning'er. Assuming she could catch up to the idiot who'd landed them in this race for their lives in the first place.

Ning'er's left foot had gone sore with exertion. Shin splints were going to be a real bitch to deal with if she lived. But it wasn't for naught. She cut across a swathe of corridor. It wasn't much, but it was just enough to shorten the distance between them.

Her hand closed around Cheng Yun's, just as she passed him. "You," she panted, yanking him along by the wrist, "are a goddamn idiot."

It probably wasn't the most compelling way to get him to follow her. For a moment, she thought he might pull out of her grasp. Then his fingers twined through hers. She chose to take that as Cheng Yun for *yes, I am, please carry on.*

Ning'er carried on.

She finally found what she was looking for around the next bend in the winding hallway. "Hey," she muttered at him under her breath. Her grip slipped sweat slick over Cheng Yun's hand, but he didn't let go. "Do you trust me?"

The shouts of the guards were growing closer. She needed an answer now.

She caught a single glimpse of his face, bathed bloodred by the reflected lights of the glass tanks around them, his expression unreadable. He looked like a monster. He looked like a dead man. He looked, somehow, still so goddamn beautiful.

Another shout, as the guards rounded the bend in the hallway. Any minute now, they'd be sighted.

"Yes," choked out Cheng Yun. "Yes, I trust you. I've always—"

That was all Ning'er needed. As booted feet rushed toward them, Ning'er kicked open the vent between one of the glass tanks. The yawning tunnel revealed behind it was pitch dark. Before Cheng Yun could react, she threw both arms tight around him, the metal joints of her elbow creaking against his rib cage.

And then she hurtled them both through that tunnel, into the black nothingness beneath.

Despite what folks said about girls like Ning'er, she had always been a good student. At the very least, she was the sort of girl who, barring disaster, always did her homework, back in those scant, early days when her father was a real father and she could still sometimes afford real schooling.

It turned out, thankfully, to be a transferrable skill.

The maze of laser trip wires hadn't been the only labyrinth the Lilium architects had built into their lab. Hidden tunnels snaked around each other at the very foundation of the building. Even with building blueprints to fall back on, you could get lost for days down there if you weren't careful. Ning'er understood why without being told. It was common to privately owned science facilities to build tunnel passageways between lab rooms for the sake of discretion. If you'd hired scientists or engineers to create something that hadn't yet been patented—or, indeed, wasn't entirely legal—you didn't want the wrong eyes on your product. When visitors were afoot, obfuscation was paramount.

The original purpose of these tunnels had been for exactly that: Not everyone who had access to the lab was meant to see everything there. On inspection days, the tunnels facilitated the quiet, unseen transfer of experiments between individual lab rooms—what those samples consisted of, Ning'er didn't know and, frankly, didn't especially want to—but now, they were a boon for thieves.

She'd memorized all their entry points. She'd even calculated for the ones with free-fall drops—she couldn't imagine leaping through a vent like this was much good for sensitive lab samples, but she was no scientist, so what the hell did she know?—and kept them logged in her notes.

That didn't change the way her belly dropped out from under her when she leapt.

It could have been so many things in this moment. The sound of security-issued boots, hot on their heels. The fall itself. Cheng

Yun's hand, hot and slick with sweat under her vise-like grip, the weight of his body tight against hers. A reminder of the consequence if she miscalculated.

She'd fallen off so many ledges, jumped through so many vents. But without fail, each time, there was just a split second of fear. And there was much more to be afraid of this time.

They slid to the bottom of the tunnel with a resounding crash. Cheng Yun yanked at her elbow, pulling most of her weight on top of him as they landed. Her head connected hard with his sternum.

"Ow," said Cheng Yun plaintively.

"Yeah." Ning'er rubbed at her forehead. Still dizzy from the drop, she squinted around, trying to get bearings for them both. This lab room didn't look like anything special—more glass tanks, more creepy red glow—but you never could really know in a place like this.

Cheng Yun emitted a faint moan. The entire focus of Ning'er's attention, to her dismay, shifted immediately toward him. "I hope you're sorry," she informed him in what she hoped was a pitiless and ferocious tone. "Since literally everything is your fault."

"Quite a proclamation from the girl who just dragged me down a chute." Cheng Yun coughed lightly.

Ning'er squinted at him. "Are you trying to make me laugh?"

"No, I'm trying to get my wind back and was testing my lungs." He blinked, looking around, as he sat up. "I don't suppose you know where we are?"

Something inside Ning'er snapped. "Any idea where—I— you—" She grabbed a fistful of his shirt. "Are you serious right now?" she hissed. "We had a plan! We were supposed to run! We could be safe outside right now with Zi'an, on our way back to the safehouse. Instead, you had to go chasing after the ghost of some half-dead dream, and for what?" She gave him a shake. "For what? For glory? Freedom? Hope?" She sneered. Rage had made her vicious. "You were supposed to listen to me, just once, and take the safe option, not the one that traps us in a glorified prison with your awful fucking father!"

"So why didn't you?" interrupted Cheng Yun.

Ning'er stared at him. She didn't let go of his shirt lapels, but he didn't seem to mind, returning her furious gaze with unblinking steadiness. Long lashes hooded his irises, darkening the hollows beneath his eyes. "Why didn't you?" he repeated. "You're right. You had a plan. You could have taken the safe option. You could have run. You could be safe, on your way home to the rest of our friends right now. So why didn't you do any of those things?"

Ning'er's tongue froze on the only real answer she could give. The wildly stupid, obvious answer.

The hint of a smile tugged the corners of his mouth faintly upward. It was at odds with the look in his eyes, soft and strangely sad. "For what it's worth," he said, "I am sorry. I didn't realize you'd follow me. I didn't think that—well." He rested the back of his head against the laboratory wall, eyes fluttering shut for a moment. Lines of telltale exhaustion painted shadows across the planes of his face. "I don't suppose what I think matters much at all right now."

Ning'er slumped over beside him, her anger spent. Without anger fueling her, the latent exhaustion from that long, awful chase crept eagerly into her bones. "Do you have any idea why your dad's here, anyway?"

Cheng Yun sighed. "Not really. I assume it's something to do with whatever favors Lilium's asking for now, but I didn't think even he would sink to . . ." He stopped and closed his eyes.

"You didn't think he'd be involved in the kidnapping of a teenage girl," said Ning'er softly. "You didn't think he'd be so far gone."

Cheng Yun remained silent.

"Are you in love with her?" she asked bluntly.

His eyes fluttered open, his mouth a little O of surprise. Hastily, Ning'er averted her gaze. She didn't dare look him in the eye now. "The Lark," she clarified, as if Cheng Yun of all people hadn't spoken her given name a million times or more, whispered into the confines of reverence and inexplicable intimacy. "Are you in love with her?"

Cheng Yun barked a quiet little laugh. "No. At least, not like you think."

Ning'er frowned. "Really? Because I can't think of another reason you'd behave with such astronomical stupidity."

"It's not about love," said Cheng Yun. "It's about need. He Bailing is a leader. She was—is—our leader. Always has been. It's how things are meant to be. What she started five years ago—"

"Oh, fuck five years ago!"

"Excuse me?"

Ning'er waved a hand, metal fingers creaking, too exhausted to bother mincing words. What was he going to do at this point, fire her? "Yes, the Lark got the country all riled up half a decade ago. She started something. She demanded accountability. And then she failed. Pretty spectacularly, as you might recall. I know Zhenyi certainly does. Even if you're insistent on changing the way things are, I don't see why you need her to lead it so badly." She hesitated. "The Red Yaksha seems to have done a fine job all on his own. Couldn't the Red Yaksha run a revolution instead? Couldn't you—"

"The Red Yaksha is a fraud," said Cheng Yun bluntly.

The interruption, cold and plain-stated, cut through Ning'er's tirade like a verbal knife.

Cheng Yun caught her gaze, smirking a little, but Ning'er knew him well enough by now to recognize an expression directed inward. "The Lark is the only reason the Red Yaksha exists," he told her. "Without the Lark, who would the Red Yaksha have been, really? The spoiled son of a father consumed by greed and hunger, oblivious to the plight of his own country. A lily-handed child who would have lived life behind the walls of a manor, waited on day and night."

"And then that same lily-handed child encountered the Lark," said Ning'er quietly, "and now he's a hero. Needing a push in the right direction doesn't make you a fraud, A'yun."

"But continuing to profit off exploitation does," said Cheng Yun. He smiled at the stricken expression on her face. "Don't dress it up. That's what I do, by continuing to be the Young Marshal. There's a word for that: hypocrisy."

"You make things sound so fucking simple," snapped Ning'er. Her old anger was returning. It felt good now. Righteous beneath her skin, like an itch being scratched sharp-nailed. If there was anything Ning'er understood intimately, it was doing shitty things for the sake of survival. "Context matters. There's a reason the army recruits their trainees so early in life. You joined the gendarme when you were too young to know better, and you stay with them because your pack of revolutionaries needs a spy as close to the inside as you can come. We'd never even have found those blueprints if you weren't the Young Marshal."

"That's only an excuse," countered Cheng Yun. The shadows in the hollows under his eyes practically glowed purple in the faint red of the tanks around them. "You of all people should recognize that. There's a reason Ruofei wanted to kill me."

Ruofei. The name struck Ning'er like a blow. The girl with the knife. The girl who'd died at the hands of Cheng Yun's unit. The girl whose poison had nearly taken Cheng Yun with her.

"You tried to save her," said Ning'er, but the words felt dull. Small consolation when the girl was still dead.

The brittleness of Cheng Yun's sad, knowing little smile told Ning'er that he knew it too. "Tell me, does that make everything else I've done better or worse?" His long hands curled into fists atop his knees. "I've raided Lower Ring neighborhoods, dragged dissenters into prisons. I've been a good little lap dog. I made myself their monster, all for the sake of espionage. For some glimmer of hope that one day we might free the Lark and name Emperor Huiming's murderers for who they really are. Maybe then this kingdom would finally start waking up and realizing that they might be better off without the throne entirely. What's the point of a good and just emperor if he can be so easily ousted by bad actors in his own government?" Cheng Yun glanced around at their surroundings: the tanks, the red liquid, the doorway they couldn't exit for fear of his father's guards. "Hope is cruel."

The force of everything he'd said struck Ning'er like a hard fall on concrete, all the wind knocked out of her sails. Her metal hand snagged the crook of his elbow. "So this is why you're so obsessed with freeing the Lark," she said faintly. "You need everything you've sacrificed to have been worth it. For her." She swallowed. "For the country."

There was a term for what she was witnessing. Ge Rong had lectured Ning'er time and again on the concept of a sunk cost fallacy, a notion that the more blood and sweat and tears you invested into something, the worthier it seemed.

Even if, in the end, it all turned out to be one big sham.

"So, what," said Ning'er, "you free the Lark, and she forces the Beiyang ministers to answer for their crimes. Corruption gets stamped out of the imperial court, and eventually, the monarchy gets abolished. You and He Bailing, side by side, usher in a brave new world. What do you do, in that world?"

"Answer for my own crimes, ideally. In a proper tribunal." He said it so plainly. Like he was talking about a grocery trip, a rent payment. "It's only right: in some ways, I'm no different from the ministers who had Huiming assassinated. The only reason a benevolent usurper wouldn't call the Beiyang Army war criminals is because the ugly things we do, we do to our own people. But that doesn't pretty them up, does it?"

"And a trial would?" demanded Ning'er.

"No," said Cheng Yun. "But a trial would be a start."

The memory struck her with casual cruelty: his voice, so tender, worn thin with illness, and bright with desperation, whispering to her like a benediction, *betray me, Ning'er. Betray me for the good of this country.*

It was like being hit again. Ning'er exhaled sharply. "Coward."

His head snapped toward her. "Excuse me?"

She had to admit, it gave her a strange satisfaction—savage, yes, but also relieved—to see a bit of that old fire in his eyes again. "You're a coward," she repeated. Her flesh hand clenched first, then her metal one. "You want to rot away the rest of your life in a prison cell or waste it on an executioner's block? Give me a break. That's not redemption. That's an easy answer to a difficult question. You feel bad about what you've done?"

She'd inched closer to him without really noticing, but they were nearly nose-to-nose now. "Guilt solves nothing. Action does. So if you feel this bad, then maybe consider doing some good."

"The Lark—" Cheng Yun began, heated.

"No." She cut him off decisively this time. "The Lark is not going to do the work for you. You—Cheng Yun, Red Yaksha, Young Marshal, whatever the fuck you want to call yourself—that's your job." She sucked in a breath. "You don't atone for your sins by sacrificing the rest of your life. You atone by living. That's the hard part. That's the work. And it's your work alone."

She sucked in a breath and gathered her own courage. "And for what it's worth," said Ning'er, "if I have any hope at all for a better world, it's not because of He Bailing. Maybe once upon a time, it would have been, but now . . . now it's you."

The hitch in his breath spoke more of his surprise than actual words would have. Bizarrely, that made her laugh. "We—your crew—we're not the gendarme, you know," she told him, then realized how that sounded. "And I don't just mean the whole oppressive authoritarian force part."

"I should hope not."

She rolled her eyes. "I mean it. You don't run us like a military. You may be our leader, but at the end of the day, the real reason people stick by your side is because you stick by ours. Shoulder to shoulder, arm in arm. You've never put yourself above us, and you're always willing to lay it on the line, even if it . . . even if it means doing some dumbass shit like getting yourself stabbed. If the rest of the country sees what I see, they'll understand how much we need you." She swallowed again, harder. "How much good you can do."

"The Young Marshal—" he began.

"The Young Marshal was a child when he became the Young Marshal," interrupted Ning'er, blunt. "You think I never did anything awful as a child? You were trying to survive and please a father who'd taught you all the wrong definitions of virtue. And still, somehow, you found yourself taking the Lark into your heart." Ning'er tried to smile. "The son of Minister Cheng, becoming a secret insurgent, all because of some Sixth Ring girl. Just think on that for a moment. It's proof that people can be more than the sum of the parts that made them. Proof that people can grow."

When he remained silent, she slipped her hand toward his. "You talk a great deal about hope, but I don't know that you're aware of how much work it takes—and how much of that work you did yourself. So if we're both going to be stuck here, in the belly of Lilium's creepy secret lab, then I say we make the most of it." Standing—and wincing at the creak in her knees—she waggled her fingers at him. "Come on. Let's get out of this room and look for your Lark."

He looked up at her from where he sat. It was a strange sight. He'd always seemed larger than life. Even physically, in the literal sense, he cut an imposing figure, standing a good head taller than her. Here, he curled up at her feet, almost childlike. The Young Marshal, the Red Yaksha, for once looking up at her instead of the other way around. Like she might be his salvation, the same way so many others saw him.

He took her proffered hand. The smile winding its way slowly across his face made him look younger than he ever had. "Let's," he said, and let her pull him to his feet.

There was the matter of getting their bearings first. Frightening tanks full of red mystery substance aside, the laboratory room appeared to function more as a filing space than anything else.

Ning'er spotted the telltale designations for blueprints, plans, schematics, all labeled neatly along the rows of cabinets.

All sitting ripe for the taking.

Cheng Yun followed where her gaze lay. "Grab them," he said. "Even without the Lark, information is power." He hesitated. "And it's free money for you, if all else fails. You don't deserve to leave this job empty handed."

Ning'er tried not to flinch. Of course he knew she'd be thinking about the money. And why wouldn't she? She was a professional, after all. It was what she was supposed to think about. It was smart. Practical. "You snag whatever files you can from the cabinets on the left. I'll go with the right."

"Done. Any idea where we are in relation to the Lark's cage?"

Ning'er had been considering just that, in fact. Thank god for her sense of direction. "I did pick us a rather opportune vent. We're not far." She hesitated. "The only trouble is—"

"The guards." He nodded, face grim again. "Right."

"Don't look so defeated," she chided. "I may not have loved you dragging us into this mess, but you should be pleased to know that you did, in fact, hire a half-decent thief. This isn't the first time I've had to shake a tail. Do you have your comm-link?"

He handed it over. It was nicer than hers, with a wider screen. Perfect. "I've always brought out Ge Rong's inner worrywart," Ning'er told Cheng Yun. Fishing a tiny wire from her supply belt, she squinted down at the screen as she hooked his device up. "Usually, it's very sweet, but a little annoying. But every once in a while, it is wildly useful."

She gave it a couple taps. The screen flared to life. "We're in business! Please and thank you, A'rong." She held the comm-link up to its owner's curious eyes. "Cameras. Its battery power is limited, so we'd best use it sparingly, but the wire lets us view security footage from the lab's mainframe. Which means we can track where the guards are at any given moment."

Cheng Yun whistled. "Thank the heavens for Ge Rong."

They were in luck. The guards, it appeared, had checked on the Lark, and finding no interlopers present, declared it safe, leaving the floor outside free. The men who'd been chasing Ning'er and Cheng Yun had retreated, scouring the upper levels for the rest of the crew, clearly hoping to ferret out the one they'd lost earlier. Ning'er didn't doubt they'd be back to retrace their steps.

The window of time wasn't large. But it existed. And sometimes, a small window was all you needed. "Let's go," said Ning'er.

The route toward the Lark's cage was a strange one. This corridor was lined with the same glass tanks they'd seen on their way in, but it wasn't just that strange red liquid inside. Ning'er wrinkled her nose as they passed. "What is that stuff?"

Cheng Yun followed her gaze, eyes narrowing as he saw what she saw. The specimens within the tank were, for lack of a better word, grotesque. Pale and bloated, they hung suspended behind the glass. Flakes of red sprouted from them in shades of the same bright crimson as that ghastly substance in the other rooms.

"Are they animals?" Ning'er asked in disbelief. "They look alien, almost—"

"Ning'er."

"No, seriously, A'yun, this stuff gives me the willies. And what's all that red stuff? It doesn't look like—"

"Ning'er," Cheng Yun repeated, more forcefully this time. She finally tore her gaze away from the tanks, toward his face.

He'd gone sheet white. A ghost in the shape of a boy, on his death bed all over again. "Those used to be human."

"That's not . . ." Ning'er trailed off as she gave the tanks a second look. Her gag reflex sprang into action before the rest of her body could account for her reaction. Her hands went to her knees as she bent, dry retching.

They were body parts: bloated and grotesque, but body parts all the same. A second look had identified the flakes of red as well. Flowers. The same bloodred flowers from which Complacency was manufactured.

Cheng Yun's hand on her spine, warm, steadied her focus. "Well," Ning'er rasped. "I guess we know now why Pirate Yang's buyer had coordinates that matched up with Lilium's lab."

The recipe for Complacency was only partially a secret. Everyone knew about those bloodred flowers. Idiot kids would pick public parks clean, thinking they could get high off the plants alone, but that shit never worked. To switch on the properties in the flowers that created Complacency—to get that perfect high— it needed to be combined with something else. The nature of the particular "something else," of course, had never been public knowledge.

And now Ning'er knew why. Her own heartbeat roared in her ears. "I always blamed the factory accidents, you know. Fifth and Sixth Ringers, we'll do anything for some spare cash, right? Every time I saw another amputee in a Lower Ring neighborhood, I'd think to myself, 'Ah, factory accident.' Fucked up one leg on an assembly line, sold the other to a lab to pay for the medical bills, will probably be dead from an oxyveris overdose inside a year." The room spun a little. "I figured the labs that bought spare limbs were probably using them to research . . . I don't know, bone regrowth or skin diseases, or something." She laughed, a little wildly. "I never guessed it would be something like this. I'm pretty stupid, I guess."

"Ning'er." Cheng Yun's voice sounded so distant in her ears. His hand grew urgent on her spine. "Ning'er, we need to keep moving. I'm so sorry, but—"

"I think I preferred that dumb rumor about palace chefs buying human limbs off the black market to cook into meals for the emperor's secret cannibal cousin." Ning'er laughed again. "That would have been easier to stomach. No pun intended." She backed away from the tanks, stumbling a little as hysterical little giggles spasmed through her body. "What's the secret ingredient that activates the chemical properties of those flowers? Why do human limbs cost so goddamn much on the black market? Amazing that none of us ever put two and two together. They've been pawning our own bodies off on us, diluted for consumption, so we can work ourselves to death and provide them with more flesh to process in their factories. Forget the emperor's cousin. We've been the cannibals, this whole time. That's what they made us into." She was swaying on her feet. It was like being at the bar, almost, off her shift and a couple bottles of cheap knockoff Tsingtao into the wee hours of the night. "Maybe we deserve to be under the thumb of Beiyang rule and their ridiculous toddler emperor. Maybe—"

Her back collided with something soft. She braced herself instinctively. For a strange, stupid moment, she thought to herself, still half hysterical: *Well, at least I haven't shattered anything I'll need to pay for.*

But this wasn't Blue Star Brewpub, and it wasn't some cheap drink she'd knocked over. Just plastic bags, filled with red powder.

One had opened slightly at the top, filling the room with its odd, earthy scent. It was that scent—as much as the bright crimson coloring—that gave it away. Ning'er reeled back.

She could see the whole stash now. Bags upon bags of pure Complacency, lining the walls of the hallway. Her first thought was the sheer horror of it—the body parts, the volume of production, the rote and awful nature of it all. The cold, hard knowledge, sitting like lead in her gut, that her arm and leg, her own flesh and bone, had created the same drug that destroyed her father. Her father. Cheng Yun's brother. Ge Rong. Even herself, before A'rong had built her limbs. So many victims and such a simple recipe. A few pretty flowers. A few pounds of human flesh.

Her second thought was that if she grabbed a couple bags of that powder, she wouldn't be hungry for months. And she'd never need another prosthetic again.

She had presence of mind, enough, to feel ashamed of that. Distantly, she registered Cheng Yun's hand, curled under the crook of her metal elbow, tugging her away from those rows and rows of red. "Come on, Ning'er, stay with me," he murmured. "It can't be that much farther. We've just got a little longer to go. Just stick here, to my side."

She stuck. It grounded her a little. She forced herself to breathe again, in and out, in and out, as they stumbled down that winding hallway, away from all that awful red: the liquid, the powder, the flowers sprouting and flaking across corpse-white body parts. Complacency, all of it.

She was just so tired of being so hungry.

"A'yun," she said softly.

He kept moving, still tugging her along on that route she'd charted for them both, but his head tilted. "Yeah." He was listening.

"Say we really do free the Lark. And say she's everything you've dreamed, and more, the harbinger of a new world. A . . . a kinder world than the one we have. If you really make it happen, A'yun, I'd want . . . I'd want . . ."

He met her eyes truly now, even as they stumbled down that seemingly endless corridor. "What? What would you want?"

There were so many things she could have said. An unlimited bank account. A nice apartment in an Upper Ring neighborhood. All the food and drink she could ever need.

"I think I want to leave Beijing," she said instead. "Go out to the countryside. See the rest of this kingdom, really see it, and make a quiet life somewhere. Maybe have a little farm, with some chickens and sheep."

Even without looking, she could hear the rise of his eyebrows in his voice: "Chickens and sheep."

"Don't make fun! Animals can be good company." Ning'er was coming back to herself a little as her fantasy unfolded. "Old Man Yu was from a village in Hebei, originally. He used to tell me that the skies are bluer outside of the city. I'd like to see it, one day. See some blue sky, drink tea, herd those sheep for company. Live a real life."

Cheng Yun was quiet for the next several steps. Then, almost shyly, "I'd like to see a bluer sky, too."

"You could always join me." The words tumbled out of her mouth before her tongue could retract them.

His gaze crashed into hers before she could try averting her eyes. Those dark eyes would never stop startling her. How intensely they could pin her in place while looking so soft around the edges at the same time. Vulnerable. His mouth parted. "Ning'er, I—"

She finally looked away. "It was just a thought." She blinked at the door at the end of the corridor. They'd arrived at last. Thoughts of blue skies and a life outside Beijing—with or without Cheng Yun—fled her mind with a snap. "This is it."

Cautiously, she pried the door open. It gave with surprising ease. It was almost an anticlimax. Even the interior of the room itself was surprisingly small: four walls, two sets of doors. It had been structured to make space for only its centerpiece: a tank, filled with pale green fluid, encasing an unconscious girl at its center, suspended in place by a riot of wires.

Ning'er paused on the threshold, staring at her. Because that really was all she was: just another girl. Around Ning'er's size and weight, at a glance. Maybe even a little shorter.

Which felt downright offensive. There had been a time when the figure suspended inside that tank had seemed larger than life. A goddess in her own right, standing ten feet tall on podiums, at rallies, commanding the mood that rippled through crowds of hundreds, thousands, with just a quirk of her mouth here, a well-placed word there.

The reality was sobering. Even unconscious, He Bailing was as lovely as Ning'er remembered: broad-shouldered and coppery-skinned, rosy-cheeked even beneath the pallor of the fluids keeping her alive. Her thick black hair floated around her amidst the foamy green. Tiny bubbles clung to the lashes of her closed eyes. She looked so peaceful. A high queen laid to rest after a long war. A thought, unbidden and possibly irrational, crept uncomfortably across the back of Ning'er's mind: what right, truly, did they have to wake her now? Why, when she looked so incongruously content, even trapped here in this awful place?

Ning'er risked a glance toward Cheng Yun. He didn't look

awestruck, or even especially shocked, to be face-to-face at last with the girl who'd nearly toppled the Beiyang five years ago. His gaze on the Lark was soft, lashes low and mouth slightly parted.

Ning'er shook herself. There was no time for either of them to be rapt, even in the face of the Lark. "Cheng Yun," she said, maybe a hint more sharply than necessary. "We have work to do."

It was the sort of reminder he'd normally be giving her. The fearless leader, executing his vision. Now, he blinked a few times, as if waking from a long sleep of his own. He settled quickly into consciousness of the situation at hand. No doubt considering the Lilium guards, prowling just a few floors above them. All the softness fled his gaze, replaced by businesslike steel, as his brow furrowed. "Right."

The tank was a good deal harder to pry open than the door to the room that contained it. Ning'er went through nearly her entire toolbelt before she finally cracked the latch. It took a joint effort to loosen the wires sufficiently and start pulling the Lark free. Ning'er's fingers splayed awkwardly over the Lark's clammy bicep to keep her body from falling, while Cheng Yun supported the bulk of the girl's dead weight over his shoulder. Without missing a beat, he tugged his own black sweater over his head, covering the Lark to preserve her modesty. Ning'er found herself grateful. She hadn't wanted to think too hard about the naked vulnerability of their would-be savior. She already seemed too fragile to be the larger-than-life figure of Ning'er's memory. Too mortal.

Too, well, human.

It was done, at least. Ning'er swayed a little on her feet, beneath her share of the Lark's limp weight, surveying their circumstances: He Bailing balanced awkwardly between her shoulders and Cheng Yun's, pale green fluid dripping off her sopping hair and pooling on the laboratory floor. The exit before them. The way out.

The way back out toward their friends, the fabled Lark in tow. The way toward freedom.

And then came the hum of the second door sliding open.

Ning'er's head jerked up in time with Cheng Yun's as her heart sank into her belly. *No,* she wanted to cry. *No, not now, not this, not after we've come so close to flying free.*

The new entrant's tread was light and slow, unhurried, a gentle clack of expensive shoes through the puddles of lab fluid puddling toward both doorways. "Well, this is a disappointment," he said. The words were soft-spoken, yet still somehow full of ice. The voice devastating in its familiarity. Ning'er's heart sank further still, curdling somewhere in the pit of her body.

Minister Cheng emerged from the shadows, languid in his movements. All the information that lived in Ning'er's head—the shady business deals, the murky nature of his climb into favor among the nobles and schemers of the decadent court, the growing horror of what hid in the bowels of a lab his corporate benefactors financed—screamed an ugly contrast to the man standing before her. He could have been someone's doting godfather, gracefully aging into his middle years, silver-streaked hair neatly styled over a dove-gray suit. The pitying smile he cast toward Ning'er revealed a dimple in the same corner of his mouth where Cheng Yun's lay.

Heaven help her, he really did look just like Cheng Yun. Those liquid eyes, bright and intense and hauntingly familiar, were downright uncanny. Ning'er's stark, irrefutable knowledge of his atrocities lay at odds with that sad, fatherly smile, with the gentle clack of those bespoke leather shoes he was ruining in the mess his son had made on the floor.

His son.

Ning'er came back to herself. Her attention snapped toward Cheng Yun. He stood rooted to the spot, trembling under the weight of the Lark on his shoulder. His eyes—the same dark, lovely eyes he shared with his father—were wide and unblinking.

Minister Cheng's gaze seemed to swallow Cheng Yun whole. The elder Cheng shook his head slowly. "Oh, A'yun," he murmured. Genuine sorrow lurked in his expression, lingered beneath that soft, cold voice. "I really did want better for you."

Ning'er flinched. Unbidden, the memory of her father's voice filled her ears: *I did it all for you, Ning'er. I needed Complacency to keep working. I needed Complacency to take care of you.*

"A'ye," Cheng Yun said at last, the word choked off. "Why are you here?"

His father's expression twisted. "I could ask the same of you. But I think we both know, don't we? It was rather careless of you, you know, to leave this laboratory's blueprints in your own bedroom under such flimsy security. Did you think I'd never grow suspicious of your absences from family events and imperial parties? Did you think it beneath my interest to unearth your tawdry little secrets? I taught you better than that." The minister's attention slid briefly toward the Lark. "Looks like we've stumbled across a little conflict of interest. I'm afraid you want to take what belongs to us. I raised you better than this, A'yun."

"Us?" Cheng Yun echoed in disbelief. "Who's us?"

"Who else?" Hesitation, faint but unmistakable, skittered across Minister Cheng's features. "There's still time for me to fix this. Go home, son. No one has to know you were here. All you have to do is leave the Lark."

"That's not going to happen," Cheng Yun said. "The Lark doesn't belong to Lilium. The Lark doesn't belong to anyone but herself."

The minister's expression hardened. "Fine. Have it your way."

Time itself closed in around Ning'er. She didn't know what, exactly, Minister Cheng planned on doing to his son. Or arguably worse, what he'd do to her.

She did know that it would be in her best interests to run. As fast and far as she could. She was good at what she did. She could probably make it, even now.

At least, on her own.

Goddammit.

Calculations ripped through her head. Choices, choices, always choices. Ning'er's gaze traveled around the lab until it landed on what she needed. She shifted the Lark's weight on her shoulders. "A'yun," she murmured under her breath.

He didn't answer, but the sudden snap of tension through the weight of their shared burden told her he'd moved. He was listening.

It was enough. "Wait for me," she whispered, and thrust the Lark into his arms.

In the same motion, she darted low, toward Minister Cheng, aiming for his legs. The base of his balance. And in an act of sheer idiocy, Ning'er flung both arms around the knees of one of the most powerful ministers of the Beiyang government, driving her body weight like a bullet into his as hard as she could.

The element of surprise was on her side. He toppled backward with a cry, dragging Ning'er down with him as he scrambled for purchase in the slippery muck of the laboratory floor. She didn't give him a chance to get his bearings. Before she could think better of it, she slammed her fist—the metal one—against the soft underside of the minister's chin.

His eyes rolled back before unconsciousness took him. He slumped over.

Instinct took over. Ning'er's fingers clamped down around Cheng Yun's wrist. "We have to run."

He followed after her, keeping pace almost listlessly, as they dragged the Lark out of that room. She kept expecting him to glance backward, toward that broken cage, his father lying motionless in that puddle of green. To second-guess himself for following her lead.

He didn't. Cheng Yun's face was worryingly vacant, but he wasn't turning around, and he was doing just fine hefting the dead weight of an unconscious girl between them, which meant he probably wasn't physically hurt. Ning'er exhaled slightly. She could take heart in that much, at least.

Her relief didn't last long. The distant echo of more boots on the ground and barked orders began to build, once more, into a steady crescendo behind them. So the guards had come to seek out the source of the commotion and discovered a minister's unconscious body. Fantastic.

Cheng Yun stopped in his tracks, his wrist slapping against her metal hand. Well, that wasn't ideal, given the circumstances.

She jerked her head at him. "What are you doing? We've got to—"

"They're going to corner us if we stick together," said Cheng Yun. He spoke in abrupt tones. In the span of seconds, a series of decisions flitted through his gaze. Gently, he laid the Lark aside, folding her hands over her chest. Then he rose and chose something from his belt, which he pressed into Ning'er's slack hands.

"A'yun," Ning'er protested weakly. It did no good against the insistence with which he pressed the derringer between her palms. She recognized the make: plasma cartridges. The good shit. Cheng Yun must have stolen it. The trigger bit cold against her hand.

Unbidden, a memory flashed through her mind: a girl with a knife, eyes wide and seeing, body torn apart by gendarme firepower.

"Take the Lark, hide, and keep her safe," said Cheng Yun. "If my father—if they come for you, the guards, you line up the sights like so." His hands covered hers, briefly, the warmth of his callused palms a jarring contrast to the cool metal of the gun. Carefully, he folded her fingers around the trigger, lifting her hands. Showing her the correct way to use it. The correct way to kill. "Aim. Pick your shot. And fire." His hands dropped from hers, warmth gone, leaving only the trigger behind. "Don't hesitate."

"And where the hell do you think you're going?"

A smile, feral at the edges, flickered across his mouth. "To lead the guards astray."

"A'yun." She swallowed. It was a preposterous thing he was proposing. "I—"

"We'll meet at the edge of the lab, where that old light-rail line is." He swallowed, too. "After. After all this."

He spoke in such certainties. As if he knew he'd survive this. As though it was such a sure and easy thing, wandering into a sea of armed guards to play decoy and emerging unscathed. A foolish, arrogant belief in a guarantee that didn't exist.

But the slightly hollow look in his eyes, the lingering hint of a shake in his hands, told a different story. Cheng Yun was a fool in many ways, but this wasn't one of them.

"The light-rail," Ning'er croaked out. "Right." The light-rail wasn't far from this point. Without guards dogging her, it would be close enough to drag an unconscious girl on her own.

"Twenty minutes," said Cheng Yun. "If you don't see me there in twenty minutes, you take He Bailing and go without me."

Ning'er opened her mouth, closed it again, choking off a protest that died on her tongue. It wouldn't do any good. Not with Cheng Yun when he was wearing that face. The bags still purple under slightly hollow eyes, still too pale, his cheekbones too sharp.

But there was a fire in his gaze now. The Red Yaksha lived in him, still.

"Go," he said. Barely a whisper.

Ning'er knelt and hoisted the Lark over her shoulders. Teetered for a moment, then took one step, and another. The other girl's weight wasn't too light, but it wasn't too hefty, either. Ning'er could carry the Lark on her own. She could do this much, for Cheng Yun's dream.

One step at a time, a half-dead girl on her shoulders and a derringer on her hip, she left Cheng Yun behind.

CHAPTER 11

A Train to Nowhere

The light-rail platform was a desolate place.

Ning'er gulped humid night air into burning lungs. At her feet, the Lark lay in an oblivious, slumbering heap, tucked away cozily inside the well-knitted bulk of Cheng Yun's black sweater. Maybe Ning'er was losing her mind—and really, she didn't think anyone could blame her, given the circumstances— she swore she could hear the other girl snoring.

A distant flicker of light and the familiar sound of machinery roaring along train tracks turned her head. The light-rail was approaching. Ning'er bit her lip. Well, that wasn't the greatest timing. She flipped her comm-link out to check the time, even though she'd just flipped it out two minutes ago. Twenty minutes. Twenty minutes wasn't so long in the grand scheme of things. Time enough for her ridiculous Red Yaksha to work another foolish, improbable miracle. But for every minute that crawled by, Ning'er's heart climbed a little further up her throat.

And now her train out—possibly the last train out for a while—was coming, and there was no Red Yaksha in sight.

Her brain ran through her options, rapid-fire. She could get the Lark aboard the incoming train, probably, even without Cheng Yun. She could find her way back to Zi'an, who'd hopefully escaped, and the rest of the crew. They could figure out where to go from there, together.

But where would they go, truly, without their Red Yaksha?

Ning'er didn't want to think about it. And was spared by the crack of a plasma shot.

Her head whipped toward the sound. Adrenaline jumpstarted old instincts. There were five men running over the cresting hilltop down which she'd dragged the Lark.

The train drew closer, its lights casting a growing glow over the grass, its progress across the tracks both warning and opportunity.

If Ning'er was going to run, too, now was the time to do it.

Instead, she squinted at the man in front. As much as Cheng Yun seemed to stand apart from a crowd, plenty of men were built like him: tall, narrow waisted, and broad shouldered, carrying themselves through the world on that long-legged stride.

She could be wrong. Heaven above, she couldn't afford to be wrong. She'd pray to every god she didn't believe in not to be wrong.

The right god-that-might-or-might-not-exist must have been listening. The thin wail of a whistle pierced the night. The lights from the approaching cars flashed over the approaching faces. It was a moment. It was only a moment. But she saw him: pale cheeked, dark under the eyes, but beautiful, and alive.

Still alive. And running toward her, the Lilium guards at his back.

There were moments, as a thief, when time itself slowed for you. Here, in the space of seconds, was the approaching train. There, all of nine, eight, seven feet from her was Cheng Yun. Between them lay the Lark, still in her slumber.

Her calculations only took those few seconds. Then the thief's instinct resurged, taking over once more. That urge to take what was yours. What you needed.

Ning'er reached for Cheng Yun in the same moment that he reached for her, fingertips brushing before her hands clamped over his arms. "The Lark," she began.

He nodded, curtly. "Got her." He hefted He Bailing carefully over one shoulder, then hesitated, eyes narrowed against the glare of the oncoming lights.

"You'll have to jump!" Ning'er yelled over the wail of the train. "Can you make it? I'll help you!"

He looked at her with serious eyes. "Give me a boost on three?"

It roared up to the platform in that precise moment.

"Three!" screamed Ning'er. He jumped. She shoved. And somehow, miraculously, he was on board, hanging to the edge of the deck with one hand. The other arm cradled the Lark fast against his shoulder.

Ning'er ran after them, heart in her throat, metal hand outstretched. *Easier to leave you behind,* whispered the cool voice of logic that lived in her head. *After all, you almost did the same to him. And now you've served your purpose. He has the Lark. He's on his way back to his friends. What possible value could be derived from going to the trouble of tugging you aboard? You're nothing to his crusade. Just a thief looking for a payday. One he won't have to make, if you—*

The hand that clamped around her cybernetic fingers—warm, human, and desperately insistent—cut off her spiraling web of thought. Cheng Yun glared at her over the clasp of their palms. "What are you waiting for?" he roared. "Jump!"

Ning'er jumped.

Her knees hit the deck of the car first, skidding along the edge for a terrifying second. Her prosthetic fingers clamped around one of the rails, sparking on contact, which gave her a moment's purchase. Then Cheng Yun's hands were under her arms. They slid over her shoulders, pulling her to safety.

"The Lark," Ning'er began faintly.

"Is fine." Cheng Yun hadn't let go. "Breathe, Ning'er. We're alive."

"You sound just like Old Man Yu." Still, Ning'er breathed. Her lungs remained on fire, lit up by the combination of the adrenaline and pushing her body well beyond its limits. Some job. Inhale. Exhale. Who knew just breathing could be agony and ecstasy all at once?

A strange sound startled her from the isolation of her own breathing. For a moment, she thought it was Cheng Yun crying. It took her a beat to realize he wasn't.

He was laughing.

She blinked at him, owlishly. "What in hell?"

Cheng Yun gasped, wiping at his streaming eyes with the back of his sleeve. "We really are in a state, aren't we?"

"Yes?" Ning'er agreed cautiously.

"I've always been the man with the plan." Another hysterical little giggle burst out of him. It would have been undignified for both the Red Yaksha and the Young Marshal, but then, the boy before her wasn't either right now. He was simply Cheng Yun. "Now I don't know what I am."

Ning'er stared past him, at the Lark's peacefully slumbering form. "You got what you wanted. Didn't you?"

"That's true," he acknowledged. "Or at least half true." He stared, soft-eyed, at He Bailing. Back in the lab, inside that tank, she'd looked like a ghost: still, ethereal, and untouchable. Here on the train, curled up and sleeping under Cheng Yun's sweater, hair still wet and sticky, she just looked like a kid. She could have been a university student, a barmaid, a farm girl. Some bright-eyed, innocent thing, still replete with idealism, dreaming sweetly oblivious dreams of a better world. Cheng Yun shook his head slowly at the sight of her, as if he couldn't quite believe it himself. "I'd banked on her being conscious when we found her, and somehow just knowing what to do. That I'd only have to keep being the man with the plan, the leader, until the better one came along."

"And I told you," said Ning'er rather testily, "that this whole thing is yours now. Not the Lark's. Not anymore." She stared at that oblivious, sleeping face, the peace in the Lark's expression. A complicated jealousy twisted her heart. "It's like I said. You don't get to leave all the work to He Bailing just because we saved her." She winced. "If we can call it saving at all. Do we know if she's even going to wake up?"

Cheng Yun sighed, his shoulders slumping. "Only time—and maybe Feifei—will be able to tell. Unfortunately, time isn't something we have much of. Especially now that we can't rely on the Young Marshal for cover. We'll have to move quickly, and carefully, in whatever we do next."

Those words struck Ning'er like a bullet. Minister Cheng had seen his son's true colors tonight. His cover was burned. The Young Marshal was as good as dead. The identity Cheng Yun had so carefully cultivated over the years, the things he'd sacrificed to sell the part, all gone the way of dust and ruin.

Well, fuck.

"Then we should circle back with the rest of the crew," said Ning'er decisively, trying to think aloud. Her brain hurt, but she wrenched her focus toward the problem at hand. Problems, she corrected herself. Problems, multiple. Cheng Yun's destroyed cover least among them, really, when considering the other threats: one, an angry Minister Cheng, who no doubt wanted his stolen property back. Two, the unconscious state of said property. Three, whatever means the elder Cheng would employ to take the Lark back into custody. Ning'er wanted to throw up just imagining it.

Cheng Yun breathed out slowly. "Let's get off before the next stop. I know a place where we should be safe, at least for a little while, owned by people I trust." He hazarded a small smile for Ning'er. "You're right. We should find the rest of the crew. It'll be easier to think when we have more brains to put together."

They jumped off right before the train pulled into the following station. It was a little awkward with the Lark's dead weight still in tow, but they managed, sliding quietly off the platform and tumbling into dry, browning grass. They were still just outside the Fifth Ring, a few miles away from the checkpoints necessary for crossing into the Fourth.

Cheng Yun led the way, taking off across the dying grass, the Lark's unconscious body slung carefully over his shoulders. Ning'er followed him. The rosy edges of dawn had begun to break through the black-blue of the night, casting the faintest glow over all three of them. This whole thing probably would have been a dream for one of Ge Rong's old art school classmates: one self-styled icon of a revolution carried over the shoulders of another, lit up by the glimmering promise of a new day.

And Ning'er, well. Ning'er simply followed.

The compound Cheng Yun had referenced wasn't far off the rail tracks, at least. It was a nondescript building, probably a warehouse that had been renovated for affordable housing and abandoned halfway through. It looked, in fact, not so different from the very nondescript laboratory building she and Cheng Yun had just barely escaped by the skin of their teeth.

It made Ning'er want to backpedal instinctively. And then she saw Zi'an.

Without thinking, she flung herself headlong into his waiting embrace. "We made it," she choked out. "We made it, we made it, we made it—"

Zi'an laughed into her hair, interrupting her idiotic stream of babble. His arms were a vise around her. She couldn't see his face with her own buried against his chest like this, pressed up against the steady thump of his heartbeat through the plain cotton shirt. Maybe this was for the best. Maybe if she couldn't see Zi'an's face, or indeed, the outside world at all, she wouldn't have to square with any of it.

"It's going to be all right," murmured Zi'an, his chin resting atop her head. "One way or another."

Now it was Ning'er's turn to laugh. "Bold statement from a man who hasn't yet been briefed on all the shit that went wrong."

"Give me the highlights."

"Good or bad first?"

He paused. "That's never a question that preceded actual good news."

"It is good news," said Ning'er, a bit defensively. She pulled herself, rather reluctantly, from his embrace to look him in the eye. "Zi'an. We did it. We have the Lark with us."

"It's true," said Cheng Yun. He'd been hanging back while Ning'er and Zi'an reunited. Now he stepped forward, the Lark in his arms, to lay her gently in the grass at Zi'an's feet. Zi'an's eyes went wide as he knelt over the slumbering girl, checking her vitals. "Is that—"

"He Bailing?" Ning'er nodded. "In the flesh."

Zi'an looked up at them both. "She's alive, if very much in need of a formal examination." He hesitated. "I have to ask. Has she—"

"Woken at all?" Ning'er shook her head. "Nope. That's part one of the bad news, though probably the least of it."

"Probably?" Zi'an's face looked, abruptly, a bit like the screen of her cheap monitor back in her studio. Like she had too many tabs open, and he simply lacked the energy to process it all. "You didn't tell me the bad news came in multiple chapters."

"It has a tendency to do that," said Ning'er.

"My cover's blown," said Cheng Yun abruptly. Ning'er winced. She could understand a need to rip the Band-Aid off fast, but you didn't want to take the skin with it too if you could help it. Cheng Yun seemed to realize as much at the same time, making faintly apologetic eyes at them both. "It's important that the rest of the crew—and our network—know that. We can't rely on the reputation of the Young Marshal to cover any further illicit activity." He swallowed, looking very much like the boy he was. "My father caught us."

It was such an absurd, teenage thing to say in light of everything else. Ning'er watched Zi'an blink once, twice. "Your father caught you," he repeated in flat tones.

"While we were breaking the Lark out, in fact," said Ning'er. "So you can see how that would be rather an enormous problem."

Zi'an winced. "Dare I ask what else has gone wrong?"

"It's less what's gone wrong, and more what's about to," Cheng Yun put in, grimly businesslike. "My father's even deeper in Lilium's pockets than we thought, for starters. He's going to want Bailing back, and he won't take my betrayal lying down."

"And as long as she's asleep, we can't rely on her to protect herself from whatever hellfire Minister Cheng spews," said Ning'er glumly, "much less help us out."

"Then lie low tonight," said Zi'an. He sucked in a breath. Ning'er could practically see the wheels turning in his head. "You're right, this is bad. But we have the Lark." He glanced between the two of them. Despite the tightness in his jaw, his gaze was warm. "And we have both of you. Alive. Unhurt. Don't knock that as nothing." He jerked his head toward the compound. "Come inside and have some hot tea. The others will be glad to see you."

"My father," Cheng Yun began, broken-voiced.

Zi'an cut him off firmly. "Your father can wait. He'll need to regroup, too, and think through what it really means to hunt down his only son. It doesn't look good for a courtier trying to establish himself to have raised a traitor instead, especially a paragon like the Young Marshal. That will take time, even for a man like Minister Cheng, to sort out. You can afford a night of rest, both of you." He paused, squinting at the pinkening sky on the horizon. "Day of rest. Whatever. Either way, some shut-eye won't kill you."

Ning'er, swaying on her feet a bit, couldn't find that she disagreed. She trailed after Zi'an, while Cheng Yun brought up the rear, once more carrying the Lark.

It really did look like a warehouse on the inside. Ning'er catalogued its contents instinctively: high vaulted ceilings, rows and rows of plasma firearms, and a few supply caches that had the look of Ge Rong's handiwork: spare prosthetics, lockpick gadgetry, projectable maps, and automatic monitors. Beyond that, down the next hall, she spotted enormous sacks of rice and other grains. Ning'er would bet the meager contents of her bank account that that wasn't the only food they'd stashed here, either. Weapons, check.

Engineering doodads, check. Sustenance, check. Cheng Yun hadn't been kidding about knowing a place where they could lie low.

They weren't alone there.

A small group of people, modestly dressed but wearing identical expressions of relief, had gathered at the edge of the warehouse's main hall. "Welcome home, Red Yaksha."

Cheng Yun strode forward, somehow still graceful despite obvious exhaustion. "I've told you a million times, Rui, it's just A'yun."

Another member of the crowd snorted. "Whatever you say, Red Yaksha." A crescendo of laughter followed this pronouncement as the crowd gathered around Cheng Yun, exclaiming, practically sweeping him away from the others.

Ning'er raised a quizzical eyebrow at Zi'an. "And they would be?"

"Original supporters of the Lark—mostly organizers and the like," murmured Zi'an. "A'yun found his way to them when he was thirteen—took him years to earn their trust. It helped that Zhenyi vouched for him." He grinned at the look of disbelief on Ning'er's face. "What? You didn't think we were working all by our lonesome, did you? You know what they say: it takes a village." His mouth twitched. "Well, a village, and the trust fund that Cheng Yun's mother left to him before she ran off to greener pastures—and presumably better parties—in Paris. I'd love to know what she'd think of her family money indirectly financing his teenage rebellion here."

Ning'er watched the scene unfolding before them: the bright, hopeful looks on the faces of the people who'd—at their own risk—once taken in a lonely thirteen-year-old from the Upper Rings. The way he so clearly belonged to them. "He really was born to do this."

Zi'an gave her a nudge. "Don't let him hear you say that. You know how he feels about the idea of birthrights and grand destinies. But yeah," he mused. He glanced at the slumbering girl in Cheng Yun's arms. "Whatever He Bailing had—that innate *something* that makes people want to believe in the same things you do—Cheng Yun's got it too."

Amidst the chorus of excited babbling, two more voices, precious in their familiarity: "A'yun! Ning'er!"

Zhenyi came jogging toward them, her face a picture of relief, Feifei on her heels. "Thank the heavens."

Behind her, Feifei's hand flew to her mouth. "Is that—"

Ning'er followed the other girl's gaze toward Cheng Yun and sighed. "Yes. The good news is that we successfully freed the Lark from her cage."

At that, the small crowd around Cheng Yun snapped their attention toward Ning'er. "You did it," said one of them, a middle-aged man with bags under his eyes. "You really freed the Lark."

Ning'er shifted uncomfortably beneath his gaze. She'd worked a crowd during happy hour at Blue Star Brewpub, but this was different. She was used to crowds who came to drink her cocktails and bend her ear. She wasn't used to a crowd that actually cared what the barkeep had to say. "That was the good news," said Ning'er. "But it behooves me to share the bad news, too."

The bad news was, unsurprisingly, the source of some distress. Ning'er found herself, for once, playing the part of the optimist. "Look," she said, a bit irritably, to the ring of worried faces crowding her. "It sucks. We knew it would probably end up sucking one way or the other. That's what contingencies are for. And this," she knocked her fist against the solid wooden paneling of the wall behind her, "isn't a bad contingency. We have food here. Supplies. Weapons, even, if it comes to that. There are worse places to lie low. But right now, all I am interested in is a hot bath and a warm bed."

Feifei, surprisingly, was the first in the group to give her a nod of assent. "That really should be the first order of business. If we want to be ready to face Minister Cheng's wrath, whenever he rains it down upon us? I prescribe sleep, first and foremost." She met Ning'er's startled gaze, the corner of her mouth lifting slightly. She jerked her head toward the back end of the building. "There are rooms with cots behind the grain stores, and hot water available in the attached bathroom. Help yourself. You too, Cheng Yun. I know you love putting on that stiff upper lip, but you're human, too." The other corner of her mouth lifted as she patted Cheng Yun's shoulder. "Go to sleep, A'yun. You've more than earned it."

Feifei glanced toward the Lark. "I'll take care of the La— of He Bailing." She swallowed. "As best I can, anyway." She frowned at the Lark's unconscious face. "I'll claim Zhenyi as my nurse on this one. I suspect a good biohack may be the ticket to waking her."

"A biohack?" Cheng Yun looked curious. "Can Zhenyi do that?"

"With some good old-fashioned medical assistance? Sure." Feifei eyed him sidelong. "And now you're stalling. Take a page out of your Lark's book. Get your beauty sleep."

"Feifei," Cheng Yun began, just this side of cajoling.

"Cheng Yun," Feifei returned, mocking his tone. She softened a bit. "Trust me. Trust all of us. Rest." She glanced back at Ning'er as well. "Both of you."

He nodded at last, attention hovering over He Bailing's still form, just for a moment. "You'll tell me if there's any change?"

"Immediately," said Feifei. Then very pleasantly, "After you sleep."

"You don't need to tell me twice," said Ning'er, already walking, zombielike, toward the back room and the promised cots. Distantly, she heard Cheng Yun's reluctant footsteps behind her. She had time to wonder, with a brief and hazy wistfulness, if this would be anything like that strange, magical night seemingly so long ago in her apartment, Cheng Yun finally resting at her side, caught in a rare moment of peace, before everything had started going to shit.

And then, quite abruptly, she was collapsing into one of the cots, eyes already shut. She stopped wondering anything at all. Sleep, blissfully, claimed her.

Sleep, unfortunately, did not last long.

The wail of the siren woke Ning'er so suddenly, for half a second, she thought herself still trapped inside a dream. The utter silence that followed, just for a few seconds, gave her heart a moment's hope that it wasn't real.

Then the second wail began. The remainder of the sleep fog cleared from Ning'er's head. Her heart sank. Then immediately kicked into high alert. She scrambled from the cot. "Cheng Yun?"

"Here." Cheng Yun was already on his feet, at the window, his body one long line of tension. His face had gone as white, a stark contrast to the darkness of his eyes as his gaze bored through the cheap pane glass. "Those are lockdown sirens. Nap time's over, I'm afraid. We need to warn the others."

"About what?" Ning'er frowned. She tried to recapture some of her earlier optimism. *Breathe, Ning'er, breathe.* Lockdowns weren't unheard of. Most frequently, the Beiyang ordered them when a protest got too rowdy. They usually didn't bother setting off the sirens unless real violence broke out, but even so, that didn't necessarily have anything to do with them. Rioting happened often enough. "Maybe we're okay," she offered cautiously. "Look, I've heard the lockdown sirens before, but with all the unrest in the Lower Rings lately, that doesn't necessarily mean—"

A deep rumble interrupted the remainder of her sentence, like the roar of some ancient beast awoken and returned to earth from the depths of hell. Ning'er started in earnest. It took another beat for her to recognize the rumble for what it was: a drumbeat, bellowing out from the towers at every Ring gate exit. She couldn't remember the last time she'd heard the drum towers in use. She racked her brain. What did they signify?

When she looked to Cheng Yun for answers, she took a step back at the expression on his face. He'd turned from the window at last, eyes wide. He looked the same way he had when they'd seen his father in the lab. No revolutionary icon, no terrifying military leader. Only a child caught out, at last.

Across from her, Cheng Yun's fists had gone white-knuckled, his eyes narrow and blank with grim resignation. "I knew it. Baba hates wasting time. His next move was only ever going to be the nuclear option. We won't last long with the Brocade Guard hunting us down."

Ning'er hadn't thought her heart could drop any further into her belly. She was wrong.

"What's this about the Brocade Guard?" Zhenyi asked.

Ning'er turned. The others, including Zhenyi, had gathered at the edge of the room, peering in from the outside, as if afraid to intrude.

"Cheng Yun thinks they're coming this way," said Ning'er.

"They *are* coming this way," said Cheng Yun. He had that brisk, cold note of finality in his voice when he was speaking to brook no argument.

Zi'an shrugged his shoulders, slouching a little in the doorway. "How bad can it be? The android patrols—"

"Are nothing compared to what the Brocade Guard in full form will do to a city district," snapped Cheng Yun. He crossed the room in quick strides. "We need to move. Pack what we can and get out of here as quickly as possible—"

"Cheng Yun," said Feifei cautiously. "Is it possible you're overreacting? The Brocade Guard is the Brocade Guard, but they're still only human. They'll need time to deploy, and—"

"Only human?" Cheng Yun chuckled to himself. It was that same giddy, hysterical sound he'd made back on the train. "Only human. Right."

"They are—" Ge Rong began.

"They're not," snapped Cheng Yun. His voice sliced through the air, whiplike. "Or did you forget that I was bred from the cradle to join them? I'm still gendarme, remember?"

An awful dead silence descended on the little room.

"That's right," said Cheng Yun, more softly. "It's easy to forget, isn't it? The way I am, planning and scheming with you. Drinking and dancing with you. It's easy to forget that I was born to be your enemy. Do you want to know what it's like, to grow up groomed for the Brocade Guard? Not merely the gendarme at large, but the Brocade Guard? The chosen elite?"

He turned back toward the window. Shouts in the distance were beginning to accompany that dreadful, deep bass drumbeat. As if it were thunder, warning of the incoming storm. "They've been conditioned since birth to serve the throne at any cost."

He shuddered. "And I truly do mean any. There was a time when becoming one of them was all I wanted in life. When you're groomed for an organization like that, the emperor could order your death and you'd be honored to oblige. Any one of us would have been proud to die, and we'd have cut down anyone in our way to hunt down an enemy of the throne. I can't even imagine how much that kind of obsessive loyalty intensifies once you've actually sworn your vows." His gaze traveled around the room, making eye contact with each of them, and landing on Ning'er last.

"So believe me," he said. His gaze like two coals, ready to ignite. "Believe me when I say that they will chase us to the ends of the earth. And when I say we need to move. I mean *move*."

No one argued further after that. They packed up as best they could, quick and light on their feet, largely silent through the process, that awful backdrop of sirens and drum towers sounding their way through it all. Cheng Yun marshaled them all so efficiently and relentlessly that Ning'er wondered how any of them could have forgotten the world he had been born into.

He was never supposed to become the creature he was now. He was never meant to be theirs. Yet watching him—striding through the compound and ordering ammunition hidden, maps and paper documents shredded and burned—Ning'er couldn't imagine him belonging to anyone else.

"I know other places we could go, people who could hide us," he mused aloud now.

"Where?" panted Ning'er, hauling a cartridge of plasma rifles into storage. "The Fourth Ring? The Third? Some place worse or better?"

Cheng Yun gave her an odd look. "Neither. Some place out-side of Beijing entirely. The whole city's going to be crawling."

Ning'er had never known a life outside of Beijing. This was absurd. "You're kidding me."

"I am not," said Cheng Yun. "We could hole up in Hebei perhaps—far enough north to be a pain to follow, and plenty of mountains for cover out in the countryside. And I have contacts in Tianjin who could give us temporary shelter. It would buy us time."

Time. They constantly seemed to be running out of it and look-ing for cheap, temporary solutions for more. Ning'er's frustration was a burning thing, wrapped around her heart. "If I ever leave Beijing—and that's a big if—it'll be on my own terms. We can't just up and leave the city without warning. This is my—this is our *home*; I won't be driven from it by glorified lapdogs. I won't do it, Cheng Yun."

"You may not have a choice," he insisted. "We—"

A great shout rose outside. Someone was banging on the doors of the compound downstairs. Ning'er exchanged a terrified glance with the other crew members before turning her attention back to Cheng Yun. "It's not them," she insisted. "It can't already be them. They barely started sounding the lockdown sirens thirty minutes ago, the drums less than that. Surely—"

She was cut off by more shouts. More insistent rapping on the doors.

"Cheng Yun!" A familiar voice, right at the door. Hesitation flickered across Cheng Yun's face before he opened it a crack.

"Cheng Yun, thank heavens you're awake." The middle-aged man from the earlier crowd stood red-faced and panting at the door. "It's happened. They're here."

The scant, desperate hope flickering inside Ning'er's heart

flickered out. Her insides turned to ice. The man didn't have to spell out who *they* were.

Cheng Yun looked back at Ning'er, weary resignation all over his face. "I told you," he said. "They'll hunt enemies of the state anywhere." His hollow smile was grim as he turned back to the man at the door. "The Brocade Guard were bred for efficiency. Luckily, I know how they think. And I did prepare, at least a little, even for this."

The man at the door nodded. "What are your orders?"

Cheng Yun didn't hesitate. "Run."

The man balked. "What about the rest of you? What about the Lark?"

"We'll handle ourselves."

"A'yun, I—"

"Please." Cheng Yun clasped their visitor around the shoulders, his gaze bright and intense as they bored into the older man's. "You take the rest of the collective and what supplies you can. And then you get out of here, through any means necessary, you hear? You're not the ones they're after. If you run now, you should be safe. They won't follow. Not when the real prize is up here. Please, please just go."

The man's face did a complicated series of things, before he gave a single, grim nod. "Heaven be with you, Red Yaksha." Without another word, true to his orders, he ran.

Cheng Yun glanced back at the crew. "Now, it's our turn." He jerked his head toward the hallway outside. "Come with me. All of you. Hurry."

The crew exchanged glances. And then they were pelting after Cheng Yun. The hall led to a passageway, barely noticeable,

practically a hole in the wall, but he swerved toward it with deci-
siveness.

She was less impressed when it led to what, by all means,
appeared to be a dead end.

Ning'er eyed the window at the end of the passageway—and
the grate of solid iron bars over the glass panes—aghast. "Please
tell me you're not thinking what I think you are."

That hollow smile grew as Cheng Yun cast his glance toward
her. The expression was almost warm. "Are you a cat burglar or
aren't you?"

Ning'er grumbled. "At least help me pry the bars off." If it
could even be done. She'd gotten her fair share of stubborn grates
off unlikely entryways into buildings before, but nothing that
looked this well-locked in.

"I'll do it," said Zi'an, fishing into his tool belt and striding
forward. He had some kind of souped-up wrench, which he pro-
ceeded to attach to the furthermost window bar. "Not my handi-
est pry bar," he admitted, "but not my jankiest, either. We'll see if
it works. Grab the other bar, Ning'er. On three."

The pry bar sparked a few times as the grate groaned. Ning'er
grimaced. Her fingers tugged, white knuckled and useless, against
the iron. "This is no good," she panted. The pounding at the doors
was growing more insistent, the shouts outside growing in a steady
crescendo.

"Like hell it's no good," Zi'an panted back. "I'll have you know
that I bought this pry bar from your pal Ge Rong. When have you
known his tools to not work?"

Somewhere at the far end of the building, a door burst
open. The rumble of heavy footsteps layered itself over the

ominous drumbeat echoing through the grounds of the city.

"They're inside!" yelled Zhenyi.

"Zi'an!" Ning'er pried even more frantically at the grate. "We're trapped."

"We're not," he snarled.

"They're iron bars, Zi'an!"

"And I'm me," he retorted grimly. He gave the grate one last good tug. And like magic, like a miracle come at last, it popped off.

Zi'an twisted his head over his shoulder, chest still heaving with the effort. "Feifei. Cheng Yun. Secure the Lark first. The rest of us can follow. Let's move."

They moved.

The street below was, at least, thankfully empty. The Brocade Guard who'd breached the compound probably still thought they were inside, which would buy them a little time, at least.

Zi'an was the first to state the obvious. "Well, we're going to need a new safehouse."

"You could come back to my place." Ning'er spoke before her brain entirely caught up with her mouth. The others stared at her for a moment. "It's not far from Ge Rong's workshop," she offered up, in hasty, self-conscious defense. "If we crash at my place for the night, that gives us time to regroup. Then we can head to A'rong's in the morning and stock up on supplies."

It was a little absurd. She had to admit that much. Her apartment was barely big enough for herself. It had already felt so small when she'd had Cheng Yun over, that tiny space just wrapped around the two of them. She winced a little at the inevitable chaos of trying to cram six teenagers and their unconscious new friend into that meager square footage. Then again, better cramped and courting claustrophobia than dead.

"I know my place isn't ideal," she began, "but it's temporary, and we aren't exactly spoiled for better options—"

"It's perfect," said Cheng Yun.

Startled, Ning'er glanced at him. "It is? I mean, you've actually *been* there before. Didn't think perfect would be the word you'd choose."

He smiled at her, a little wry. "For a vacation getaway, maybe not. For a usefully forgettable hiding spot? As I said. Perfect."

That settled things.

They took the longer but more careful route, back alleys and near-abandoned train tracks from the Fourth to the Sixth Ring. They chose uncrowded areas, affecting nonchalance and casual cheer for the benefit of the few bystanders they encountered. The Lark, swathed in borrowed clothing, became just another drunk college student, being carried home after one too many shots. The rest of them were simply her friends, laughing and joking among themselves, careful all the while to keep her long hair draped over those poster-perfect, dangerously identifiable facial features. Right now, they were anonymous. If they didn't stay that way, they were done for.

Every time they stopped at a checkpoint, no one breathed. And every time a bored border guard waved them through, the oxygen gushed out of their lungs all at once.

Ning'er practically burst into tears as her shoddy little apartment came into view. It must have said something for the sheer exhaustion permeating their crew that no one so much as blinked at the scant size of Ning'er's Sixth Ring hovel. They simply stumbled in, one by one, single file, collapsing without a word on various surfaces like wrung-out little heaps of humanity. Feifei took an arm of the threadbare couch while Zhenyi went directly to the floor, Zi'an beside her, his eyes already squeezed shut. The Lark had been laid carefully at the center of the room, hands folded over her chest, a fairy-tale creature in the guise of a girl. The legend herself come back to life, hidden away here in Ning'er's nowhere apartment. It had to be the universe's idea of a joke.

Ning'er looked at Cheng Yun. He was the only member of their crew left without a spot claimed in the meager space. Cheng Yun looked back at Ning'er. The side of his mouth curled upward.

She was already crawling into her bed. "Well, what are you waiting for?" Amazing how even now, even under these circumstances, blood was still rushing right to her cheeks. She patted the space beside her on the mattress. "Climb on in."

Cheng Yun laughed softly as he obeyed. Ning'er tried to ignore the sense of déjà vu that washed over her as his weight settled in beside her. It had felt like a turning point in—what, exactly? What did they call what they had? She'd had enough boys in her bed to recognize that she could probably give name to that awkwardness, should she choose to, but there was a time and a place for these things.

On the business end of the Brocade Guard's shit list was, most definitively, not the time or place at all.

It was the last thing she thought of as she drifted, once more, into sleep.

A cacophony of banging at her door woke Ning'er so abruptly she wondered for half a second if she'd really been sleeping at all. She glanced around the room, heart skittering in time to the insistent knocks at the door. The others were also slowly startling awake, faces a mix of terror and exhaustion. Ning'er wondered if any of them had gotten any real rest at all.

"The Brocade Guard again?" Feifei's voice was hoarse.

"The Brocade Guard again," Cheng Yun confirmed. He sat up beside Ning'er in the bed. How he could seem so alert—so much more awake and ready to hit the ground running than anyone else in the room—was beyond her. Ning'er didn't feel alert or awake at all. Maybe Cheng Yun was a robot. Maybe he was the latest in android technology.

Ning'er's mind had gone strangely fuzzy even while her pulse skyrocketed. They couldn't keep doing this. Running for hours on end, sleeping, waking, running, running, running again until some eventual, inevitable collapse. It wasn't sustainable.

Cheng Yun was shaking her shoulder. "Ning'er. I know you're tired—beyond tired—but I need you to snap out of it. Please."

Slowly, she turned toward him. That once uncannily beautiful face had become so familiar to her over the course of this stupid job. The sharp bones, the wide dark eyes and long lashes. And now, those seemingly permanent purple shadows hollowing out the planes of his face. They were darker than ever now, belying his own exhaustion, even as his voice held steady. "Ning'er," he repeated. "Listen. Can you get the others out of here?"

Ning'er dug her nails hard into the palms of her hands, trying to force her brain to catch up with her heartbeat. "I think I can," she said after a moment.

Wait. She could, actually. Ning'er blinked, a little surprised at her own realization. There was another way out of the studio, so familiar to her she thought nothing of it. But it wasn't going to be pretty. If they survived this, the rest of the crew would be having words with her about her methods. Probably.

"Trash chute," said Ning'er. Then louder, pitching her voice to be heard over the murmured panic filling her apartment.

"Hey! Everyone shut up! We need to go down the trash chute."

For a moment, the others just stared at her.

"You're serious?" asked Feifei faintly. Her nose wrinkled.

"As serious as the Brocade Guard soldiers currently trying to break my door down," Ning'er snapped. "We can either die clean here or stink to live another day. Your choice."

That decided them. Zi'an went down first, the Lark tucked in a fireman's carry over his broad shoulders. Zhenyi and Feifei followed, Feifei's nose wrinkled and eyes squeezed shut the entire time.

Ning'er and Cheng Yun were next. She stepped toward the chute, angling one leg in, before meeting Cheng Yun's gaze. It was a weird moment. She wasn't entirely sure how she'd have described the look on his face at that moment, the full mouth slightly parted, his gaze soft on her. Hopeful, if she wanted to read him optimistically. Fearful, if she didn't. Maybe it was both. It was increasingly easy to be both.

Her leg buckled against the chute. Instinctively, he offered a steadying hand, reaching toward her. It was another déjà vu moment in a day full of them. In another time and place, he'd offered her that same hand when she'd danced with him. Her fingertips brushed his.

Someone knocked thunderously on the apartment door.

The world slowed down. Cheng Yun's eyes went wide for a fraction of a second. Then an expression of something like relief stole across his face. The shouts of the soldiers, so loud a moment ago, dimmed into background noise. Cheng Yun's fingers tightened painfully on Ning'er's as he hauled her close. They were on a dance floor again, his hands on hers, his lips at her ear.

She could feel every puff of his breath, hot against her ear, as he spoke. And this, she heard, far more clearly than the chaos in the room: "Thank you, Ning'er. For everything."

"What do you mean?" Her chest was tight.

"I'll buy you as much time as I can." A hint of a smirk returned to his face. A ghost of the Young Marshal he'd spent most of his life pretending to be.

"Don't you dare," she snarled. "Remember everything we said back at the lab? About redemption?" Her voice hitched on a sob. Everything in her chest compressed. "You have to take a gamble on what's *right*."

"I am," he said. He smiled at her. One of his real smiles, secret and genuine and awfully, heartbreakingly lovely. The smile that made him look simply like Cheng Yun. "I'm gambling on you."

She hadn't realized how much of her weight he'd been holding up. All it took was a gentle little shove. A slip of the fingertips. And suddenly, she was falling down into the darkness of the chute. Alone.

Ning'er screamed. She couldn't help herself. It was the shock of the fall as much as the loss of his hand, that final contact point between them. She was still screaming when she hit the soft cushion of the garbage bin.

The others were on her almost immediately. "Are you hurt?" Feifei demanded.

"Where's Cheng Yun?" asked Zhenyi, more quietly. As if she already knew. As if she could guess what he'd done.

Ning'er stopped screaming. Instead, she just sat there and cried. Big, ugly crying that robbed her lungs of oxygen. Sobs that felt like little earthquakes vibrating down the spent cavern of her body. "We have to go," she managed at last, gasping a little. "He's—he's holding them off so we can get a head start. So we have to run. We can't—we can't let him have wasted. Wasted"— with an effort, she stopped blubbering and stood—"wasted his life."

The world tilted around her. The faces above her blurred in and out of focus, expressions of concern melting into nothingness. She heard Zi'an give an alarmed shout, heard Feifei yell, "Catch her!"

And then Ning'er's world went black.

CHAPTER 12

A Tale of Two Revolutionaries

T he first thing Ning'er recognized upon waking was the scent of Ge Rong's studio. She inhaled sharply, sense memory stirring to life. It was that unique, a faint blend of paint fumes and mechanical oils which probably would have smelled disgusting to anyone else but always felt like safety to Ning'er. She lifted her head slightly, wincing at the echoes of a headache pulsing through her temples. Slowly, her bearings returned as the familiar walls around her swam into focus. She was on a makeshift cot, set up smack-dab in the middle of the workshop.

Ning'er propped herself up on her prosthetic arm and started slightly. The movement was smoother than she remembered, the joints operating without a hint of a creak. She peeked down at the arm, examining the freshly polished metal casing and flexing newly rewired fingers. Someone had given her an upgrade while she was asleep.

"So you're awake, too."

Ning'er blinked sleep crust from her eyes, trying to make out the blurred figure standing across the room from her. "I know you," she croaked.

"Do you?" The figure strode closer.

It was the same voice. That was what Ning'er recognized first. She'd heard it a million times, on the radio, blaring from

TV screens, tinny through the filter. But never had she heard it directed toward her just so, in real time.

Ning'er sat up on her elbows, suddenly wide awake. "You're the Lark."

"Don't call me that." The girl standing before Ning'er certainly looked like the Lark: striking and lovely and imminently recognizable, even with the shadows exhaustion had carved into her features. It reminded Ning'er painfully of Cheng Yun.

Ning'er frowned. "But you're . . ."

"I said don't call me that!" barked the girl. With terrifying speed, she was in Ning'er's face, panting hard.

"Ning'er!" Feifei arrived in the room, Zhenyi and Zi'an in her wake.

Dumbly, and uncertain how else to react, Ning'er pointed at the half-feral girl practically sitting on top of her. "Look who's awake."

The Lark leapt from Ning'er's bed, the movement strangely animalistic. "Who the fuck are all of you?"

"Your rescuers!" snapped Ning'er. "We broke you out of that Lilium facility—"

"No," the Lark interrupted, shaking her head. "No, no, no, this is all a trick, they're trying to get me to give it up again—"

"Give what up again?" Zhenyi asked softly.

The Lark's attention zeroed in on her. "You," she rasped. "I know you, don't I?"

Zhenyi bowed her head. "I followed you once. Into the First Ring."

The Lark's posture crumpled. "Pan Zhenyi," she whispered. "I remember your face. I remember all their faces."

Cautiously, Zhenyi approached the other girl. When He Bailing didn't flinch away, Zhenyi took her hands. "This isn't one of their tricks, Bailing," said Zhenyi. "It's me. I'm real. You were imprisoned by Lilium for five years. We broke you out with the help of"—her breath hitched, before she steeled herself—"our friend. A boy named Cheng Yun."

The Lark's head tilted. "Cheng Yun?" she asked suspiciously. She glanced past Zhenyi's shoulder at Zi'an. "You?"

"No," said Ning'er before Zi'an could answer. She swallowed hard. "Cheng Yun is—he's gone." Her eyes burned. "He was captured by the Brocade Guard."

"Oh," said the Lark. "Then he's dead. Or as good as."

"You don't know that," snapped Ning'er.

The Lark gave a raucous laugh. "I'd know that better than anyone. If he's lucky, he's dead. If he's not, he'll end up like me."

"Then we'll save him, too," said Ning'er stubbornly. "You could help us," she barreled on.

"Ning'er—" Zhenyi began quietly, a warning note in her voice.

Ning'er ignored her, throwing caution to the wind. "You're the Lark—"

"I told you not to call me that!" He Bailing screamed. Her frantic gaze swept across them all, darting back and forth. "The only reason I have to believe a word any of you say is her." She jerked her head toward Zhenyi. "But for all I know, Zhenyi's a traitor, too. Maybe you're all in Lilium's pocket. Maybe they're finally ready to kill me. Maybe—"

"I saved you from Lilium!" Ning'er screamed right back. A dam had broken inside of her. "I stole you out of that lab because you were supposed to save all of us." Hot tears rolled down her cheeks. How could this be the same girl who'd once graced every broadcast in Beijing, the girl who'd once taught Ning'er to find hope in the shards of her own broken heart?

It was like the Lark had died all over again, only this time, Ning'er was the one who'd killed her.

"All I'm asking now is for you to save one person," Ning'er sobbed. "Just save Cheng Yun. Please."

Bailing shook her head frantically. "No. No, no, no. He could be Lilium, too. Just like the rest of you."

"We're not Lilium," snapped Feifei. "And we're not going to hurt you. Just tell us what you want!"

He Bailing gave a shuddering little sob. "All I want is to go back to sleep. There's nothing for me here anymore. There never was." She buried her head between her hands. "Now, please, please, if you're not going to kill me, then just leave me alone."

They did as the Lark asked. He Bailing was locked up once more, in one of the spare rooms of Ge Rong's workshop. Meanwhile, her rescuers conferred heatedly on what to do next.

"You could go home," Zi'an offered Ning'er. "Cheng Yun left your money with me. You did your job. You'll be paid."

"For what?" Ning'er snarled. "You heard the girl in there. That's no Lark anymore." She shivered. "I don't know who the fuck she is."

"I don't think she does, either," said Zhenyi, dull voiced. "I think that's what happens when Lilium Corp kidnaps and tortures you for five years in an attempt to get you to give up the location where you've stashed evidence of all their collusions. Tell me, Zhong Ning'er, would you particularly want to be the Lark if that's what it earned you?"

Ning'er relented, abruptly ashamed of her own anger. "If she doesn't want to be the Lark anymore, fine." She looked around at them all. "But I'm not going home. Not until we get Cheng Yun back. We may not have a Lark anymore, but we still have a Red Yaksha. We can't give up on him."

So began the thankless, awful process of monitoring the newsreels. It was pure agony. The newscasters covered the usual talking points: shifting weather patterns and grain shortages, a clinical little nod to the protests still being put down all over the kingdom. Nothing that lasted. Nothing that seemed to leave any real impression. But, more critically, there was no news either of a break-in at a government facility nor news of the Young Marshal or his disgrace.

It left them all in a state of awful, nebulous uncertainty. Word of his death would have been better, in some ways, than waiting for some hint in the news, some whisper of the Young Marshal's fate. Death was a concrete data point. At least it would have meant knowing something for sure. Instead, all they had going for them was amorphous dread.

"We should go to his father's house," said Feifei at last, when their collective anxiety had become too much to bear. "I know families like his in the Upper Rings. Political types. My family sometimes gets commissioned to do print work for them." Her full mouth thinned. "They'll do everything in their power to keep their only remaining heir. Besides, the court will be inclined to protect the Young Marshal's reputation—he's too valuable as propaganda. Which leaves them one option, pretty much: house arrest. It's not a sure thing, but it's better than nothing. Either way, there's no way to know unless we stake out Minister Cheng's manor."

"And how do you propose we go about doing that?" Ning'er asked. "It's not as though we can just waltz into the Second Ring."

The side of Feifei's mouth quirked. "I seem to recall a certain

244 · ANDREA TANG

thief who breached those demarcation lines more than once."

"'More than once' is an exaggeration," said Ning'er. "Even at my most daring, I tried not to press my luck too often. Besides, half the reason I did so well as a thief was that I was invisible. Now, though?" Ning'er shuddered. "We've spent too much time running; too many Beiyang authorities have probably seen my face, or at least my general size and shape, along with distinguishing physical features. Like this." She waved one metal hand in front of Feifei's face. "And if you say something like 'why not just get special dispensation to cross the Rings legally,' I will eat my own arm, metal and all."

"Please don't, that was a very expensively illegal job," muttered Ge Rong from his corner. His expression was one of weary resignation. "Then again, I suppose that's the least of my concerns, isn't it? Now that I'm harboring a pack of wanted criminals in my place of work."

A pang of guilt slithered through Ning'er. "A'rong, I'm sorry to have dragged you into this—"

"You dragged me nowhere. I dragged myself," said Ge Rong. Beneath the exhaustion, a hint of warmth clung to his voice. "Truly, harboring wanted criminals is the least I can do. But I agree: dispensation to cross the Rings—wanted as you are—is going to be a tall order."

"We don't need to get special dispensation to cross the Rings," said Feifei.

Ning'er sucked in a long breath. Heaven grant her patience. "Did you just hear anything I—"

"We don't need special dispensation," Feifei repeated, looking increasingly smug as she spoke, "because I already have it." She reached into her purse, producing a laminated student ID. "I attend school in the Second Ring, remember?"

"What about the rest of us?" asked Zi'an. "Our dear thief here has a point, 宝贝儿. Not all of us are Second Ring medical students."

"I've thought about that part, too." Feifei offered him a grim smile. "I have a plan. Did I ever tell you guys about my weekend volunteering shifts?"

"I can't believe you let Feifei talk us into this." Zi'an's teeth rattled as he scowled pitifully across the scant, dingy space between his body and Ning'er's. He rubbed the back of his neck, cramped beneath the low ceiling of the truck as they careened through the city streets. Probably. The back of the truck had no windows, so light was scant. Ning'er had to take it on faith that they were going the right way at all.

"Me?" Ning'er was indignant. "I seem to recall you agreeing quite meekly when she pitched this plan."

Zi'an chose to ignore this. "And how come Ge Rong gets to stay home and relax?"

"He's not relaxing," Zhenyi pointed out. "He's babysitting the La— babysitting He Bailing, or did you want to leave a traumatized and unstable political prisoner alone in the closest thing we have to a safehouse right now?"

Well, when she put it that way.

"Let's just focus on the job," said Ning'er.

They'd embarked on their journey into the Second Ring in the wee hours of the evening. The plan was reasonably simple. Feifei, the magnanimous medical student, would be driving a borrowed medic truck. She was a bleeding heart returning equipment after a late-night shift at the free clinics of the Lower Rings, seeing to those poor unfortunate souls who couldn't afford the quality medical care of Upper Ring hospitals.

The rest of them just had to stay in the back, hidden, and keep quiet at the security checkpoints.

It went smoothly enough. Feifei was an old hand on the regular volunteer crew, and most of the guards at the entry gates recognized her. She laughed and joked with them, asking after their families, and if any of them noticed the slight strain in her tone as she wished them well, none were rude enough to remark on it.

It wasn't until they finally disembarked—to muffled groans of relief from Zi'an and his long limbs—that Ning'er actually began worrying in earnest. She'd only been in the Second Ring a scant handful of times, and tried to minimize recklessness whenever she entered the uppermost domain of Beijing's elite. It wasn't unusual, in neighborhoods this ritzy, to see the odd security vehicle here or there. But Ning'er hadn't been ready for the current reality of the Second Ring—the streets were packed with gendarme on seemingly every corner. She could spy blockades on major avenues, and curious little bubbles of the well-dressed whispered among themselves as they scurried past.

Minister Cheng's manor, though, was near impossible to miss. Patrolled by android sentinels and covering the equivalent of several city blocks, it stood at the edge of the Second Ring like an enormous, ostentatious monument to decadence. While the rest of Beijing's populace had been forced into cramped high-rises, traditional manors remained the sole privilege of ministers and businessmen.

All Ning'er could think of as she scouted the route past the sentinels' blind spots was the truth of what financed it all. How many grams of Complacency had Minister Cheng helped manufacture to pay for that lovely siheyuan or the artfully manicured gardens inside? What percentage of human blood and bone had Cheng Yun's father sold back to their owners to pay for the symmetrically sloped rooftops and flawless green-accented walls?

It made her want to throw up. She fought down the urge. Instead, she kept moving forward, careful to signal to the others which way to turn to avoid the patrols. It was all about precision. She had to think of this as just another job. She couldn't keep thinking about the true cost of this place or the life of the boy who hung in the balance of it all. Otherwise she'd never get them safely through the manor grounds.

And then they'd truly never see Cheng Yun again.

It felt like a lifetime had passed when she finally found herself underneath his bedroom window. It boasted a second floor, perfectly situated over one of the sentinel blind spots on the property, with a little staircase leading down to the somber stone courtyards. Practically made for the Red Yaksha to sneak in and out undetected.

Ning'er stood beneath the balcony for a long moment, breathing slowly in and out as she looked upward toward her destination. The bedroom—Cheng Yun's bedroom, please let it be Cheng Yun's bedroom—had a light on. If he was there, he was awake.

If he was there.

Her crew stood silent around her. Feifei met her eyes first. The side of her mouth tilted up. "You ready, thief?"

"Does it matter?" Ning'er shrugged, ignoring the drumbeat of her heart. "It's now or never."

That seemed to satisfy Feifei and the rest of them. As one, with Ning'er in the lead, they hurried up the little staircase to the balcony. Ning'er got to the top first. She cleared the last step and practically ran for that window.

Her heart almost climbed into her throat. There he was, sitting inside at a long oak desk: Cheng Yun, alive and conscious, his gaze a little distant as he fiddled with a pen between long callused fingers. He had a fading bruise under the left side of his jaw, and exhaustion still painted purple shadows under his eyes, but they were his eyes, still, big and dark and glittering with purpose, even now.

And they were staring right at her.

Neither of them moved for a moment. Then Cheng Yun scrambled toward them. He got the window open with a little effort. "Ning'er," he breathed. "Oh, Ning'er, what are you doing here?"

"What am I doing here?" Ning'er demanded. Her hands clamped down on the edges of the windowsill as she leaned toward him, trying to drink in his presence. Alive, alive, alive. "What are you doing? Where the fuck is the door to this balcony?"

Cheng Yun jerked his head to the side. "Locked and bolted." Sure enough, a tiny little side door had been padlocked several times over. Ning'er had nearly missed it under the tangle of chains. Cheng Yun tried to smile at her as she raised her eyebrows at him in disbelief. "My father has to put some effort, at least, toward making this house arrest look legitimate," he informed her.

"So Feifei was right." Ning'er breathed out, a long, slow whistle. "He really does have you locked up here."

"Cheng Yun?" Speak of the devil. Feifei scrambled into place beside Ning'er, Zhenyi silent on her heels but just as eager. "Cheng Yun, are you all right?"

"I'm fine." Cheng Yun pressed his fingers against the window ledge, surprise sitting gentle in his features. "Truly, Feifei. I've been kept here while the Beiyang decide what they're going to do with me, and . . . nothing has happened." His jaw tensed briefly. "I'm surprised to see you here, honestly." He glanced at Zhenyi and Ning'er. "All of you."

"Why?" The question fell out of Ning'er's mouth, blunt, edged in hurt. "Why would you ever think that we wouldn't . . . that we wouldn't come for you?"

"Ning'er," Zhenyi began. "We can discuss this later—"

Cheng Yun shook his head, forestalling Zhenyi's defense with a gently raised hand. "Change is rarely bloodless. There are worse people to lose than me."

"Not in my view," said Ning'er. "I don't believe in acceptable sacrifices. Not human ones. Not . . ." She trailed off, steeled herself, and continued: "Not people we love." She barreled on before she could give him too much time to process that last bit. "So we're taking you home, princess." She twisted her head over her shoulder. "Zi'an. You got explosives on those padlocks yet?"

"What do you take me for?" Zi'an grinned at her over the tops of his glasses. "After all that trouble I went to procure special components, my feelings were hurt when I never got to use them back in Minister Cheng's lab."

Cheng Yun's eyes widened slightly. "You brought explosives?"

"Not my favorite method," Ning'er admitted thoughtfully. "Even with silencers, I've never loved the mess. Still, there's always a time and a place."

"Discretion is overrated, 宝宝," said Zi'an around a piece of twine stuck between his teeth. He bit it off, securing the tie on the explosives he'd set at the door. "But for what it's worth, these babies are pretty precise. Still, Cheng Yun, you'd best stand well back."

Cheng Yun did, backing away from the rest of the crew, hands up.

Zi'an turned to the rest of them. "Ready?"

"Do it," said Zhenyi grimly.

There was a pause, then a tiny little burst of sparks around the chains on the door. The door jolted on its hinges. When Zi'an strode cautiously forward to pry the knob, it swung wide open. Silently, he waved Cheng Yun through.

For one split second, as Cheng Yun emerged from the small puffs of clearing smoke, Ning'er reached toward him. It was instinct, more than anything else, a thief's simple greed. He was, after all, the prize who kept slipping through her fingers. Three times now, she'd nearly lost him: once to Devil's Mark, once to those labyrinthine tunnels where they'd opened the Lark's cage, and finally to the Brocade Guard. Three times, she'd reached for a hand that vanished from hers like a ghost's fingertips fading with the dawning of the morning. Now, she reached again, her fingertips, metal and flesh, pressing briefly into his outstretched hand. Reassurance that he was here. Reassurance that he was real, after all.

And then they were flying down that spiraling staircase. Ning'er scrambled down first, leading the way, Zi'an at the rear with Cheng Yun. They hit the grass at a sprint, taking off toward the fence. They would make it. For just a little bit, in half-hopeful disbelief, Ning'er really, truly believed that stealing Cheng Yun back from right under his father's nose would be that simple.

Which, of course, was right when Minister Cheng strode across the grounds from the opposite end of the yard, hulking androids at his back. He looked like a man out for an evening stroll. As if he'd simply been going about his business and found himself caught unaware by intruders on his property.

The cold, careful smile that snaked across his mouth, though, told a different story.

"Father," Cheng Yun breathed. He'd stopped. They'd all stopped. Even Ning'er had stopped. Her feet rooted themselves in that perfectly cut grass as she stared at Cheng Yun's father. They looked so alike: the same long lashes and glass-cut cheekbones, the same expressive, too-full mouth. It struck her harder now, here in the open air of a beautiful summer's evening, than it ever had in the belly of that awful lab. She hadn't noticed all the intricacies of the resemblance there, but now she couldn't escape it. The way Minister Cheng curled that lovely mouth—the mouth so like Cheng Yun's—upward in contempt at the sight of her knocked the wind right out of her body and sent chills running down her spine.

"A'yun," said the minister. "What's all this, then?"

It was a rhetorical question. It had to be. Any idiot could see what 'all this' was, from the residue dusting Zi'an's fingers to how Zhenyi went immediately for the blaster holstered under her coat to the way Feifei backed up, pressing her spine into Cheng Yun's chest, as if this was one more thing she could protect him from, like his father was a disease that could be eradicated. Minister Cheng knew that his son's real family had come for him.

It was why, perhaps, when he next spoke, he deployed the ugliest weapon he could: "A'yun," he repeated, more softly now. "What would A'wei say if he could see his little brother now?"

They all heard the way Cheng Yun's breath hitched at the mention of his dead brother. Cheng Wei's name was still a bullet after all these years, sure to find its target.

But Cheng Yun didn't crumple. He didn't flinch or fall. With careful hands on Feifei's shoulders, he prodded her gently aside as he strode forward. Toward his father and those hulking androids. The Red Yaksha reduced to nothing but a boy, looking inches smaller and years younger than he was, beseeching giants.

"I don't know," said Cheng Yun, blunt voiced. "But guess what, Father? Neither do you. Neither of us ever will."

His father's face twisted itself up. "All I've ever done is try and protect you both. I already lost A'wei. Don't make me lose you, too." The grief clinging to Minister Cheng's voice was an alien thing. Ning'er had never wanted to think of Minister Cheng as a man who could grieve. She'd never wanted to think of him as a creature capable of human emotion at all. It was so much easier to make him a monster and nothing else.

"A'wei died of a drug overdose," said Cheng Yun. His eyes glittered. "Oxyveris. The same stuff your cronies at Lilium peddle."

"And you think that was an accident?" Minister Cheng had gone sheet white. "Didn't you ever wonder why it was oxyveris? Why, when A'wei never touched Complacency?"

Cheng Yun's brow furrowed. "He was always wild."

"With fine wine and pretty girls and long nights out at expensive parties, yes. But never with Complacency. Never that. It was the only thing we couldn't agree on. Lilium Corp plucked our family from ruin the day they awarded me that scholarship. My support for them has kept us out of poverty, and worse. He knew all that. He understood. I made sure he understood, or I thought I did." The minister shook his head, like he was shaking off an old ghost on his shoulders. "But A'wei could never bring himself to stomach the cost of oxyveris: the way it forced its users to rely on it for strength, while chipping away slowly at their minds and bodies and hearts."

The minister paused, and looked at his remaining son, dead

in the eyes. "And you know something? For a time, he almost got me to see things his way. I thought to myself, 'Why not? Lilium has enough ministers in its pockets, and you've served them well enough over the years. Why not bow gracefully out of your arrangement? Why not make your son happy?'" His mouth twisted. "And do you know what happened, two nights after I announced as much to the executive board?"

Cheng Yun had gone as pale as his father.

"That's why I was so careful about protecting their lab, you know," the minister continued. "After they killed one son, they made it abundantly clear that I needed to prove my renewed loyalty so I wouldn't lose the other. One more manufacturing lab hardly matters to Lilium, but they needed a facility that could do double duty as a prison. And for that, they needed imperial allegiance."

"The Lark," Ning'er blurted out, aghast. "They asked you to help cage her, didn't they? So she couldn't publicly expose how many imperial ministers they bought. So she couldn't expose *you*."

"You can still do right by him, you know," said Cheng Yun quietly. "A'wei. You can do what he would have wanted. It's not too late to cut ties with Lilium now." He swallowed. "All you have to do is let me go."

Ning'er heard a peace offering for what it was. She'd been there herself with Baba far too many times. She stopped breathing. For that scant moment, stuck between Cheng Yun and his father and years of dead history, maybe they all did.

Minister Cheng walked toward his son. Ning'er wanted to step between them. She wanted to put a halt to the slow, dreadful inevitability of the long-shattered thing unfolding before her eyes. Cheng Yun had broken from his father so long ago, and watching them now only made obvious all the places where whatever twisted love may have once lain between them had healed up ugly.

Cheng Yun's father leaned forward, one hand reaching for his son. It was an odd mirror of the way Ning'er kept finding herself reaching for Cheng Yun, grasping for something that always managed to slip just an inch out of reach. For the space of a heartbeat, Ning'er thought that coming from Minister Cheng, this too might be a gesture of tenderness. Some small, shriveled sign of a love so long buried.

Then the minister whispered, "You foolish, foolish boy." He cupped the side of Cheng Yun's cheek. Again, that ghost of what would have been tenderness. Then the minister's hand dropped to Cheng Yun's shoulder. He gave his son a careless little shove, no real force behind it. The way you might shove an old pile of hand-me-downs out of the way while cleaning a house. A gesture that did not speak of love or hate, but of indifference. Cheng Yun's father pushed Cheng Yun aside and turned away from his son. "I will never, ever let you go. Hate me tonight if you must. But one day, you'll thank me for protecting you from yourself."

It was as if the air had been sucked out of the evening. Cheng Yun had gone utterly still, his spine rigid. Ning'er had seen Cheng Yun hurt before. She knew, intimately, in more detail than she'd ever wanted, what Cheng Yun's breaking point looked like. She'd seen him in the throes of feverish agony. She'd seen him ready to face gunfire rather than let his Lark die. She'd seen him on the business end of his would-be comrades in the Brocade Guard. Too many times, she had witnessed this boy on the brink of so many almost-deaths, both little and large.

This was a new kind of death, though. Ning'er didn't need

to be told what she was witnessing: the last choking embers of a boy's hope that a parent's love might be enough to save them both, snuffed out for good. She turned away, unable to keep watching the terrible thing Cheng Yun's face was doing. A firing squad would, perhaps, have been kinder.

She should have run right then. Every last member of Cheng Yun's beloved, disaster-courting crew should have turned tail and run. Instead, they stood numb and wordless, like idiots, around the boy who'd once been their leader and his awful, grieving father.

Which meant they all heard it, loud and clear, when Minister Cheng spoke, cold and clear into the darkening night: "Androids, attention. You have a new order protocol. Escort young master Cheng Yun back to his quarters. And then kill the intruders."

CHAPTER 13

Prodigal Son

Ning'er should have known that stealing Cheng Yun back from his father's clutches wouldn't be so easy. Some disaster would ensue. You simply couldn't break into the private home of a man like Minister Cheng, whisk his only living son away into the night, and not expect something to go horribly wrong. She hadn't quite guessed at the shape of this impending doom, but she'd known it was inevitable, the way things like neck cricks and sprained ankles and paper cuts were inevitable. It would simply be a matter of adapting and pushing past it.

She had not, in any universe, expected that this particular doom would consist of getting slowly beaten to death by Minister Cheng's killer androids. Ning'er was a little insulted. She was a burglar from the Sixth Ring, after all. Who better to consider themselves an expert on the art of ducking android patrols? She'd evaded them just fine on the way into the Cheng property.

But this wasn't a patrol. This was three hulking machines on spindly legs with mean, glittering eyes. They weren't operating on surveillance orders anymore. They were operating on an attack protocol. And that, Ning'er had never truly dealt with before. She was a thief, not a fighter.

She dodged the scything arm of the first. "Run!" she screamed at the others. Too little, too late. They should have been running five minutes, an hour, a day ago.

A second android closed in on her, trying to box her up against its friend. Ning'er flinched away, cowering as she searched for space between them. Some semblance of an escape route. Any escape route. She ducked between their legs, going down knee first to make the gap. Her own legs skidded hard against the lawn as she scrambled back to her feet.

It was no good. They were on her again.

And then, quite abruptly, someone else was driving it back. Ning'er backed up instinctively as Zi'an and his disproportionately broad shoulders crowded into the space between her body and the android's. "Hey now," he drawled. "That's really rather rude, don't you think?"

It answered by charging at Zi'an. Ning'er clapped a hand over her mouth before she could scream.

Zi'an simply grinned. Then he dove low. His arms pinched around its spindly legs as he twisted his hips, rising back to his feet. The momentum of the collision—and gravity—did the rest of the work for him. It crashed hard into the grass. Zi'an wasted no time, stomping one booted foot hard against the android's head. It jerked once, circuits firing wildly. Zi'an stomped again. Then again and again, until the glowing eyes dulled.

Ning'er twisted her head to look for the other two androids and found them entangled with Zhenyi and Cheng Yun. Zhenyi had made surprisingly short work of her android, armed with what appeared to be one of Ge Rong's wire cutters. She'd been bruised up a little for her efforts, but in the process had managed to snip away the cables at several joints, leaving it an unsteady hunk of metal teetering around in its attempts to land a blow on her. She sidestepped it, then kicked the knees out. The hulking mass fell, rattling and sparking along the grass.

Cheng Yun, meanwhile, was having far worse luck. It had wrestled him to the ground, hooked itself across his back, and had powerful metal arms clamped around his throat. The more Cheng Yun struggled against its power, the harder the metal arms squeezed. Cheng Yun gagged, eyes rolling back.

"Cheng Yun!" Ning'er pelted forward. What could she do? Distract it, maybe, or control one of the arms.

Before she got there, something collided hard against its metal skull with a heavy crash. To Ning'er's amazement, Feifei strode into view, carrying a smoking hunk of the first android Zi'an had destroyed.

Zi'an gave a mighty whoop. "That's my girl!"

Ning'er yelped, jumping back, as the wiring in the damaged head sparked while the metal limbs spasmed. The spasms gave Cheng Yun just enough space to escape. He wrenched himself free, sucking down air as his chest heaved. As soon as he cleared its arms, Feifei brought her makeshift weapon down hard a second time. Its eyes flickered, then went dead and dim.

Ning'er scanned the premises, frantic. "Where did the minister go?"

Zi'an grabbed her by the elbow. "Don't know, don't care!" he yelled. "We've got to run!"

"He could still be here with a fresh crop of machines waiting for us," snapped Ning'er, "or worse, ones bearing actual weapons. We need to assess—"

Zhenyi gave a cry, interrupting the argument. "Look out!"

They looked. Across the minister's perfectly manicured lawn, the sparks from the ruined wiring had caught the edges of the grass. Several small fires were licking their way to life across the green.

Soon, they'd grow.

Ning'er tried to stomp one out, frantic. The smell of smoke was slowly filling the once clean night air. "Cheng Yun!" she cried. "Help me!"

The boy shook his head, one hand at a still bruised throat. "Leave it, Ning'er."

"But the fire," she began, and trailed off when she saw the look on his face.

His gaze was fixed somewhere past her, past the growing promise of a full-blown fire. "Let it burn," said Cheng Yun. With the glow of those little flames reflected in his irises, he looked like some ancient god, deceptively youthful, returned to life.

You had to squint to see the slow tracks of tears running down his cheeks.

"Let this whole damn place burn," said Cheng Yun.

None of the news outlets knew precisely how the fire on the Cheng property got started, but the blaze was, by all accounts, a great and terrible thing. The minister was left unaccounted for. Perhaps he perished in the blaze. Perhaps he escaped.

But in the remarkable days that followed, as it turned out, those same news outlets would have far bigger fish to fry.

The crew's return to Ge Rong's studio was not quite the triumphant homecoming they'd been hoping for.

Their first hint that something had gone awfully wrong was the broken window. Even during the protests and gendarme raids, even during the worst of the tumult that overtook the city, Ge Rong had taken pains to keep his workshop meticulously safe. The broken window was as symbolic as it was anything else.

It sent Ning'er rushing inside. The door was unlocked.

Ge Rong lay unmoving near the entrance. Ning'er screamed at the sight.

This, thankfully, moved Ge Rong. He stirred, then rolled over, groaning, hands against his ears. "Heavens above, please stop that racket."

Ning'er stopped screaming. She inhaled slowly. Exhaled again. "I thought you were dead."

"I'm impressed you could tell it was her," remarked Feifei, kneeling at Ge Rong's side. She looked up at Ning'er. "He's not dead, by the way."

"What remarkable bedside manner you continue to develop, Feifei," groaned Ge Rong. Slowly, her hands aiding him the entire way, he sat up. "Did you guys save Cheng Yun?"

"In a sense," said Feifei.

Ge Rong's nose wrinkled. "Why do you all smell like smoke?"

"That's a long story."

"What happened here?" asked Zhenyi. She entered the workshop cautiously, flanked by Zi'an. "It looks like a break-in."

"The opposite, actually," said Ge Rong. "A breakout."

Ning'er's heartbeat paused. Her insides went cold. "Ge Rong," she said slowly. "Where's He Bailing?" The answering look on his face told her everything she needed to know. Ning'er dropped to her knees beside him, heavy hearted, her bones like lead. "So she's gone. She ran. I don't suppose you have any idea where she went, either."

"She kind of knocked me unconscious before I could ask her for a forwarding address, so no," said A'rong, a little testily. He rubbed the back of his head.

Ning'er winced. "Point taken. My bad."

"Maybe this isn't as bad as it seems," said Zi'an. "Bailing didn't want to be the Lark anymore. What was she going to do, live here in this workshop forever?" He spread his hands. "We planned that whole silly little heist assuming that she would still be the same girl, interested in setting the same fires she did half a decade ago. It was foolish on our part. There was no contingency plan. If He Bailing is no longer the Lark, then maybe it's for the best that she strike out on her own. Build her own life, far from the people who wanted so badly for her to be something she's not." He looked away for a moment, jaw tight. "Far from us."

"That's not all," said Ge Rong. He rubbed his temples. He looked at Ning'er. "It's a very fortunate thing that you and Cheng Yun made off with as many of those file drives from the lab as you did."

Ning'er's heart pounded. "Why? What's on them?"

"Precisely what the Lark has been hiding all these years." A'rong shook his head. "All this time, the evidence they tried to torture out of her was hiding in plain sight. She just hid it among their own files. The one place they wouldn't look. I decoded what you dug up, just to be sure." He hesitated. "It's not everything. You couldn't pick up every single file in the building. Of the ones you grabbed, from what I could see, I wouldn't call it decisive evidence of regicide. I think that would have been an impossible stroke of luck, even for Cheng Yun. But it's enough to raise eyebrows. Enough, at least, to get people asking questions again."

Ning'er's pounding heart sank again. "But without decisive evidence, we can't prove anything for sure."

"Maybe not." Ge Rong's smile was grim. "But murder isn't the only dirty little secret the Beiyang ministers have been harboring." He looked around at them all. "One of those drives has the names of every minister ever bought and paid for by Lilium. A little more digging, and it won't be hard to find the skeletons in the closet that put them in Lilium's pocket."

Ning'er's entire body was strung tight. It was like being back in the belly of that lab, an inch from being caught, an inch from victory, her heart rattling hot inside her chest. "Then we can't give up."

Zi'an looked at her, shock temporarily overwhelming his obvious frustration. "I'm sorry, did I just hear Zhong Ning'er encourage us *not* to give up?"

"Okay." Ning'er exhaled slowly. "Okay, you're right, I deserved that. But think about what we have. The names of dirty ministers. A paper trail to prove it." She shuddered. "And don't forget, we know what Complacency is made of now. I'd say that puts us in a solid position to get back on track."

"Us, huh?" Cheng Yun spoke quietly, but his voice could still fill a room. He was leaning against the door frame of the workshop, arms folded, but the corners of his mouth had turned upward. "You counting yourself an insurgent now?"

Ning'er met his gaze head-on. "I'm counting myself one of your friends." She swallowed. "And I'm counting myself as someone who would fight to see a world where teenagers don't get locked up and tortured. If that makes me an insurgent, then so be it."

Cheng Yun tilted his head carefully. "You have a plan." It wasn't a question.

Ning'er shrugged. "Not a good plan, probably. And not a particularly safe one." Here came the hard part. She bit her lip. "We do still have a few cards left." She didn't want to play this particular hand. She didn't. Oh, how badly she didn't. But at the end of the day, that wasn't her call to make. The choice had never really belonged to her. She closed her eyes and made herself continue: "This particular play, though, it won't . . . it won't work without you, Cheng Yun. I know you've lost an awful lot in the past twenty-four hours." His father. His home. The carefully assembled bricks upon which the Young Marshal had built his life. "But I'm afraid that if you want to see this through, I'll have to ask you to sacrifice just a little more."

Ning'er watched the series of expressions flit across Cheng Yun's face before his features settled into a quiet sort of understanding. For the first time she could remember, he looked at peace. Her heart thrilled. Her heart sank. He knew what she meant. How foolish of her to assume that telling him aloud would be anything but a formality. Of course he'd know what she meant. He'd known ever since that long-ago, delirious night when he first informed her, fever-hot and somber as a prophet, that one day she would betray him.

"Anything," said Cheng Yun. He was bright-eyed, lucid, and utterly present. There was no mistaking his intent now. "I'll give anything."

It was what Ning'er had expected him to say. And it was what she'd been afraid of. But then, that had always been Cheng Yun in a nutshell. A tragedy, without rhyme or reason, caught in the shape of a beautiful boy. A beautiful boy who'd break her heart to save his kingdom from itself.

CHAPTER 14

We Who Set the Fires

The story of the boy named Cheng Yun ended the way Ning'er had always believed it would: like so many of the young, luminous revolutionaries who came before him, he set himself ablaze.

In the days that followed the Lark's disappearance, an unprecedented information leak trickled its way through the grooves of the city, into café gossip circles, the parlors of the Upper Ring taitai, the whispers along the train lines between neighborhoods poor and wealthy. They were all documents concerning the mysteriously missing Minister Cheng: ugly records of the prison he'd built for a girl formerly known as the Lark at the request of his corporate benefactors. The way those benefactors had milked her blood for the business that padded their coffers. The way Lilium Corp had bankrolled more than half the ministers who'd sat the exams, and in exchange, those ministers had allowed them to bleed Complacency from human bodies for the many long years preceding Emperor Huiming's short-lived reign.

You didn't have to be a genius to guess the source of the leak. There was only one person who could orchestrate something so devastating. Only one person who'd dare, and it was anyone's guess if he was a person at all. Maybe the Red Yaksha really was a spirit. A servant of Varavasa, protector of the righteous. Some strange, eldritch creature summoned by all the dead whose bodies had been bled dry, each as disposable and consumable as the next.

The Red Yaksha had always treated his information leaks as his gift to the people, but some among them—the cautious, the conservative, the ones who'd had fear successfully beaten into them—had to wonder if maybe this one was a curse, in truth. There was such a thing as knowing too much, after all. There was such a thing as knowing what you would rather forget.

Protests burst once more to life in the streets, this time buoyed with renewed vigor. The ministers, clearly panicked, did what they always did and sent the gendarme back into the neighborhoods, hoping they'd nip discontent in the bud with electric batons. When ordinary troops faltered, the Brocade Guard were deployed next.

This was no ordinary discontent, though, and these were not like any of the protests of the past century. This time, the people fought back. Even against tear gas and poison. Even against the terror of the Brocade Guard. Too many remembered the girl they'd known as the Lark. Too many had lost family, friends, lovers to Complacency overdoses and addiction. Too many had simply been so hungry for so long. And sometimes, sheer numbers were too much, even for the brutality of the Beiyang court.

Soon, the city ran thick with whispers of two men. The first man was the Young Marshal. Wherever the gendarme were deployed, Minister Cheng's son had never been far behind. A true model of the perfect Second Ring boy, flawlessly loyal to emperor and kingdom. Yet now, at the height of their need, he was nowhere to be seen. Speculation exploded throughout the city. Perhaps he had perished along with his father. Or perhaps the elder Cheng had survived, and escaped, and spirited his son away. To nearby Japan, perhaps, or farther afield to Australia. Where was he, the boy who should have been the salvation of the imperial court, the last trump card of the gendarme? Had he really been a coward all along?

The second man was the Red Yaksha. That flood of damning information aside, the people's hero had lain low for months, through famines and earthquakes and protests. Now he emerged, just once, to make a single announcement. It had been a simple message, but every outlet had seized on it immediately:

"I am and will always be a servant of the people," the masked man had said. "I have shared everything that I have, everything I know, based on the belief that people who have been starved and beaten deserve tools with which they can fight back. I have shared everything, of course, except my face. That hasn't been fair of me. To you." He added, almost an afterthought, "It hasn't been fair to either of us, really." He gave a pause there. It didn't sound planned. It sounded precisely like what it was: a moment of uncertainty. Anxiety. Fear. It sounded like a young man, still mortal, still flesh and blood, preparing to take a risk he'd never dared to before. And that was what made at least a few rapt listeners wonder if perhaps, just perhaps, the Red Yaksha might be human after all.

"If you want to know who I really am," continued the Red Yaksha, "then meet me at the southern gate of the city wall tonight, at sunset. I've hidden for far too long from my own people. It's time we meet each other in the light."

Ning'er met Cheng Yun—Cheng Yun as she'd known him—for the last time on the steps of Ge Rong's studio. He was dressed as the Red Yaksha, dramatic in that magnificent red cloak of his, but he had the hood pulled back and stood barefaced before her.

Without the hood, the clothes looked strange on him. They'd been tailored to fit his frame perfectly, yet when Ning'er saw him this way—those intense dark eyes soft on her, the full, familiar mouth parted slightly as she stepped up to meet him—she couldn't help but think the cloak was too big for his shoulders. Even ones as broad as his. The cloak was too big for anyone's shoulders, really.

She began to laugh before she could help herself. Better than crying, she supposed. "It was always going to end this way, wasn't it?"

Cheng Yun blinked at her, placidly confused. "What kind of way was that?"

"Me," said Ning'er pointedly, broken-voiced, "betraying you. I should have known you'd always get what you wanted, in the end. Of course I'd end up helping you burn your aliases. And of course I'd be the one leaking all the documents to back it up."

His gaze softened on her. "Those files we stole from the lab aren't just about me. They're about the secrets the court kept from the people they were supposed to protect, for over two hundred years." He hesitated. "Ning'er, if I've pushed you too far—"

Violently, Ning'er shook her head. "Please don't infantilize me. You know me better than that." She cut him off as he began to open his mouth. "And don't tell me I didn't have to do it. Don't tell me I had a choice. I never had a choice, you understand? Not when it came to you. And not . . . not when it came to the truth." *Not when it came to doing what you needed from me, in the end.* She gulped in one shaky, steadying breath, then another. Old Man Yu would have been proud. Then, in a shameful little voice, she said, "I felt dirty, you know, taking your money for this job. Nothing turned out the way we'd planned it."

"Maybe not." The side of his mouth pulled upward. "But

technically, you did fulfill the conditions of our arrangement. You set the Lark free."

"But—"

"But nothing," said Cheng Yun. "You're right. You've been right, this whole time. It was never really about her." His chuckle was rueful. "In a way, even I was looking for a figurehead. But I don't regret breaking her out, Ning'er, and I don't regret helping her fly free." A bit more dryly, he added, "Even if I do wish she hadn't concussed A'rong in the process."

Ning'er gave a watery little snort. "What do you think will happen to her? Out there, in the city?"

Cheng Yun hummed. "I don't know." Honesty colored the edges of his voice, pulling vulnerability to the surface in its wake. "But I do have faith that whatever path she chooses, she'll find her way."

"Like you did," said Ning'er softly.

Cheng Yun gave a darkly amused little huff. "I'm not so sure that I'm the best example. None of my plans turned out as I intended."

"Maybe not," Ning'er allowed. "But isn't this better, in some ways? When has a revolution ever been anything but messy as hell?" She shook her head. "Hope—and the will to do something with it—isn't just a feeling, A'yun. Hope is work. It's the hardest work I've ever done, and at the end of the day, none of us can ever be sure of its outcome. But we can persist. I think maybe that's enough: knowing that the odds are always stacked against us and playing them anyway, every time, for as long as it takes."

"And how do my odds look to you now?" asked Cheng Yun.

The corners of Ning'er's eyes burned. "Worthy," she said. "They look worthy."

He glanced toward his comm-link. It was time. They could both feel it, a shift in the air between them, tension drawing taut as the minutes ticked down.

He smiled at her. Her heart twisted inside her chest at the sight. "Thank you," said Cheng Yun. "For taking a chance on me."

He turned to go.

"Wait!"

She had one of his hands caught between hers before she could help herself. Even now, she was still reaching for him, still the greedy little thief, hungry and wanting and trying so hard to put her hands on a prize that was eternally slipping just beyond her grasp.

"You don't have to do this, you know," she blurted out, his hand clutched between hers. "You could stay. Here, I mean. Let them all think the Young Marshal died with his father, that the Red Yaksha was a ghost all along. You could just stay here and be Cheng Yun. No Young Marshal for the Upper Rings. No Red Yaksha for the Lower. Just plain old A'yun. Isn't that what you've always wanted to be, at the end of the day? A boy without masks, seen for who he really is?"

Cheng Yun looked at her over his shoulder, gaze drifting to their entwined fingers. He didn't say anything, but he didn't take his hand from hers either. He didn't leave.

"It's just," Ning'er struggled for the right words. She blinked hard, several times, her eyes hot. "It's just, if you go now, if you do as the Red Yaksha promised and show your face to all of Beijing, plaster it on every news camera at the South Gate, you'll never be able to undo it. You'll . . . you'll never come back, not truly. The Young Marshal will be well and truly dead. The Upper Rings will never accept you back into the fold. The Cheng Yun you are now, the one we all know will just . . . cease to exist. You'll become something else. I don't know what."

"Neither do I," said Cheng Yun. Quiet and bluntly honest. The side of his mouth tilted upward. "But I think I'd like to find out."

Ning'er swiped angrily at her eyes. Stupid tears. Stupid sentiment. Stupid, stupid, stupid. "Aren't you afraid?" she asked him. She didn't have to tell him that she was afraid. He could probably read it all over her face: her reddening eyes, the tremor in her lip.

Yet this had been her idea, hadn't it? She'd simply seen what was necessary and let him make his choices. She'd known he'd choose correctly.

Just, oh, how badly the selfish thing inside her, the greedy little thief, wished that for once, Cheng Yun would make the wrong choice. The selfish choice. The choice that would let Ning'er keep him, a secret prize she could tuck away for herself, safe from the uncertainty of an angry nation that loved tearing its martyrs apart at the seams.

"I'm terrified," said Cheng Yun. Remarkable, how someone could speak so gently and so bluntly at the same time. "I don't think I've ever been more terrified."

She bowed her head over their twined fingers. "But you're going to do it anyway."

He still hadn't let go. "Yes."

"Even though you might be captured. Or jailed. Or killed. Or—"

He laughed. "Ning'er. When have you ever known me to do anything by halves? Yes, everything you just said is possible. But it's as you said: hope is hard work. And you can't have hope without courting a little fear. A cat burglar would know, hmm?" He sobered abruptly. "You know, I always thought A'wei would be the one to make something of himself. Sometimes, I think my life since his death has just been one long series of auditions to fill his shoes. To fit inside a family that never quite had space for me." Cheng Yun shrugged. "Well, it's over now. I may not truly belong anywhere at all, and I may not matter, but I'm still a Cheng, at the end of the day. And the country deserves to know the kind of family we are."

"A'yun." Ning'er dropped his hand at last. "You're so much more than that. You have always been so much more than what your family made·you. You're right. You don't belong to them because they don't deserve you. And I . . ." She trailed off, looked away for a moment, blinking hard.

Courage, Ning'er. If he can have courage right now, then so can you.

"Even before I knew your face, when you were just the Red Yaksha, you gave me pieces of myself back that I thought were lost forever," said Ning'er. "I didn't know who you were, but you were already mine. You made yourself a part of my life from the moment you decided to give a shit about people like me. You will always matter." She inhaled. Exhaled hard. "Fuck your family. I don't care if this is a selfish thing to say. You're *mine*. Do you understand? I'll always think of you as mine, even after you've given yourself away to the rest of this broken, beautiful country. The part of you that's mine is mine alone."

His eyes went wide. For a moment, her brain flashed bizarrely back to the night she'd taken him home with her, his cheeks red with liquor, his body warm against hers. That dark liquid gaze of his, strangely innocent, as he whispered in her ear that he'd never shared a bed with someone else before. That hers was the first body that had ever curled up against his.

How badly she'd wanted him, even then. Even then, when

she knew, surely, that he'd never really be hers. Not when he was so intent on belonging to a world so much wider than the confines of that narrow, rickety bed.

But she'd wanted him, all the same.

She wasn't sure who closed the distance first. The last rays of the dying sun had half blinded her, as it sank slowly beneath the cityscape horizon. *Fuck it*, she thought to herself, squinting hard against the sting of light. And then her hands were tangling in his hair as she pulled his mouth down to meet hers.

He kissed her back with the kind of intent that only Cheng Yun seemed capable of, his hands careful at the nape of her neck, cradling her head with gentle and reverent fingers, as though she was something precious. As though for once he was the thief and she the prize, just out of reach.

Always just out of reach.

She closed her eyes and dropped her forehead against his chest. His heartbeat thumped steadily against her cheek. Maybe he was still afraid. But his body was prepared for what his mind had already decided to do.

"Go," she told him. "It's time. Give yourself away to all the rest of them."

In the end, Ning'er watched the boy she loved set ablaze from behind the clinical distance of a TV screen. It felt fitting in some ways. After all, this was how she'd seen the Lark fall, half a decade ago: a broadcast, flooding every screen in the city, the helpless onlookers separated from the martyr by nothing but that thin layer of glass. And yet that layer of glass may as well have been a million miles of distance. Maybe that was the fate of all great revolutionaries.

She sat curled between Zi'an and Ge Rong in the workshop, Feifei at her back, Zhenyi huddled at her feet, all five of them glued to the monitor in the window. Together, they watched as the boy dressed as the Red Yaksha climbed to the top of the massive city walls. The newscasters were speaking, trying to report it all live, but the shouts of the gendarme nearly drowned them out. "Stand down!" they screamed. "Stand down!" Their guns were trained on him, but not a single shot was fired. Maybe they too were afraid. Or maybe they, like the rest of Beijing, simply wanted to see the human face, hidden all those years beneath that bloodred hood and demon's mask.

He reached the top. Immediately, soldiers swarmed forward to arrest him.

It wouldn't be so easy as all that. The gendarme weren't the only people on the wall. Protesters swarmed the scene, mixing with members of the gendarme, tussling with their shields and weapons, creating a wall around their hero. Their Red Yaksha. They'd never even seen his face, but now, any one of them would die for him.

"Oh shit," breathed Zi'an. He craned his neck toward the TV. "You see that?"

They all saw it: The pair of officers shouldering their way through the wall of protesters until, at last, one of them reached the boy in the mask. The crowd's roar reached a fever pitch.

The boy in the mask didn't seem to care. "People of Beijing!" he roared. "I made you a promise. I'm here to make good."

Before the gendarme could lay hands on him, he stripped his own mask off.

It was as if a conductor had silenced an orchestra. Silence descended on the square as the city took in the famous, beatific smile of the Young Marshal, the Red Yaksha's mask resting between his hands. Cheng Yun stared into the cameras, face like a burning brand over the Red Yaksha's swirling red cloak as the wind howled and tugged at him. "There," he said, more quietly. "Now you see me. Now you know."

A great crack split the air. Someone screamed. Maybe it was a gunshot. Or maybe someone's transport simply backfired. Cheng Yun turned, startled, before the crowd roared back to life. The camerawork went sloppy after that, the lens out of focus as pandemonium erupted. There was one shot of Cheng Yun being pulled into the throng of gendarme as the people gathered in the square poured, shouting, into the rest of the city. Then it was just flailing hands and feet, the unintelligible shouts punctuating the air as everyone ran.

"Do you hear that?" Zhenyi asked. She wasn't looking at the TV. Her gaze was fixed past the screen at the window outside.

Ning'er tilted her head. Sure enough, not all the shouting was coming from the monitor speakers. It was muffled, faint still, but some of it was happening right outside the workshop, out on the street.

"Shit," said Feifei. She rose to her feet and hurried to the window. "Guys, look at this."

Ning'er and the others followed after her, pressing their faces against the glass panes. Outside, people poured into the streets in waves. Some sported yaksha masks, while others carried bright red banners, visible even in the dying light of the day, painted all the redder by the glow of the sunset. The floor rumbled beneath Ning'er's feet.

She looked at the others. They looked back.

"He's done it," she told them. "Cheng Yun. He's really done

it." As the world quaked around her, Ning'er began to laugh. Half-giddy, half-terrified. "Come on, let's go see what all this talk of hope has wrought."

She reached for someone's hand and wasn't sure whose she grasped. She wasn't sure it mattered as they all stumbled through Ge Rong's workshop door, out into the teeming streets outside. Everywhere Ning'er looked, she saw red: a mask here, a flag there, someone's jacket passing in a flash. All of them like little sparks of flame. Not so different from the ones that had set Minister Cheng's estate ablaze. Not so different, indeed, from the fire that Cheng Yun had been courting ever since he'd buried his brother, learned to love the Lark, and picked up the Red Yaksha's mask.

Ning'er stood witness. One of her crew-mates was holding her metal hand. Another was holding her flesh hand. For just a moment, squinting through the chaos around her, she thought she saw Cheng Yun's face—his true face, the private, vulnerable one, bare of masks or hoods—flash through the crowd. For just a moment, she pretended it was really him and not just a trick of her own longing. That some stranger in the crowd was Cheng Yun, escaped from the gendarme and returned to her, his dark eyes soft on hers, full mouth parted for a kiss. For that fleeting moment, Ning'er let herself pretend that the boy she loved was still hers and hers alone.

Then she closed her eyes and waited to be set ablaze like all the rest.

ACKNOWLEDGMENTS

I cannot open these acknowledgments without expressing the deep debt of gratitude I owe to my brilliant editor, Alyza Liu, without whom this book would literally not exist. Alyza, thank you for pushing me to be the best writer I could be, even when I was tired and uncertain and dragging my feet creatively—and thank you for going above and beyond the call of duty in ensuring that the story we've created together is something I am so truly, deeply proud of.

Thank you also to the rest of my brilliant publication team at Simon & Schuster, including Morgan York, Chava Wolin, Elizabeth Mims, Anna Elling, Justin Chanda, Anne Zafian, and Kendra Levin: you all do such tremendous work, and I'm very, very lucky to have you on my side. Special shoutout to my cover designer, Chloe Foglia; interior designer, Hilary Zarycky; and illustrator Bastien Lecouffe-Derharme: I am in awe of your incredible visuals. Thank you for building such a beautiful book for my little story.

To my authenticity readers, Jessica Burkhart and Jennifer Owens: I have such admiration for your empathy, attention to detail, and generosity in sharing your knowledge. I've learned so much from working with you both, and I firmly believe that my book is better for having passed through your hands.

To my tireless super-agent, Thao Le: thank you for continuing to be my best and strongest advocate, and for encouraging me to chase the opportunity to tell this very special story. Having you at my side always makes me stand a little taller as an author!

To my author friends who have supported me along this journey, including Grace Li, Amélie Wen Zhao, Becca Mix, Victoria Lee, Gina Chen, June Tan, Em Liu, Axie Oh, Amanda Quain,

Anna Bright, Cameron Thomson, Alexander Darwin, Jade Feng Lee, and so, so many others: you guys are proof that writing really can be a team sport, in the best of ways. Thank you for your excitement, your encouragement, and most of all, for continuing to inspire me with all the amazing words you write!

To my non-author friends who nonetheless somehow continue to endure my antics, up to and including letting me write furiously in the middle of their living room floors, namely Melody Lee, Alex Lupp, Raphael Baseman, Morgan Tornetta, Spencer Pretecrum, Perri Moeller, and Tara Ohrtman: you guys are among the true unsung heroes of the literary world.

To bookseller extraordinaire and one of the best friends I could ask for, Allison Senecal: thank you for hosting a much-needed DIY writing retreat that got me where I needed to be with this book (i.e. drafting literally entire swathes of this novel to the dulcet sounds of video games and anime in your house). That trip to Colorado remains one of my fondest memories!

To my long-suffering roommate, Becca Hurd: I'm sorry I kept hogging the couch at weird hours in the middle of the night and stress-eating more than my fair share of our snack stash during deadline weeks. You are an angel, and I love you very much.

And last but not least, to Mom, Dad, and the rest of the Tang family: I'm always thinking of you guys when I put pen to paper, and am always hoping to make you proud. Thank you, always, for your love, support, and patience.